THICKER THAN

BLOOD

Also by John Lutz

Novels of Suspense Featuring Private Investigator Nudger

Diamond Eyes
Time Exposure
Dancer's Debt
Ride the Lightning
A Right to Sing the Blues
Nightlines
Buyer Beware

Other novels of suspense

Dancing with the Dead
SWF Seeks Same

Short story collection

Better Mousetraps

THICKER THAN
B L O O D

JOHN LUTZ, 1939-

ST. MARTIN'S PRESS
NEW YORK

Design by Junie Lee

Library of Congress Cataloging-in-Publication Data

Lutz, John
    Thicker than blood : a novel of suspense featuring private
investigator Nudger / John Lutz.
        p.   cm.
    "A Thomas Dunne book."
    ISBN 0-312-09922-3
    1. Nudger, Alo (Fictitious character)—Fiction. 2. Private
investigator—Missouri—Saint Louis—Fiction. 3. Saint Louis
(Mo.)—Fiction. I. Title.
PS3562.U854T48   1993
813'.54—dc20   93-24382
                                                         CIP

First Edition: November 1993

10 9 8 7 6 5 4 3 2 1

With thanks to
Don Koch

Sailed on a river of crystal light
Into a sea of dew.
—Eugene Field, *Wynken, Blynken and Nod*

THICKER THAN
BLOOD

CHAPTER ONE

Nudger felt guilty.

Was guilty.

The five MunchaBunch doughnuts he'd eaten ten minutes ago still lay heavy in his stomach, but they weren't as heavy as the single Dunker Delite his friend Danny Evers of Danny's Donuts was trying to foist off on him for breakfast.

Danny had just finished the morning's baking and the doughnut shop was warm. The heat, the sugar-and-grease baking smell, the very sight of the Dunker Delite, made Nudger's delicate stomach twitch. Traitor he might be, but he wouldn't wound Danny by letting him know he'd developed a fondness—no, to be honest an addiction—to the delicious miniature doughnuts sold by Danny's recently opened competitor down the street, MunchaBunch Donuts.

Behind the counter, full-size doughnut in hand, Danny let gravity gain control of his basset-hound features and sad, concerned eyes. "You've been skipping breakfast a lot

1

lately, Nudge. I'm worried you're maybe sick or something."

"I'm okay, Danny," Nudger lied. "Been eating late-night snacks and I'm not very hungry in the mornings."

"Late-night, huh? You been sleeping okay?"

"Sure." He hastened to change the subject. "Anyone been in looking for me?" His office was directly above the doughnut shop, and when he was out, the sign on his door directed prospective clients to the shop, where Danny acted as his sort of polysaturated secretary.

"Oh, yeah!" Danny slapped his forehead. "There's a woman up there waiting for you." He let the Dunker Delite thunk back on its display tray, where it lay like an unexploded Scud missile.

"She mention what she wants?"

"Wants to hire an investigator, she said. I told her she came to the right place. Gave her a doughnut. Sent her on up. That was half an hour ago, but I never heard her come down. So she's still up there in the outer office waiting. I switched on your air conditioner so's she wouldn't sweat too much."

"Ever the gentleman," Nudger said. "She have the look of a process server?"

"Nope. But then process servers don't."

Danny had a point. Lately Nudger had been hearing ominous rumblings from his former wife Eileen. Or rather from her lawyer, Henry Mercato, whom she was sleeping with these days. They wanted more of Nudger's money.

They always wanted more of Nudger's money. Eileen's annual income from her barely legal, home-product pyramid-sales scam was double that of Nudger's, but she enjoyed threatening to drag him back into court now and then to squeeze a little whatever out of the turnip. It gave her life meaning. Whatever he paid her, she'd hinted to him once, went into a legal fund that was used to ream him regularly for more money, kind of like plowing profits back into a business. "Look closely at your money," she'd told him not long after the divorce, "and you'll see my picture on every bill."

It wasn't as if they'd had children. Child support he would gladly have paid, and on time. But alimony? How many women received alimony these days? Nudger was sure someone in the legal system had been paid off by Eileen to influence the judge. And maybe the fix was still in. Nudger was afraid that if she ever got him back into court, she might be able to have him drawn and quartered. On the other hand, that might be too quick for her. The woman was vindictive.

"Said her name was Norvella," Danny said, drawing Nudger back from dire musings. "Sounded like she was from the country." As he spoke, he held a large Styrofoam cup beneath the spigot of a huge stainless-steel urn. There was hissing, gurgling, glugging, and then a dark, dark sludge oozed into the cup. "By 'the country' I meant this country, of course. What I was trying to say is she's got this accent like she was raised way out in the country. I mean—"

"I get you," Nudger interrupted.

"I didn't wanna call a lady a redneck," Danny said.

Nudger nodded. "It's best to be politically correct."

"At least have a cup of coffee, Nudge." Danny turned around and set the cup in front of Nudger on the stainless-steel counter. "You ain't too proud to accept a free cup of coffee, are you?"

Nudger said no, he wasn't. He picked up the cup and took an obligatory sip. "Thanks, Danny," he said, managing not to grimace.

Carrying the Styrofoam cup, he pushed out through the

doughnut shop door into the morning heat, made a sharp U-turn, and went through another door that led to the narrow stairwell leading up to his office door. It was miserably hot in the stairwell. In the winter the stairwell was miserably cold. "Seasonal," the landlord had called it, as if architects had carefully worked it out that way.

She stood up when Nudger entered. She looked country, all right. Red hair, freckles, green eyes, wearing jeans and a sleeveless blouse that showed off a trim, if angular figure. She had even, slightly protruding teeth, a receding chin, a long, long neck. Though there was a wise, haggard air about her, she somehow looked very young. She was attractive, though Nudger couldn't figure out why. The way it all hung together, he supposed. He took into account the beginnings of crow's-feet at the corners of her eyes and figured her age to be about thirty. A rough thirty.

She tried a smile on him. It made her nose crinkle in a way he liked. "I'm Norvella Beane," she said. "With an *e*. Nobody calls me Norvella, though. I go by Norva." She sounded as country as she looked.

"Nudger," Nudger said. "I go by Nudger."

"No first name?"

"None to speak of."

He ushered her from the anteroom into his office, then excused himself for a moment while he ducked into the tiny half-bath and poured the coffee down the drain. He came back and sat down behind his desk. Considerate Danny had switched on the window unit in this room, too, and cool air evaporated perspiration at the top of Nudger's collar, making his neck cold, though the rest of him was miserably hot. He reached back without looking and angled the vanes on the plastic vent so the stream of cold air flowed off to the side. When he straightened out to sit facing forward, the swivel chair *eeeked* and Norva Beane

4

with an *e* swallowed hard, sending her Adam's apple careening up and down her long neck.

She said, "I got me a problem, Mr. Nudger." He placed her accent as southwestern Missouri, a flat Ozark drawl.

"A man or money?" Nudger asked.

She grinned at him as if dazzled by his perception. She was growing on him. "Started with a man, I guess. Now it's money." She raised both rough, oversized, yet oddly feminine hands palms out, like a child about to play pattycake. "Not that I can't pay for your services. You'll surely get whatever I owe you. Don't you worry a second about that."

"You haven't hired me yet," Nudger pointed out. "I don't even know what you want."

"Want somebody followed," she said.

Ah, it was coming clear, the old story. The heart and the groin kept Nudger in business. "Your husband causing a problem?"

"Stockbroker," she said. Full of surprises. "You ever hear of Fred McMahon?"

Nudger said he had. McMahon had been in the news lately when McMahon Investments, his financial consulting firm, had folded after it was discovered he'd been using clients' money for his own investments. He was out on bail and awaiting trial while his lawyers petitioned for a change of venue so he'd be treated fairly. Maybe someplace where barter was used instead of money. McMahon had influential friends, but Nudger didn't figure he could sidestep prison on this one.

"White-collar crime," Norva said, looking ready to spit. "Betcha he's outa the penitentiary and swindling somebody again in less'n a year."

"Why do you want him followed?" Nudger asked.

"I don't. He didn't do nothing to me. It's that bastard

Rand I want followed. Wanna see him strung up by his—"

"Who's Rand?" Nudger asked.

"Dale Rand. He's a stockbroker who cheated me outa my life savings, only I ain't got proof. He talked me into buying junk bonds that defaulted on payment, companies that went belly-up a matter of months after I paid my money. I mean, it was all too quick and convenient to be legitimate."

How do you mean?" Nudger asked, leaning forward in his chair. Eeek! He rested his elbows on the desk and studied Norva.

"I mean I figure he wasn't investing my money at all, just holding it and telling me he'd bought bonds he knew all along was gonna turn worthless. Then, when they did go bad, I think he kept my money and told me it was my loss."

"Don't you have sales confirmations? Dates, numbers?"

"Not that he wouldn't have had a chance of doctoring. Something else: I'm sure I heard him one day talking to that Fred McMahon on the phone. Now, all I want you to do is follow Rand and see if he contacts McMahon. If he does, then that'll prove he's crooked."

"Not in court, it won't."

"I ain't so interested in court as I am in satisfying my curiosity. In at least letting Rand know I know. Just 'cause I'm from Possum Run—"

"Where?"

"It's a little town down in the Ozarks, not far from the Arkansas line. I came into a bit of money by way of inheritance, and when I came here to Saint Louis last year and picked a stockbroker outa the phone book, I wound up with Rand. I know now he figured me for some dumb hick and set out at the git-go to take advantage of me. I don't like that, Mr. Nudger. I can't stand to let it be. You see my point?"

Nudger could. Still, he had to caution her. "If your money's gone, and Rand technically hasn't done anything illegal, you'll be dropped off at the end of this exactly where you are now, at the beginning. Less my fee, of course."

" 'Course. But money be damned, Mr. Nudger, it's the satisfaction I'm interested in. Country folks ain't all rubes to be taken advantage of, but I'm afraid that's just how that Dale Rand saw me. Sees me. But if he figures I'm a little yokel know-nothing who won't have gumption enough to come after the money he stole, he's wrong as piss in the wind." Anger and determination sparked for an instant in her green eyes, flint striking flint. Then she blushed. " 'Scuse my language. I get mad sometimes and sorta let fly. Let's just say he's wrong as berries in January."

Nudger said, "You can get those in the frozen-food aisle over at Shop-n-Save."

She fixed those unblinking green eyes on him, a tough little bird down deep where it mattered. Dale Rand had probably made a mistake if he'd actually diddled her out of her inheritance money. She said, "You siding with me or with Rand?"

Nudger thought, What is this, the Civil War?

He said, "Well, you're the side that's willing to pay me."

Norva gave him her slow, toothy smile, crinkling her nose again as she fished her checkbook out of her oversized vinyl purse. "Then that settles that." She might be a simple country girl, her look told him, but a hillbilly accent didn't matter when money talked.

She and Eileen had nothing and everything in common.

CHAPTER TWO

Nudger cleaned up old business, then started work for Norvella Beane the next morning.

Dale Rand was easy enough to find. He was in the phone book. Nudger was pleased when investigative work turned out to be that easy. It lent the illusion that all of life could be a cinch. Hah!

The Rand address turned out to belong to a luxury home in the Saint Louis suburb of Ladue, where new money lived sometimes uncomfortably among old. The Rand house looked like new money, especially with its aluminum window trim and expansive glasswork gleaming in the hot, brilliant sunlight. It was a two-story brick modern, large enough to be a terminal building at a small airport. The roof was red tile and most of the face of the upper floor was darkly tinted glass, which mirrored the tops of trees lining the base of the circular driveway. Here and there angular, rough-hewn beams were allowed to show through the brickwork, an incongruous pass at appearing rustic. Well behind the house, Nudger glimpsed a four-car garage, which seemed to have been built fairly recently. Its brick-work was paler, and the mortar looked almost white. On the garage's roof was a small cupola, which sported a black piece of modern sculpture, a minimalist sort of bird that turned out to be a weather vane. So this was what the rooster had come to. An overhead door was open to reveal the trunk and rear bumper of a shiny black Cadillac.

Nudger backed out of the driveway, pretending to be a disoriented driver who'd nosed in only to turn around. Then he found a spot down the street where he could park in the shade and watch the house.

He knew he couldn't stay there long. The Ladue police might regard his rusty fifteen-year-old Ford Granada as litter. Might regard Nudger himself that way. Take him in and conduct a strip search with rubber gloves. Ladue might have a law against wearing J.C. Penney underwear, might toss him in a cell, and throw the key into the manicured bushes.

He didn't have to wait long. Within ten minutes the black Caddy eased out of the Rand driveway and made its way along the tree-lined streets to Ladue Road.

It was a new Cadillac. They were building them big again, and easy to tail. Nudger followed in the land yacht's wake as it turned south on Hanley, then east on Highway 40. They were headed toward downtown. Not once did Rand seem to glance at his rearview mirror. Nudger dropped three car lengths behind anyway. He was sure he knew Rand's destination, so there was no reason to play in close.

Rand exited at Seventh Street and drove north into the heart of downtown. At Chestnut he made a sharp left into the underground parking garage of the Medwick Build-ing, one of those pale concrete-and-glass skyscrapers, which look like stacks of ice-cube trays. It was the kind of maximum-profit architecture that bloomed like fields of tulips during Reagan's Morning in America.

Nudger found a parking space on Chestnut, fed the meter a quarter, and jogged across the street. He entered the garage instead of the building and stood by the elevators with a couple of women dressed in business suits. Rand had parked the Caddy and was approaching. Nudger hoped the elevator wouldn't arrive too soon for him to make it.

Rand was wearing an elegant gray suit and was taller than he'd seemed sitting behind the steering wheel, probably an inch or so over six feet. He was slim, with sandy hair combed sharply to the side to disguise the fact that it was receding. His features were what used to be called patrician, with a long jaw and aquiline nose. Blue eyes peered out from behind oversized gold-rimmed glasses. His complexion was pale and smooth, like a woman's, though his appearance wasn't at all feminine. He glanced at Nudger as if he owned him and was considering selling, then settled his weight to patiently wait for the elevator, his right hand wrapped around the handle of an expensive, black, leather attaché case, thin as the creases in his tailored slacks.

Norva Beane had told Nudger where Rand worked, but he wanted to verify it. Wanted, if nothing else, to be sure this was indeed Dale Rand, who fit Rand's description and who'd emerged from Rand's house and driven to the building containing Rand's office. Nudger had been mixed up in a mistaken identity case before and had found himself embroiled in a stew of murder and suicide. Now he was cautious. But then, he was cautious about most everything. Even so, life often took him by surprise. That made him even more cautious.

The elevator arrived and everyone got in. Small talk ceased as elevator etiquette took hold. Nudger pushed 30, the highest numbered button, and leaned against the back wall, staring straight ahead and slightly above eye level, like everyone else, as if waiting for a film to be shown on the surface of the closed doors.

At lobby level, half a dozen more business types squeezed in. Someone's stomach growled loudly; Nudger was sure it hadn't been his. Reasonably sure, anyway. A man in a chalk-striped blue suit hummed "When the Saints Go Marchin' In" beneath his breath.

At 17 the two women got out. One of the men exited at 19.

" 'Scuse me," Rand mumbled when the doors glided open at 24, and he slid between two other passengers and out into the hall.

Nudger hesitated a few seconds, then followed him, barely beating the closing elevator doors. He turned in the opposite direction, and stood staring at his palm as if reading instructions on a slip of paper. From the corner of his vision he saw Rand open a door near the end of the hall. Suddenly turning direction, Nudger walked toward it.

The door was heavily grained, polished oak, and lettered "Kearn-Wisdom Brokerage" in brass. Nudger gripped the gleaming brass handle and eased it open.

Ah! This was working out fine. Kearn-Wisdom was one of those brokerage firms with a space and chairs provided where speculators who played the market daily could sit and watch "real-time" quotes crawl past on a lighted screen. Behind a waist-high oak divider were six desks where brokers' agents sat before computers. Nudger was just in time to see Rand walk past the rows of desks and enter one of three doors to what were presumably offices.

The market had opened less than an hour ago, but already there were half a dozen players seated in the chairs and gazing transfixed at the quotes rolling past. Putting on his "I belong here" attitude, Nudger made his way to an empty chair and sat with them, staring at the screen, and even now and then recognizing what corporations some of the symbols represented. There was General Motors, Anheuser Busch. And IBM was easy enough. Maybe there wasn't much to this stock-market thing, after all.

After about five minutes, Nudger only seemed to watch the crawling symbols and numbers on the digital screen, while he actually watched the office door Rand had closed behind him.

An hour passed, and there was little activity at Kearn-Wisdom except for the reps who were seated at desks with computers taking orders by phone. Occasionally one of the traders seated near Nudger would get up and talk to a rep to place an order.

An old man next to Nudger, wearing a thick blue suit that smelled of mothballs, poked him in the ribs and said, "That Facile Industries got a P/E ratio high as outer space. Sold that one short yesterday and it's already down two and a half."

"Hm," Nudger said.

"Bull market, shit!" the old guy said. "This many bulls around, I gotta sell against them." He seemed angry. "You a contrarian?"

"Presbyterian," Nudger said. It was what he usually said when pressed about religion. He didn't actually attend church.

The old man said, "Oh," and fixed his attention on the glowing numbers.

Finally Nudger realized that the time on his parking meter had expired. Nothing was happening here, and he was tired of smelling mothballs and listening to occasional comments he didn't understand. (What was the "broad tape"? And why hadn't the feminists neutered that terminology?)

He decided to change tactics. No one seemed to pay much attention to him when he stood up and walked out.

The meter's time had just expired, but there was already a parking ticket tucked beneath the Granada's windshield wiper. Nudger sighed. He wasn't really surprised. Murphy's law. He wished he could find Murphy. Kill him. But the police hadn't had the car towed. A break there.

He waited until a parking space opened up where he'd be in a position to see the entrance of the Medwick Building as well as its garage. Then he shot the Granada out into traffic, provoking the ire of a grandmotherly sort of woman in a van, and maneuvered his way into the space. The woman glared at him, then made an obscene gesture, and drove on. Nudger hadn't even suspected she wanted the parking space.

He got out of the car, snatched the ticket from beneath the wiper blade, and stuffed it into his shirt pocket. Then he crammed a quarter in the parking meter and got back in behind the steering wheel. Settled in to wait. The woman in the van drove past again. She'd apparently circled the block in search of a parking space. When she noticed Nudger still in the car, she gave the horn a light tap and made the same obscene gesture. She sure was combative.

A little after ten-thirty, Rand's Caddy emerged from the Medwick Building garage and turned west on Chestnut. Nudger managed to get the Granada started on the third try and followed, vowing to use some of the fee for this job to have the carburetor rebuilt. He knew that when the weather turned cold he'd have to open the hood and use a screwdriver to get the car started, as he had most of last winter.

Right now though, sweating profusely as he stayed a discreet distance behind the black Cadillac, he wished it were the air conditioner that worked.

His hopes rose as the Cadillac headed west on Highway 64, still and forever referred to by its old designation, "Highway Forty," by St. Louisans, who generally tended to cling too long to the past. Rand drove toward the kind of high rent district where he'd be most likely to meet the infamous McMahon. If Nudger remembered correctly, McMahon lived in Clayton, which was only a kiss away from Highway 40 as it bisected the St. Louis metropolitan area.

But Rand didn't drive anywhere that made it easy for Nudger. Instead he traveled out beyond the suburbs, pulled into the lot of the Chadwood Country Club, and hoisted a red golf bag out of the Caddy's trunk.

Chadwood, a span of level greens and fairways beyond an English Tudor clubhouse nestled among tall oaks and spruce trees, was the kind of exclusive place where Nudger couldn't follow. His car alone would have disqualified him, or at least made him a handicap golfer.

He drove along a road bordering the course until he could see a red pennant, then parked, and glanced around.

It was a secluded enough place, and he was parked in the shade. He got his binoculars from the glove compartment and fixed them on the pennant. He'd bought the binoculars from a mail-order catalogue, which also sold inflatable hair curlers and Elvis collector plates, and he had difficulty focusing them, but finally he made out a 2 on the flag.

Obviously Rand intended to play a round of golf, so he should come into view soon.

Nudger raised the binoculars to his eyes again, directing them on three men who'd just dismounted golf carts and walked onto the green. He could make out their faces all right, so he'd have no difficulty identifying McMahon if he was one of Rand's golfing partners.

Half an hour and several foursomes passed before Rand and two other men appeared on the green. They stood aside while a fourth man's chip shot landed ten feet from the hole, then the taller of the men walked up to the hole and removed the flag. He stood patiently, leaning his weight on the pole, while the chip shooter sank his long putt. The guy could really golf. Had a great short game, anyway.

Nudger studied each member of Rand's foursome as they putted out on the second green. Rand left his easy putts well short, pretended to break his putter over his upraised knee, then finally sank the ball after long and intense concentration while the other three men stood by with polite, serious expressions.

Nudger moved the binoculars from one to the other. None of them was Fred McMahon, whose photo Nudger had seen plenty of times in the news media.

A nearby voice said, "Fore."

Startled, Nudger dropped the binoculars in his lap and turned to look out the window.

He was staring into the muzzle of what he knew was a small, black automatic. Only it didn't look small to him.

The man holding the gun said, "Fore's what golfers yell just before somebody gets hit."

CHAPTER THREE

Nudger swallowed his heart and inched down a bit in the seat so he could look up at an angle and see the man's face.

A black guy with straightened and oiled-back hair and a barely visible Errol Flynn mustache. Wearing dark slacks, a green shirt with the collar open to show off a gold chain. A single gold earring, a small swastika dangling on the end of a three-inch chain, glinted beneath his left ear. Nice looking guy except for the gun and the flatness of the eyes. Eyes like that could watch what happened if the trigger got squeezed, and never take on a hint of expression.

"My God! A holdup!" Nudger said, trying to convince fate.

The gunman laughed. "You wish." He hunkered down slightly and let out a long breath. "We both know what this is, and it ain't a stickup."

"You must have the wrong man," Nudger said in a voice that sounded as if he'd just inhaled helium.

The gunman said, "Hmm," as if that might be a possibility. "You the man following Dale Rand around, right?"

"Uh, not actually."

"No shit? Then it could be I *do* have the wrong guy. Listen, let me apologize, sir. Hey, *you* wanna shoot *me?*"

"At least you've got a sense of humor," Nudger said, as if that were a desirable characteristic in killers. His stomach was kicking against his belt buckle and he wondered if his heart might actually beat hard enough to crack a rib. "So let's talk about this, why don't we?"

"Gotta have a sense of humor for what I do." The man backed away a short step, so Nudger couldn't reach the gun, and glanced up and down the road to make sure nobody was around. Bad sign. "Takes two to have a conversation, though, and in a couple seconds there's only gonna be one of us."

He moved in close again. Nudger picked up the acrid scent of the oil and bluing of the gun. The shooter took care of his equipment; he was a pro who wouldn't miss, a craftsman, not a sadist who'd make death as painful as possible. Odd, what somebody could be thankful for at a time like this. Also, if he left Nudger only badly wounded, an invalid, Nudger was behind on his Blue Cross insurance. Another point in favor of a quick death.

"Hand me your wallet," the man said.

"Huh?"

"Don't get the idea this really is just a holdup. I wouldn't want you starting to hope. I wanna know who you are—were. Before you get all messy and your driver's license gets hard to read."

Nudger was reaching carefully into his pocket when he heard something. The crunch of tires on the gravel road shoulder.

His eyes darted to the rearview mirror. A car had pulled up close to the Granada's back bumper.

Nudger glanced at the gun barrel, then again at the rearview mirror. The car behind his was a big one, an American luxury model, too close for him to discern the make. An elderly woman sat on the passenger side. A man was climbing out from behind the steering wheel.

The gunman angled his body to conceal the automatic, then slid the weapon into his pants pocket, leaving the hand in the pocket. Leaning very close to Nudger, he said, "You play it right or I kill the old man, the cunt, and you."

The man who'd gotten out of the car was tall and was wearing expensive casual clothes, a white leather belt. He was bald but for a fringe of gray hair. Probably in his late sixties. He shouldn't have stopped but Nudger was gloriously grateful that he had.

"Problem, huh?" he said as he approached Nudger and the gunman, wearing a big smile to go with his big mistake. He looked like a glad-handing Shriner doing whatever they do between conventions. Nudger went from praying he'd escape this alive to praying somebody would.

The gunman returned the old guy's smile, then he glanced down at Nudger.

"Oh, car trouble," Nudger said. "It died on me all of a sudden and I pulled over and parked."

"I saw him stranded here and thought maybe I could help," the gunman said.

Still with the big dumb smile, the old man propped his fists on his hips and looked around. "Where's your car?" he asked the gunman.

The gunman patted his pockets, as if he'd forgotten and left something at home, making a joke of it. "Don't have it with me. I was out walking. Doctor's orders."

"Bad heart?"

"Hypertension. Something in me causes a lotta that."

It was an unlikely place for a black man to be out for a

18

stroll, but the old man seemed satisfied with the explanation. Didn't have much choice, really. "Well, you fellas are in some kinda luck," he said. "I retired last year from running a Pontiac dealership. Been working on cars since I was a kid." He grinned at Nudger. "Pop the hood and I bet I can get you running again in a New York minute." That was what Nudger wanted to do, run. "Let me try it one more time," he said. "There's a little life left in the battery." The gunman stared hard at him, but with a tight little smile. His eyes hadn't changed expression—rather, lack of expression.

Nudger tapped the accelerator and twisted the ignition key.

The Granada's engine sputtered but refused to start. Nudger's stomach started, though, diving and zooming like a drunken bat at twilight. This was terrific—his car was in cahoots with his killer.

"Careful! Don't flood it," the old guy said, kind of testily.

The gunman was still smiling. Nudger didn't necessarily regard that as a good sign. But he didn't figure the man would murder him in front of two witnesses. And he'd surely walk away and bide his time before he'd kill three people in a fouled up hit, stirring up the news media and the law. That wouldn't be professional. It might cost him future business.

But Nudger knew that if he called attention to the danger, the gunman wouldn't have much choice other than to make it a triple killing. Probably he'd do it, not liking it, then forget about it by dinner, and sleep soundly tonight.

"Just pop the hood latch and I'll take a quick look," the old man urged.

Instead, Nudger twisted the key again. He wanted out of there as soon as possible. *Sput, sput, sput* . . . The engine seemed to be mocking him, siding with the man with the gun and rubbing it in.

"Sounds like it needs a tune-up," the gunman said with a grin.

Nudger's stomach was tying itself into every known knot. He was sweating hard, as if he'd just broken a fever.

The old guy shook his head. "No way to tell for sure about a tune-up until—"

This time the engine turned over. Nudger tromped the accelerator to keep it running, then backed his foot off to a point where the idle was rough but fast.

"You were right," the old man said. "She sure as heck does need a tune-up."

"Better get that taken care of," the gunman advised Nudger. "You had a close call today. It could happen again and not end so nice."

"Well, thanks to both you fellas," Nudger called above the clatter of the motor, putting the car in Drive.

"Want me to give you a lift someplace?" the old man was asking the man with the earring and gun.

"No, I better continue my walk." His right hand finally came out of his pocket. Without the gun.

Nudger couldn't help it. He winked at the gunman as he fed the Granada gas. Gravel rattled off the insides of the fenders as he drove away.

In the rearview mirror, he saw the old man ambling back to get in his car.

The gunman was standing still on the side of the road, a hand raised to his forehead to shield his placid, killer's eyes from the sun, staring after Nudger.

CHAPTER FOUR

Norva didn't answer her phone. She hadn't given Nudger an address, so he thumbed through his crisscross directory and got it off her phone number. It was on Virginia in South St. Louis, in an area he knew was mostly low-rent apartments.

After going down to the doughnut shop and telling Danny he'd be away for a while, and to keep an eye out for anyone going up to his office, he got in the Granada and drove to South St. Louis. Most of the way there, he chewed antacid tablets.

The building on Virginia was even worse than he'd expected, a mottled brick, six-family apartment with peeling, gray-wood trim and rusty, green-metal awnings, which had been dragged low by years of heavy snowfalls. Everything about the building suggested it had given up. Not even gentrification could save it.

Nudger parked the Granada across the street, behind a battered pickup truck with a dented and rusted hot-water heater propped in its bed. That was as valuable a cargo as anyone with good sense would leave parked unattended in this block. He stretched awkwardly to reach into the back of the Granada and got Car Guard from where it lay on the floor. It was one of those gadgets that clamped on a steering wheel and locked with a key, making it impossible to turn. The theory was that no one would steal a car they couldn't steer. Car Guard advertising claimed it was made of a space-technology alloy so hard it could only be sawed through with a diamond blade—something your run-of-the-mill car thief wouldn't have in his kit.

After locking Car Guard firmly onto the steering wheel, Nudger climbed out of the car and locked it behind him. He ignored the hostile stare of a deranged-looking old woman seated on a concrete stoop, crossed the street, and then the brown and barren lawn to reach the entrance to Norva's building.

The vestibule needed a fresh coat of gray paint to cover the graffiti, though it probably wouldn't entirely eliminate the stench of urine. The floor was a yellowed hexagonal tile, dirty but glittering here and there with an odd beauty where crack vials had been stepped on and ground to fine-glass filings beneath heels and soles. A small tricycle no one would bother stealing lay on its side in a corner, near the bank of mailboxes whose ancient brass doors were missing. A crudely printed card in the slot above one of them, near a doorbell button that somehow had survived, simply read, "Beane, 2B." Nudger pressed the button, heard what sounded like the distant buzz of an angered insect, then trudged up creaking wooden stairs to the second floor.

The door to 2B was open a few inches when he got there, and Norva was peeking out from behind a tarnished-brass chain lock. When she saw Nudger, the door closed, the chain clattered loose, and she reopened the door and smiled at him. "Gotta be careful in this neighborhood," she explained. Then her gaunt features took on a pained expression and her green eyes got hard. "That Dale Rand took all my money and put me here in this place." Her country drawl somehow added intensity to her words. The Hatfields had probably sounded like that talking about the McCoys.

She stepped back to let Nudger inside the apartment. She was wearing faded Levi's, which were baggy on her angular figure, and a sleeveless red T-shirt with "Go Fish!" printed in washed-out black letters across the front. No shoes or socks. Her toenails and blunt fingernails were painted a matching red brighter than the T-shirt.

"You like to play?" Nudger asked, staring at her chest.

Her green eyes narrowed with surprise and suspicion. "I ain't sure exactly how you mean that, Mr. Nudger."

He pointed to the T-shirt. "Fish. The card game. You play?"

Her face softened with relief. "No. The truth is I don't know how. I got this shirt at a garage sale for a quarter." She suddenly seemed embarrassed. "Sit down, why doncha?"

Nudger walked over to a sofa covered with a blue bed-spread and glanced around. The place was cheaply furnished but clean and orderly: An old console TV in a corner, a low coffee table with cork coasters and a glass ashtray on it, an oval braided rug on the scarred and waxed hardwood floor. Shelves supported by stacks of bricks stood on one wall, holding an old aluminum-cased stereo with a record player on top. A dozen or so albums stood leaning on the bottom shelf. On the top shelf was a vase of plastic roses and a row of small stuffed animals. Bears, mostly.

When he sat down on the sofa, Norva said, "Get you a lemonade?"

"Sure. I could use one of those."

She went into what he assumed was the kitchen and clinked and dinged things around for a few minutes. The window shade that partially blocked sunlight made one side of the room dimmer than the other. Nudger sat listening to the fan in the front window hum and cluck about the heat. Its metal grille vibrated and rattled every ten seconds or so. The apartment wasn't air conditioned, but it was comfortable. The fan was enough.

Norva returned with a tall glass in each hand. She gave one to Nudger before sitting down opposite him in a wicker chair that had been enameled dark green.

"You learn something?" she asked, settling her weight and making the chair creak.

He sipped lemonade before answering. It was delicious, chilled with ice cubes and sweetened with real sugar, some of which lay in a residue at the bottom of the glass. The glasses had a pattern of plaid cows on them; they'd once contained cheese spread, but you wouldn't know it now. "Actually I came here to learn something," he said. He sipped again. Swallowed some pulp and a lemon seed but didn't mind. "You know a black man about thirty, average size, good-looking, thin little mustache, gold chain-and-swastika earring in his left ear?"

"I believe I'd remember him if we'd met, but I don't. Who is he, anyways?"

Nudger told her, watching her face grow serious and more haggard, somehow more attractive. Like one of those country-western singers who sold character lines as well as big boobs and high cheekbones as ideal womanhood. The kind of woman who would be great in bed and then wouldn't mind going out and clearing some weeds.

24

When he was done talking, she crossed her legs the way a man might, ankle to knee, and said, "Don't what you just told me prove Dale Rand's a swindler?"

"Not exactly."

"Does to me."

"So far the only incriminating thing I've seen him do is pull up short on an easy putt."

Norva chewed on her lower lip with her slightly protruding teeth, making Nudger wonder why that came across as sexy. Then her green eyes darkened and narrowed, crinkling the flesh around the corners. She said, "So!" As if accusing Nudger of something.

"So?" Nudger asked.

"So you gonna quit on me?" A different kind of "so" that time.

"You mean just because somebody threatened to kill me?"

She wiped at her eyes, though they appeared to be dry. "Men been quitting on me, doing me wrong all my life. Why should you be any different?"

"Because you're paying me." Because my work is all I've got and what I am, he thought. Not giving up is all I have left of what I started out with, the only thing they can't take away from me if I don't let them. But he didn't say it, because he doubted she'd understand such a concept. Women usually didn't. Women had better sense.

Norva's eyes brightened and blood rushed to her face. The change in circulation somehow made her freckles much more noticeable. "Then you're still gonna follow Rand?"

"Still am."

She seemed barely able to restrain herself from leaping from her chair to give him a big hug. He wasn't sure if he wanted her to restrain herself. It would be nice to get something out of this other than a bullet.

But then there was Claudia. And guilt.

"Mr. Nudger," Norva said, suddenly calmer, "I realize what I'm asking you to do. I mean, money ain't everything, and I want you to be sure you wanna go on with this. If a man was to point a gun at me, I'd be a scared rabbit just like you."

"It isn't that I'm scared," he said, too quickly, feeling angry and embarrassed, wounded in the machismo. Scared rabbit? "I'm just trying to be logical. You hired me to do a job, so I should do it."

"Money don't seem a logical reason to risk your life."

"Well, the truth is, I'm doing it for the love of a woman."

Freckles came out like stars again, a vivid dusting against a ruddy sky. "Now, Mr. Nudger—"

"My former wife, Eileen," Nudger said, keeping the conversation in bounds.

She cocked her head to the side and looked at him with an air of surprised discovery. "So you're a romantic."

"Sometimes. If there's nothing good on television."

"But you must still love Eileen a lot."

"Far from it. If I don't come up with the back alimony I owe her, she'll become twice as dangerous as the guy with the gun."

"That kinda talk don't fool me." Norva finished her lemonade and placed the glass on the edge of the oval rug, near her chair, so it wouldn't leave a ring on the wood floor. She wiped her damp hand on her T-shirt and said, "Love's one of the most powerful forces in the world."

Nudger said, "So's hate."

She aimed her emerald eyes straight at him, like lovely

lasers. "They can be exactly the same force, Mr. Nudger. Didn't you know that?"

He had known, actually. It was one of the things that complicated life and made it such a trial.

CHAPTER FIVE

"What kind of gun was it?" Hammersmith asked.

Nudger said, "The kind that was pointed at the bridge of my nose." He threw up his hands. "How should I know who manufactured it? All I saw was the muzzle. It looked as big as—"

"I know, I know."

They were in Hammersmith's office in the Third District station house on Tucker and Lynch. Hammersmith was Lieutenant Jack Hammersmith, who in another world in an earlier time had been Nudger's partner in a two-man patrol car. This was when Nudger's nervous stomach was just beginning to give him the idea that he was in the wrong occupation, and when the now-corpulent Hammersmith was still thin and handsome and could wheedle the most secret information out of charmed prostitutes and addicts.

"The description you gave me," Hammersmith said, "fits a kazillion guys in this city. If you knew what kinda gun he carried, that might narrow it down. That is, if he's a well-known badass."

"If I had some mustard and some bread, I'd have a ham sandwich, if I had some ham," Nudger said.

"Sure, I get your point. But as it is, you could search through mug books for days and still not find this character, even if he does have a record."

Nudger couldn't argue with that. Average-height black men with average builds and pencil-thin mustaches were all over the city. They were . . . well, average. "What about the earring?" he asked. "Can't be a lot of people running around with swastikas dangling from their ears on gold chains."

"You wouldn't think," Hammersmith admitted. "But it can be removed. Maybe he's wearing some other kinda earring now."

"Might it be some sort of identifying jewelry? I mean, maybe he's a member of a gang."

"Possible but not likely. I know most of the gang colors and tattoos and whatever. But I'll check on it. My guess is your guy was simply trying to make a fashion statement."

Nudger sat silently and chewed on the inside of his cheek.

"Maybe you'll see him again, Nudge," Hammersmith suggested with straight face and sadistic humor.

Nudger didn't give him the satisfaction of reacting.

"My feeling," Hammersmith said, "is that this guy wasn't really going to kill you. If he had been, he wouldn't have walked up and started a conversation. It was a scare tactic, that's all."

"It worked well." It annoyed Nudger that Hammersmith didn't seem to take the incident seriously. He said, "What's the story on Fred McMahon? Is he gonna get nailed for stock manipulation?"

"Not exactly," Hammersmith said. "There was no stock to manipulate. He sold clients over-the-counter stocks that didn't exist, stocks too small to be listed in the newspaper. He even supplied them with phony stock certificates. Gave them phony quotes when they called his brokerage firm to see how they were doing. They were always doing well. McMahon didn't want his clients to sell. The word is the prosecutor's got a locked-in conviction. Plea bargaining's probably already begun.''

"Is there anything on Dale Rand?"

"The guy you were following?"

Nudger nodded.

"I can check, Nudge. Get back to you." Hammersmith leaned far back in his desk chair and meshed his hands behind his head. His smooth-shaven, pink jowls spread over his shirt collar like balloons bloated with water. "You're gonna drop this case, right?"

"Wrong."

"I thought you were a coward."

"Poor and a coward."

"Is Eileen after you again for child-support payments?"

"Alimony," Nudger said testily. "We didn't have children."

"Whatever."

"There's an important distinction," Nudger said.

"Not if you don't pay what you owe." Hammersmith had always liked Eileen and considered the dissolution of the marriage to be Nudger's fault. "I thought only rich guys paid alimony, Nudge."

"Guys pay it whose ex-wives have Henry Mercato for a lawyer." Mercato and Eileen had stripped Nudger of all dignity and assets, and now they were partners in lust. That was Mercato. That was Eileen. Still, Hammersmith couldn't see it. He liked Nudger's present lady love, Claudia Bettencourt, even more than Eileen, or it would have been a problem. Before Nudger had met Claudia, Hammersmith had tried to maneuver him and Eileen back together. Big old matchmaker Hammersmith.

"While I'm finding out about Rand," Hammersmith said, "I advise you to stay away from him. That should help you avoid the man with the gun of indeterminate make."

"I'll steer clear of Rand as much as possible," Nudger said, standing up. "I think I know a way to do that."

Hammersmith was looking at him speculatively. As Nudger was leaving, he said, "Nudge, please don't tell me what you got in mind."

"Not unless it's a must."

Nudger made an appointment with the bug man. His name was Charlie Roache, but that wasn't why he was called the bug man. He was an expert in planting listening devices, and finding those planted by others. Often he did this for illicit reasons. Sometimes it wasn't as profitable as one might imagine. Now and then he did work for Nudger. The bug man had a sliding scale.

As Nudger approached his booth in the Howard Johnson's restaurant on Lindbergh, the bug man looked up and smiled. He was a wiry little guy about fifty, always moving, with ears that stuck out like shutters in a storm, and jet-black hair always cut unevenly and badly mussed, as if squirrels had been rooting in it. He constantly chewed on his writhing lower lip, as if trying to kill it and make it be still, and he had glittery little dark eyes that were slightly mad. He loved to take chances and not get caught.

"Clams tonight," he said, as Nudger slid into the booth to sit across from him.

"Huh?"

"Clams are the special tonight. You gonna get some? I already ordered."

Nudger told him he'd already eaten, which wasn't true. His stomach was still roiling from looking into the barrel of the gun. It had looked as big as—

"Ready to order?"

He told the waitress who'd interrupted his thoughts just coffee and sat back and watched the bug man light a cigarette. They were in the No Smoking section. The bug man touched the cigarette to his lips, barely drew on it, then slipped it out of sight beneath the table. He squinted at Nudger, eyes like onyx. "You mentioned a job."

Nudger told him what was required.

"I can do it," the bug man said. He swallowed some smoke.

The waitress arrived with coffee and clams and a glass of iced tea. After placing everything on the table, she sniffed the air, shook her head, and walked off.

"There's Rand, the wife, and the daughter," Nudger said, "so there might be somebody in the house all the time."

"I can do it," the bug man said again. "Everything you asked, I can do. I'll call you."

The smell of the deep-fried clams was making Nudger nauseated, so he laid a dollar bill on the table to take care of the coffee, then got up and left.

As he was climbing into the Granada out in the parking lot, the bug man glanced over at him through the window and waved with one hand, forking in a cluster of clams with the other. He must have extinguished the cigarette under the table, or maybe had it balanced on the vinyl seat so it wasn't quite setting the booth on fire.

Nudger waved back. He hadn't even touched his coffee.

It was a little past six, so he drove down Highway 44 to South St. Louis and parked outside Claudia's apartment on Wilmington.

Claudia was home from teaching summer-school classes at Harriet Beecher Stowe girls' school out in a west county suburb. She'd already changed clothes and was wearing red shorts and a black blouse when she let Nudger in. She was slender, with long dark hair, lean, delicate features, and a perfectly straight nose that was maybe a little too long and gave her a look of nobility, like somebody in a medieval painting. She had beautiful legs, and was all in all a beautiful woman, but in a subtle way. The kind of woman who got more attractive with each glance, Nudger thought.

After giving him a peck on the cheek, she walked toward the kitchen. "I'm making spaghetti," she said. "Want some?"

The spicy, garlicky smell was better than the clams. "Sure," he said, and followed her into the kitchen to help. Not too closely, though. He loved to watch her walk.

He got a can of Budweiser from the refrigerator, popped the tab, and stood leaning on the sink counter drinking it, watching her snap uncooked spaghetti into lengths of about six inches and drop them into a big pot of boiling water.

"How were your students today?" he asked.

"Feisty as hell." She finished with the spaghetti and turned on the burner beneath a pot of sauce she must have made yesterday. "They don't like diagraming sentences in the middle of summer. I don't blame them. How was your day?"

Nudger told her about the man with the gun, how he'd aimed it right between his eyes from only a few inches away.

"It must have looked as big as a mine shaft," Claudia said, her own eyes as wide as Nudger's must have been looking at the gun.

"Now that you mention it," Nudger said, moving to the

refrigerator to get out the wine he'd brought Claudia when they'd had dinner here two nights ago. He unscrewed the cap to let it breathe. Thinking, at least as big as a mine shaft.

"That must have been scary as hell," Claudia said, working at the sink and glancing over her shoulder.

"A little bit scary." He nonchalantly sidled over and kissed the nape of her neck. This spaghetti business could wait, and at the price he'd paid, it wouldn't matter how long the wine breathed, even if it hyperventilated. "I've got an idea."

But she didn't share his idea. She handed him a spoon to stir the sauce.

She'd feel different about him later, he thought, stirring. After he'd relaxed her with the wine. It might be cheap, but it had a pretty high alcohol content.

Sly Nudger.

CHAPTER SIX

The jangling phone next to Claudia's bed pulled Nudger up from a deep sleep. He fought it, the way a fish fights the line. Finally he opened his eyes.

The bedroom was bright and warm with soft morning light. He reached out a hand to prod Claudia to ask her to pick up the phone. It was on her side of the bed.

His fingers found smooth, cool sheets.

No Claudia.

Nudger groaned and slid over to the other side of the mattress, groping for the phone. He dragged the plastic receiver to his ear, then mumbled a hello that sounded like someone strangling.

"Nudger?"

"Yeah. Who?"

"Charlie Roache here. It's done."

The bug man. "You. So soon?"

"I told you Nudger, this was a simple enough job. I set up a voice-activated system with real-time indicator, so if you need—"

"Wait a sec," Nudger said, trying hard to wake up all the way.

"Who's on the phone?" Claudia lip synced, walking in from the bathroom. She was fully dressed in her navy-blue skirt, white blouse, white high heels. Crisp and attractive and ready to leave for work.

"Bug man," Nudger said.

"Huh?"

"Yeah?" said the bug man.

"I was talking to someone else," Nudger said into the phone. He wriggled his eyebrows at Claudia in a silent signal for her to put her questions on hold until he was off the phone. She smiled.

"Claudia?" the bug man said.

"She's about to leave for work."

"You mean an exterminator?" Claudia asked.

Nudger shook his head no. Wriggled his eyebrows again.

"I don't wanna talk to her," said the bug man. "I just wanted to make sure she was the someone else you were talking to, so I could know it'd be okay for you to talk."

"How'd you know I was at Claudia's?" There were certain aspects of his work Nudger didn't want her involved in, like securities swindles and folks with guns.

"I called you, Nudger, remember? I figured you were at Claudia's if you weren't at your apartment or office, so I looked up her number."

Claudia moved toward the door, waving good-bye to Nudger.

"I'm barely awake," Nudger said. "We better talk later, maybe meet someplace."

Claudia had paused at the door, mouthing "me?" and tapping her chest between her teacup-sized breasts with her forefinger.

"Bug man," Nudger said.

"What?" asked the bug man.

"Not you," Nudger said.

"Not who?" Claudia whispered.

"Let's meet at Danny's in an hour," Nudger suggested, violently shaking his head no at Claudia. Not her at Danny's. She glared at him angrily and left.

"If you promise I don't have to eat any of them lead-and-lard doughnuts," the bug man said. "That guy Danny forces them on people."

"It's a promise."

As he hung up the phone, Nudger heard the apartment door to the hall open and shut. Claudia on her way. He lay still for a few minutes, until he picked up the muted sounds of her car starting down on Wilmington and driving away.

His teeth felt huge and fuzzy and he had a headache. He'd drunk too much wine at dinner. Then after dinner. He'd fallen asleep on the sofa while watching the Cardinals play the Mets on television. He didn't know who'd won the game. He vaguely remembered Ray Lankford striking out. Nudger had struck out, too, with Claudia. Dozed off, for Christsakes, like some kind of middle-aged husband in a TV sitcom. Well, he wasn't anybody's husband and he wasn't in a sitcom, even if he was into his forties. He'd make it up to Claudia soon. Make it up to himself. He wished the bug man had phoned an hour earlier and she was still here getting dressed. Undressed. Ah, well.

After a shower and the last inch of black liquid from Claudia's Mr. Coffee, his headache was gone and the morning light no longer hurt his eyes.

He locked the apartment behind him and drove the Granada west. The old car seemed to feel pretty good this morning, accelerating away from traffic signals without its customary wheeze and clatter, charging with spirit into its own elongated shadow.

The bug man was already at Danny's Donuts when Nudger arrived, sitting hunched over at the counter explaining to Danny how he'd already had breakfast and wasn't hungry. A white Styrofoam cup full of coffee was sitting in front of him. Danny had gotten that far.

"Ah, Nudger," the bug man said, swiveling on his stool. "Let's go up to your office where we can talk." He made frantic expressions with his eyes while he chewed his lower lip.

"You can talk private business here if you want," Danny offered. "I got work to do in back. That office'll be hot as Madonna, Nudge."

Nudger had never compared his office to Madonna. He didn't think the analogy held up.

"Besides," Danny said, "talk here'n you can have breakfast on the house."

The bug man slid off his stool and stood tucking in his silky, perspiration-stained shirt. He was already out the door when Nudger said, "I'll be back down later for a doughnut and coffee, Danny."

"Wait!" Danny said, bustling out from behind the counter. "Your friend forgot this." He handed Nudger the cup full of the truly horrible coffee, which oozed from the giant steel urn every morning, then wiped grease from his hands onto his white apron. "He mize well take it upstairs with him."

Nudger thanked him and hurried to catch up with the bug man, who was waiting outside his office door at the top of the stairwell.

When he tried to hand the bug man the coffee cup, the bug man sneered and crammed his hands deep into his pockets. He rocked his weight from leg to leg while Nudger keyed the lock and pushed the door open. Nudger hadn't needed the key, actually; he'd forgotten to lock up again when he'd left. He did that too often. Under present circumstances, he decided to be more careful.

Danny was right about the heat, but probably wrong about Madonna. Nudger switched on the air conditioner in the window near the desk. Like all things mechanical, it did not respond well to Nudger. It clattered, hummed, whined, then settled into a state of mechanical resignation and emitted a stream of reasonably cool air. Who knew how long it would last?

"Hotter'n Kathleen Turner in here," the bug man said, dropping into the chair in front of the desk and twitching around in discomfort.

Nudger excused himself, then went into the little half-bath and poured the coffee down the drain. He didn't run any water. Danny might hear it in the pipes and suspect.

The office was beginning to cool down, he noticed, when he returned and settled into his squealing swivel chair behind the desk. He saw that the glowing little window on his answering machine said he had two messages. Something to cope with later.

"So what's the deal?" he asked the bug man.

"I didn't let one of them doughnuts near me, but the coffee's even worse than the last time I was here."

"I mean about the Rand house."

"Oh. Like I said, the job's done. The place is wired for sound, every room. Voice-activated. The receiver's stashed nearby and will record everything that goes on in there even if it's mice making love. You got a real-time indicator so you know when what was said."

Nudger wiped his perspiring hand down his face, trying not to imagine what mice might say to each other if they could speak during intercourse. "Real time as opposed to unreal time?"

"Exactly. It'll all run together in unreal time on the tape, but you'll also get a reading of actual time. I mean, like, if Rand says something at ten o'clock, then nothing else till noon, the two things he said'll be one right after the other on the tape, seconds apart, but you can look at the real-time indicator to see what times he said them, how much time there was in between."

"So there's nobody personally monitoring what's being said in the house?"

"That'd be godawful expensive, Nudger. You want that?"

"No. How do I get the tape?"

The bug man reached into a pocket then laid a key on the desk. "The receiver and recorder are in the trunk of a blue Chevy parked in the block behind the house. Four hours' worth of tape, which should be enough since we're working voice-activated. Every evening you drive by there and open the trunk, take out the old cassettes, then insert fresh ones from the box in the trunk. There's a recorder in there for you to take with you and use. It'll give you the times the conversations took place. I want it back when this is over."

Nudger swiveled a few degrees in his chair and stared out at some pigeons on a ledge across the street. He thought the setup the bug man had described would do okay. He swiveled back to face the bug man and said so.

"I got the most sensitive listening devices on the market in that house," the bug man told him, "and the same goes for the recording equipment in the car trunk. You'll be able to hear a pen drop."

"A pin?"

"That I doubt." That bug man had apparently forgotten

about the amorous mice. He stood up. It was impossible for him to stay in one position very long, and the office was still uncomfortably warm.

"You're sure the bugs are planted where they won't be found?" Nudger asked.

"Don't ask such a thing, Nudger."

"But the family was home. You had to work fast."

"Fast is how I work anyway. And I like it when somebody's home and asleep where I'm doing a job. I know right where they are, so they ain't gonna come traipsing through the front door and surprise me. And I can hear their breathing and monitor it while I do my work. I know how sleep-breathing sounds, Nudger. If it changes and they're awake and listening, I'll know right away and get outa there. I can't be fooled."

"I didn't mean to question your competence," Nudger said. "It's just that this is a sticky matter."

"Hey, I understand. Another thing you might wanna know is your girlfriend's phone is clean. I got equipment that picks it up if the unit on the other end of the line is tapped, so our conversation this morning was private."

Ah, microchips! Nudger had a sudden thought. "What about my office phone?"

"Clean, too," the bug man said.

"How do you know?"

"This is where I called you from this morning, right there sitting in your chair. I only talk on clean lines. I mean, I got something at stake here, too."

"Now I know I need to remember to lock my door when I leave."

The bug man smiled. "You didn't forget. Locks ain't nothing to me but turnstiles." He told Nudger the license number of the blue Chevy, to prevent him from maybe tampering with the wrong car. Then he eased out the door.

Nudger heard his soft but rapid footsteps as he took the stairs down to the street door.

For the next half hour Nudger busied himself with paper work, shifting unpaid bills to the past-due pile, past-due bills to the final-notice pile. It made him feel better, getting a kind of overview of his finances.

He punched the Message button on his answering machine with some trepidation.

The first message was from Eileen, who had taken time out from her busy and profitable day as sales manager for the thinly disguised pyramid scam that sold household products, to call Nudger and threaten litigation if he didn't part with the twelve hundred dollars he owed her. He felt a surge of futile anger. It was only nine hundred. She knew that.

The second message was also from Eileen, threatening more litigation . . .

He fast-forwarded the machine, then erased both messages. He'd pay Eileen if he could possibly afford it; he knew she and Henry Mercato could use the money to buy more mutual funds. But he didn't have an extra nine hundred, or even an extra hundred, after paying his creditors who would actually turn off services or show up to repossess things. So he simply wouldn't think about Elieen. What was the use?

He knew what he was going to do, really, though his stomach kept trying to talk him out of it. Thanks to the bug man, he could stay clear of the Rand residence, but he had to keep a watch on Rand away from home. It was the only way he could do his job. Which was the only way he could get paid. Which was . . .

Well, the endless cycle of the common man.

He stood up from the squealing chair and grabbed his

sport jacket and tie from the closet and slung them over his arm.

In case the uncommon Dale Rand led him somewhere upscale.

And in case, if he got seriously injured along the way, he might be mistaken for somebody with medical insurance.

CHAPTER SEVEN

Nudger didn't go into the Medwick Building this time. Instead he sat across the street in the Granada where he could watch the entrance. Chestnut Street was crowded with pedestrians as well as vehicular traffic, so he didn't think he had to worry about the man with the gun and earring doing a rerun of the scene out by the golf course. Besides, Nudger knew Hammersmith was probably right; the guy was trying to scare him off the case rather than kill him, or there would have been no conversation and now there would be no Nudger. The problem was, he couldn't be sure it would be the same the next time. That left adequate room for fear.

His stomach twitched against his belt buckle as he thumbed an antacid tablet off the roll and popped it into his mouth. He got a little aluminum foil with it and spat it out, but not before it came into contact with a silver filling and caused a galvanic reaction that gave him a tiny but painful shock. He chewed while time crawled.

A little after one o'clock, Rand came walking out of the

Medwick Building and started up the sidewalk toward Nudger but on the other side of the street. He had on a terrific blue suit today, and a great shine on his shoes, and the intrepid bearing of a door-to-door evangelist who knew he was right by divine decree. All in all, he was bright as a new dime. Even on the teeming sidewalk, he strode in a straight line. Folks got out of his way because it was obvious he knew they would.

Nudger waited until Rand had passed, then climbed out of the Granada and walked a few steps behind him, on the opposite side of the street. He had difficulty keeping up. People kept bumping into him. A large woman juggling several shopping bags said something to him that he didn't understand, but that was unquestionably venomous.

Finally Rand stopped outside Miss Hullings, an upscale cafeteria, which had been in the same downtown location for decades. He glanced around, then went inside.

Nudger debated with himself about staying outside and waiting for Rand to emerge. Then he noticed he was perspiring, and he was still getting bumped by pedestrians even though he was leaning with his back against a brick wall. Also, he was hungry.

He crossed the street toward the cafeteria.

The pungent, mingled scents of the hot food increased his appetite. The restaurant wasn't crowded, though the serving line was still long. Many of the diners had already finished lunch and left to return to their offices.

Rand was at the other end of the line, near the cash register, when Nudger picked up his tray. While waiting for his meatloaf special to be served, he kept an eye on Rand to see where he'd sit.

As Rand walked away from the cashier, carrying his well-stocked tray, Nudger noticed for the first time that he was with the man who'd been behind him in line: a short, stocky type, bald on top but with a lot of frizzy gray hair around his ears. He was wearing a brown business suit, so Nudger didn't recognize him at first. Then, as he watched the two men sit down at a table, he realized the gray-haired man had been one of Rand's golf partners yesterday.

" . . . gravy or doncha?" a woman's irritated voice asked.

Nudger turned back toward his food. A tired looking server was standing with a ladleful of rich brown gravy poised over his mashed potatoes, her eyebrows raised inquisitively.

"Just a tad," Nudger instructed, remembering his cholesterol count from one of those free readings at Walgreen's Drugstore.

The woman emptied the entire greasy content of the ladle on his plate and handed it to him. He started to protest, but she was focusing all of her attention on the woman behind Nudger in line, another meatloaf special, asking the gravy question again. Nudger continued toward the cashier. On the way, he selected a large wedge of apple pie for dessert to console himself. If he was going to eat all that gravy, the additional cholesterol and calories of the pie could do scant additional harm. And it figured that Rand and his companion would be quite a while at lunch, the way their trays had been laden with food.

He thought he might be able to get a table close enough to overhear what they were saying, but as he was moving toward the last one within earshot, an old man in a golf cap and colorful flower-pattern tropical shirt took it. Nudger sat at a table behind him, angling his chair so he could see Rand and his lunch companion.

When the old guy in the flowered shirt had finished eating and was picking his teeth, Nudger was mechanically consuming apple pie, watching the balding gray-haired man remove a sheet of paper from his briefcase. The man brushed crumbs from the table, then laid the paper on it sideways so both he and Rand could see it. He talked to Rand about whatever was on the paper for about ten minutes, now and then tapping it with the tip of a silver pen he'd unclipped from his suit jacket's breast pocket. People didn't usually do that, carry pens clipped where fancy handkerchiefs sometimes rode. Nudger had carried a pen like that once and ruined a jacket with ink.

Rand folded the paper and slipped it into an inside pocket, and both men finished lunch in what appeared to be thoughtful silence.

As he followed them out of the restaurant and watched them shake hands and then part, it seemed no mystery to Nudger where Rand was walking—back to his office at Kearn-Wisdom Brokerage. The man with the halo of bushy gray hair seemed to be the most interesting to shadow.

Safest, too.

With an energetic, bouncy stride that made it difficult for Nudger to keep pace without breaking into a trot, Rand's lunch companion bounded north on Eleventh Street, then west on Washington, where he entered an old and ornate office building.

Breathing heavily, Nudger followed and watched him step into an elevator.

The lobby featured marbled walls, tarnished brass, and a tile floor marked with smudges where cigarettes had died beneath heels. Still, it was clean and in good repair; old as it was, the building was well maintained, as if waiting for better times.

The ancient brass arrow above the elevator door lurched to the 7 then stopped. Started. Retreated. Stopped again and remained frozen. It had made up its mind.

Nudger was alone in the lobby, which exited both on Washington and the next block, Lucas. There had once been small shops in the lobby, but now they were closed, their windows soaped over. He walked to the directory and saw that there was only one business on the seventh floor: Compu-Data Industries. He got in the elevator and rode.

Compu-Data Industries didn't occupy the entire floor. All of the offices appeared to be vacant except for the ones at the far end of the hall. Nudger walked toward them, his soles making soft sucking sounds on floor tiles softened by the heat. He hoped Compu-Data's offices were air-conditioned.

Two doors near the end of the hall had block lettering on their frosted glass. One read, "Compu-Data Industries," the other, "Dr. Horace Walling." So, a business not yet on the lobby directory. Maybe the doctor was a new tenant. Maybe he was, in fact, Dale Rand's physician. Or psychiatrist. This might prove interesting.

Nudger chastised himself for letting his imagination roam. His was the business of facts, and it was time to add to what he knew instead of standing in the hall speculating. He opened Dr. Wallace's door and stepped inside.

He found himself in a large, cool anteroom, alone. There was a grouping of black vinyl furniture around a low coffee table with a scattering of news magazines on it. A wide desk with a computer on it sat near another wide desk, which held only a green felt pad and an answering machine. There were framed, modern museum prints on the walls, the kind that made Nudger dizzy and slightly nauseated if he stared at them too long.

A woman said, "Oh!"

He turned and saw that a short, dark-complexioned woman in a tailored business suit had come through one of several doors on the back wall. She was about forty, plain looking except for exotic dark eyes that were heavily made up.

She said, "Sorry, I didn't realize someone had come in. Generally I'm behind my desk to greet visitors."

"Are you Dr. Walling's receptionist?" Nudger asked.

The woman gave him a smile that took away her plainness; the eyes had been right all along. "Generally speaking, yes."

"Is he, er, seeing patients today?"

She stared at him. "Patients?"

Nudger didn't know quite how to respond. "This is Dr. Walling's office, isn't it?"

"Sure it is. Generally speaking."

"What is he," Nudger asked in frustration, "a general practitioner?"

The woman smiled. "I meant, this is his office like it's his business."

"Well, isn't that how it generally is?"

She pursed her lips, then said, "Ah!"

"That's what I assumed the doctor might ask me to say," Nudger told her.

"Not likely. Dr. Walling isn't a medical doctor. He's a doctor of economics, and the chief executive officer of Compu-Data."

Nudger understood then. The directory had been right. There was indeed only one business on the seventh floor.

"So this is an economist's office—like a think tank? That what Compu-Data is?"

"No, sir. We create custom computer software." She went to the almost-bare desk and sat down, then folded her hands and looked up at him with her large dark eyes. The mascara made them seem bruised, as if she were recovering from a beating.

He decided it was time to retreat, but first he wanted to make sure of something.

"Isn't Dr. Walling a tall man with red hair? Walks with a limp?"

"You must have the wrong floor," the woman said. "Dr. Walling is average height with gray hair, and he certainly doesn't limp." Nudger was obviously making her uneasy now, wasting her time. She bent low from her chair and slid open a drawer. "If you'll excuse me . . ."

"Sure," he said. "Sorry. I must have been given wrong directions."

He backed to the door, then out into the uncomfortably warm hall.

Okay, he thought, walking slowly toward the elevator, a computer whiz with a doctorate in economics. Brilliant guy. But then, Dale Rand was probably no fool. It wasn't surprising he'd have friends he could talk to without getting them confused.

It occurred to Nudger that if the man with the gun and earring had been following him, the sparsely occupied office building would be a likely place for a confrontation. He actually felt the beat of his pulse in his throat.

He dropped to the lobby in the lurching old elevator, then walked quickly outside where there were people and sunlight. He might have heard echoing steps behind him in the lobby, but he couldn't be sure.

For the next few hours he sat in his car outside the Medwick Building, waiting for Rand to emerge again.

It was past four o'clock when the blue Caddy flashed from the shadows of the parking garage and turned west. Nudger started the Granada and followed.

Rush-hour traffic was building, and keeping Rand's car in sight wasn't so easy this time. There were too many vans and pickup trucks blocking Nudger's view, until Rand drove south on Tenth Street and got on the Highway 40 ramp to go west. By that time Nudger's nervous stomach was letting him know again he was in the wrong business. Antacid tablets didn't help much. Maybe because of the heat.

Or the fear.

Nudger thought Rand was probably going home, and he didn't want to park again on a secluded street in the county where the man with the gun might show up. The earring didn't seem very memorable now, only the gun.

Sure enough. Rand drove to Ladue and steered the Caddy into his driveway on Houghton Lane.

Nudger didn't even slow down as he drove past the house. It wasn't that he was afraid, he assured himself. He'd hired the bug man so there'd be no need for a stakeout here. The guy with the gun would inform Rand he wasn't being watched at home, and Rand might let down his guard elsewhere.

That was the strategy, anyway, so why mess it up just so Nudger could assure himself he was macho and unafraid? Like some insecure teenager who'd been challenged outside school.

"You don't have to prove yourself," a voice inside him said disdainfully, as he fought the impulse to defy the gunman. "For God's sake, grow up!"

Another, softer interior voice said, "Grow old."

He heeded them both and drove to his office.

CHAPTER EIGHT

Nudger set his alarm for 12:30 A.M., lay down on the bed fully clothed except for his shoes, then sat straight up as the alarm screeched at him.

Could this be? So soon?

Surely there was something wrong with the alarm.

But the clock actually read twelve-thirty, and the darkness and dearth of noise outside the window suggested twelve-thirty. Twelve-thirty, all right. He'd been asleep for more than three hours.

He slipped into his shoes and adjusted his wrinkled and twisted clothing; it knew that hours had passed. After rinsing off his face and combing his hair so it only stuck out on one side, he left his apartment and drove the Granada through the hot, humid night to the block behind Dale Rand's house in Ladue.

The houses here were on large, woody lots and set far back from the street, and there were few cars parked at the curb. The blue Chevy the bug man had described was parked near the cross-street where a small-strip shopping center anchored by a Quick Stop market sat in an oasis of light. The nondescript vehicle would attract little attention there.

He pulled the Granada in behind it, glanced around, then climbed out and walked to the back of the Chevy. The night was quiet but for the shrill scream of crickets, a primal background noise that settled in the depths of the mind like suppressed panic. He used the key the bug man had given him and opened the trunk.

The bug man had painted over the trunk light so it revealed the contents in a soft glow. There was the receiver and recorder, rectangular black objects with dim, pinpoint red lights to show they were in operation. Another recorder lay by itself on the left side of the trunk. A box of cassettes sat between them. Nudger saw a small white placard near the receiver and squinted at it to peer through the darkness. "Property of U. S. Government."

His stomach jumped. It took him a few seconds to realize that the bug man had placed the placard there to cause confusion if local authorities for some reason happened to look in the trunk. His contacts in law enforcement would tip him off, and he might have time to remove the equipment while various bureaucracies were still trying to sort out which government agency might actually have planted the devices. In government, the right hand seldom knew what half a dozen other hands were doing, or holding.

He had no trouble removing the dual cassettes in the master recorder and replacing them with fresh tape. The used cassettes and the smaller, spare recorder he slipped into his sport coat pocket. Then he shut the trunk and got back in the Granada.

There was a little activity down by the Quick Stop market, two guys talking alongside a pickup truck. One of them held an open can of soda or beer and waved it around while he talked. A blond woman was seated on the passenger side of the pickup, patiently waiting for them to finish their conversation. No one seemed to have seen Nudger, or paid any attention to him if they had.

He backed the Granada a few feet so he could clear the Chevy, cringing at the idea of trying to explain the contents of the trunk and his jacket pocket if he rammed the car from behind and the police arrived. Then he swung the dented red hood of the Granada out toward the center of the street and accelerated away from there.

He knew he wouldn't be able to sleep when he got home. He'd have to listen to the tapes.

Back in his apartment on Sutton, Nudger settled down on the sofa with the recorder on the cushion next to him. Balanced on the sofa arm was the box of MunchaBunch doughnuts he'd stopped for on the way. Danny would never know. He held a can of Budweiser in one hand, and with the other pressed the Power button, watching with satisfaction as the little red light winked on.

He pressed Rewind and ate a miniature doughnut while he waited for the tape to spin out, then pushed Play.

The real-time numerals on the recorder indicated that this conversation had taken place at 11:03 A.M., Sydney Rand calling the liquor store down by the Quick Stop market for a delivery. Two bottles of Gilbey's gin. The bug man had rigged his equipment to pick up both ends of phone conversations. They seemed to know Sydney at the liquor store, and assured her the delivery would be made within the half hour.

It was. Real time was 11:27 A.M. when the recorder played the brief conversation between Sydney and the delivery man at the door. Nudger reluctantly admitted to his subtle thrill of being secretly present in other people's lives. He didn't like that about himself, but there it was.

Then, almost immediately, real time read 5:12 P.M., when Rand had arrived home from Kearn-Wisdom. The Rands didn't greet each other like June and Ward Cleaver. Rand's wife, Sydney, spoke first:

" 'Bout time. Let's go."

Rand's voice: "Christ, I just walked in the—"

"I'm hungry, damnit. I wanna go out and get some supper."

"Hungry or thirsty?"

After a long silence. "I'll take my car. You can come along or stay here and eat by yourself."

"By myself suits me fine."

"It would. You do everything else by yourself."

"It seems that way sometimes. Where's Luanne?"

"Out. I figured you might know where."

"What's that supposed to mean? She's your daughter, too. Right? Right, goddamnit?"

"I haven't forgotten. Have you?"

"No. Even though she's . . . difficult."

"Oh, I'll just bet she is."

"Why don't you talk to her about it?" There was sadistic amusement in Rand's voice.

"You bastard! You know she won't talk to me."

"She's seventeen years old. It's natural she has her secrets."

"Natural, is it?"

"Why don't you take your car and go to a restaurant. I'd rather have a sandwich here at home."

Silence. Then Rand's voice again.

"And try not to have an accident on the way home."

* * *

Click. Whir. The real-time indicator read 7:24 P.M. A phone ringing, not in the room with Rand, but on the other end of a connection. The phone was answered, and a voice said, "Yes?"

Then Rand's voice, on the phone and in the room:

"Me, Horace. Can you talk?" Nudger assumed Rand was addressing Dr. Horace Walling.

"Until I'm interrupted. Did you act on the information I gave you?"

"All of it. We have nothing to sweat about. They're solid stocks with plenty of room to go up in price. How are you doing on the software?"

"Not to worry about the rest of the software, Dale. It'll be ready well before Labor Day."

"Then we've got no problem."

"You positive about those stocks?"

"Horace, Horace . . . Synpac is a sure thing by almost any standard. Fortune Fashions is a lock, too. The returns on their new spring line will drive the price way up within the month. It's the word from people who know, the kinda fairies who follow that stuff, sleep with the models and designers figuring to get rich by selling what they learn to the competition that needs it most. These people know book value like they know their phone numbers. Everything I learned confirmed your information. Believe me."

"I do believe you, or I wouldn't be doing this."

"We're getting the diversification we need. And in some cases I'm calling in favors, acting on inside information that'd make the SEC's hair curl if it knew."

"That's the kind of edge we can use."

They talked about stocks for another five minutes, then Rand said, "I can get away for a game of golf tomorrow, maybe have some more recommendations for your kind of research, see if they fit our pattern."

"Golf it is. Afternoon?"

"Afternoon."

"Uh, Dale, how are things with Sydney?"

"Up and down. Depends on how much she's drinking at the time."

"Yeah . . . well. How about Luanne?"

"I don't know where she is right now. I hardly ever do. That's Luanne these days."

"Be cautious with Luanne, Dale."

"What's that supposed to mean?"

"Just what I said. You know how it is with teenage girls."

"Everything's under control, Horace. Don't sweat any of this."

"Best be careful what you say. I don't trust the office phones."

"Nobody's gonna tap your phone, Horace. When would they get a chance, the way you spend your evenings there?"

"But why take the chance?"

"So don't take it. Call me from a public phone when we need to talk."

"You might laugh, but I intend to do that from now on. I'm a prudent man, Dale."

"That's why I bet against you when we golf."

"You're the one who leaves your putts short."

A laugh, more resentful than amused. "See you tomorrow at the club."

The connection was broken.

Nudger took a sip of beer. The real-time indicator flashed to 10:01 P.M.

"You still up?" Sydney had returned home. Her voice was slow, unsure. She sounded drunk.

"I was waiting for you."

"Well, I'm goin' up to bed."

"If you do that you'll pass out within two minutes."

"Tha's the idea. What the bed's for. Our bed, anyways. Sole purpose."

"For Christsake, Syd."

"Night. Fuck you."

Flash to 12:25 A.M., less than an hour before Nudger had removed the recorder and cassettes from the blue Chevy's trunk: moans, bedsprings creaking, a rhythmic knocking sound, probably the headboard banging against the wall.

Embarrassed and feeling like the tawdry P.I. some people thought him to be, Nudger listened for a few minutes, then fast-forwarded.

The rhythmic knocking ceased, as did the moans. Now there was soft sobbing.

That was the end of the recording.

Nudger punched Rewind and rested his head on the sofa back, listening to the cassette whir. There hadn't been much conversation in the Rand household; two cassettes hadn't been needed. But maybe tomorrow would be different. Though it didn't sound as if the talk would be any friendlier, even if the absent Luanne showed up. This was obviously one of those unhappy families miserable in its own way.

The recorder clicked. Nudger glanced down and saw that it had finished rewinding and had switched itself off.

He decided the recorder had the right idea, so he ate the last doughnut, took a last sip of beer to help him sleep, and went to bed.

He didn't sleep, though. He lay there sweating with the

air conditioner on high, trapped in slowly passing real time and thinking about Fortune Fashions. And Synpac. And book value.

Whatever that was.

CHAPTER NINE

Claudia wasn't scheduled to teach until noon, so Nudger met her at the Bradmoor restaurant, near Clayton and Big Bend. They ate breakfast there occasionally, when Nudger simply had to escape the obligatory Dunker Delite and acidic coffee. After all the MunchaBunches he'd consumed last night, he didn't want a Dunker Delite anywhere near him.

When he arrived a few minutes before ten, Claudia was already in one of the orange vinyl-upholstered booths by a window, sipping coffee and gazing out at the bright morning. She looked up at him and he saw surprise and mild curiosity on her face.

"What happened to you?" she asked.

"Happened? Me? Oh, I was up most of the night. It shows?"

"You look like you were in an accident."

He slid into the seat across from her. She looked fresh and put together, her dark hair swept back off her fore-head, her deep brown eyes tugging at something in his heart. His weariness and the edge of his excitement fell away. Being in Claudia's presence did that; he often thought inanely that she had the same relaxing effect as a warm bath. He never had mentioned that to her, though; she might not take it the right way.

"Why did you want to meet here so late?" she asked. He'd phoned her at eight o'clock and awakened her. "I was hungry an hour ago."

"This is my second stop."

A pretty young waitress of apparent Indian descent arrived and took their orders. Claudia asked for her usual Number Seven on the menu. Nudger oddly enough wasn't hungry, so he requested only a bagel with cream cheese and jelly. The waitress wrote all this down, then topped off Claudia's cup and poured some coffee for Nudger, spilling a little, and glided away.

Claudia held her cup but didn't drink from it. Instead she leaned back and smiled faintly at Nudger, waiting. She obviously knew he'd been up last night because of the case he was working on, and the time had come, as it often did in his job, when he needed to share. Claudia always listened, and often provided insight.

Nudger told her about last night and the contents of the tape. She sat quietly without interrupting, now and then sipping coffee, tapping a red-enameled fingernail on the table.

When he was finished, she said, "Look out."

He flinched, thinking the dribbling waitress had returned with more hot coffee. But when he glanced around there was no one within twenty feet. "Look out for what?" he asked.

"I don't know exactly, which makes it all the more difficult to look out for. But there might be something explosive in the Rand family. Didn't you sense it when you listened to the tape?"

"I sensed it even before that," he said, "when that guy pointed a gun at me."

"These are not happy campers, Nudger."

"They must get along to some extent. Remember how the tape ended, in their bedroom?"

"I thought you said it ended with her sobbing."

"Tears of joy, maybe. Some women do that."

Claudia grinned at that one. "Did he tell her he loved her?"

"No, but they've been married a while."

"What you described sounded to me like marital rape."

"I didn't hear Sydney say no."

She gave him a look that suggested he could only guess at his hopelessness.

"Anyway, they have a teenage daughter. My impression was they were trying to keep their lovemaking quiet out of habit, even though she wasn't home."

She shook her head. "Nudger, Nudger, maybe she was home."

"What does that mean?"

But he had to wait for an answer because the Indian woman arrived with their orders. He placed his chin in his palm and stared out the window at the cars waiting for the traffic light to change. The intersection was in Clayton near the city line, and there were always attorneys who worked in Clayton driving past on the way to their offices. Or attorneys who lived in Clayton but worked downtown, going the other direction. That's where most law offices were, downtown or in Clayton. Lots of expensive cars, and more people talking on car phones than at any other intersection in the metropolitan area. Nudger sometimes wondered who they were talking to, sitting staring at the traffic signal with their phones glued to their ears. Maybe they were talking to the guy in the next car. Nudger thought he might be able to afford a phone for the Granada soon, call Danny from anywhere and see if anyone had been by, or was waiting upstairs in the office. Actually, it wasn't such a dumb idea.

The waitress had gone, leaving behind a machine-gun stitch pattern of coffee spots on the table. She'd barely missed Nudger's hand. He began spreading cream cheese on his bagel, and Claudia said, "That furtive sex you heard might mean something else."

He stopped what he was doing and set the knife down on the edge of the plate. She was looking knowingly at him. He didn't like what he was thinking. "You suppose it's possible?"

"I teach school. I know it's not only possible, it happens more than most people imagine. It could be that Rand was in bed with the daughter and didn't want to wake his wife."

Nudger hadn't considered it. He had to admit that Sydney had sounded unapproachable when she'd gone up to bed. And judging by the weariness in her slurred voice, she'd probably fallen into a deep alcohol slumber. Which might have encouraged Rand to sneak into Luanne's room.

He began spreading cream cheese again. "You might be right."

"I'm not saying that's how it is," Claudia said, "just how it seems. Maybe when you listen some more, you might find out for sure. Then, if it's true, you're going to have to do something about it."

"That complicates everything," he said, knowing that what she'd said was true, he'd have to act on that kind of information.

"And makes it more dangerous. Men do anything to keep that kind of information secret. Anything."

Nudger was thinking of Norva Beane, how she'd take that kind of news. Maybe she suspected it. Maybe Sydney suspected, too. If it happened to be true. He couldn't be sure. It was certainly something else to fret about and twist his intestines into complex knots. He was beginning to wish he hadn't come here and had instead braved the double threat of a Dunker Delite and Danny's coffee. It would have been free, and without the side order of worry.

Claudia said, "You mentioned this was your second stop this morning. What was your first?"

"My stockbroker."

Claudia raised an eyebrow. "I didn't know you had one."

"I didn't until this morning."

Her eyes flared in alarm. "Nudger—"

"I bought some great stocks," he said. "Benny Flit told me they were bound to increase in value. I'm getting the inside info on these securities from some real pros doing their own investing. Since they don't know anyone's listening, the information's all the more valuable."

"Flit? He's your broker?"

Nudger nodded.

"Who's he with?"

"With?"

"Which brokerage firm?"

"Just Flit. He's in business for himself. He's Danny's cousin."

She stared out the window in apparent disbelief. "Well, he's certainly made Danny a wealthy man."

"I'm not relying on his advice," Nudger said. "And I'm not telling him where I'm getting my recommendations, or even that I have access to inside information. The SPCA has very strict rules against that."

"SEC," Claudia corrected. "The SPCA is the Society for the Prevention of Cruelty to Animals. Come to think of it—"

"I don't see how I can miss," Nudger interrupted. "Fortune Fashions is supposed to have a dynamite new fall line, and I found out on my own that Synpac Industries manufactures guidance systems for nuclear missiles."

"Isn't the government destroying nuclear missiles?"

"That has nothing to do with the price/earnings ratio of the manufacturer. And Fortune Fashions is reintroducing the feather boa. Flit thinks, anyway."

She leaned toward him and placed both her hands over his. Gently. "SPCA, price/earnings ratio . . . Nudger, you have a little amount of knowledge, which is the dangerous thing. Please don't invest in these enterprises."

"I told you, I already have. This morning. My retainer for this case will cover the check."

"What about the back alimony you owe?"

He was getting exasperated. She simply refused to understand that a small risk could mean a great gain. "Damnit, that's the main reason I'm doing this—so I can pay off Eileen and get her and Henry Mercato off my back!"

Claudia released his hands and sat back, an expression of weary resignation on her lean features. "Okay, I'm convinced."

Nudger grinned. "Good."

"Convinced that you're beyond reason." She spread strawberry jam on her toast, then took another bite of egg. "How much have you gambled?"

"Invested. Twelve hundred dollars. At least that was the value of my holdings this morning."

"Uh-hm. Well, it could be worse." She sighed and

smiled and patted his wrist. "It could work out. You might double your money." Swinging over to his side now. Finally grasping the possibilities.

Feeling better, Nudger finished his coffee and signaled the waitress for more. Only half a cup. He intended to drive downtown and make sure Rand's car was in the Medwick Building garage, then follow him when he left the office for lunch and his golf game.

Maybe Rand would meet Horace Walling for lunch before they played golf, this time someplace where Nudger could work into position to overhear their conversation. It wasn't out of the question that Nudger would purchase more stock. He could borrow some money. Or write some Visa and MasterCard checks on his charge accounts, invest the money, then pay it back with a neat profit left over even after paying off the balance due on the accounts. It should be easy to come out ahead that way, as long as he settled the accounts in full within a reasonable amount of time; those credit-card interest rates were criminal.

Rand was doubtless in his office at Kearn-Wisdom, which meant he wouldn't be going anywhere for a while. So Nudger had some extra time this morning.

He smiled at Claudia. "Suppose after breakfast we drive to your apartment?"

She shook her head. She seemed angry at him for some reason. "No, I'm going out to the school early. It's cool and quiet there and I can grade some papers without interruption."

"You could grade them tonight."

"They have to be ready for today's English class." She forked the last bite of her Number Seven into her mouth, chewed, swallowed, then downed the rest of her coffee. "In fact, I'd better get going or I won't have time to finish." She slid gracefully out of the booth and stood up, fishing in her purse for her wallet.

"I'll take care of it," Nudger said, picking up the two checks and moving them to the far side of the table, well out of her reach.

"I forgot," she said, "you have investments and can afford to treat." Keeping her legs straight, she bent low from the waist and kissed his forehead.

"Soon we'll be having breakfast someplace with table-cloths," he assured her.

As she was walking away, he heard her say, "I promise to buy a feather boa, but I have more use for a nuclear missile."

CHAPTER TEN

At 11:45 A.M. Rand's fancy black Caddy peeked shyly from the cavernous entrance of the Medwick Building parking garage, as if checking to make sure a wicked summer shower wouldn't mar its glossy wax job. Then the car emerged into benign sunshine and headed like a parade down Chestnut.

Nudger followed in the rusty Granada, like the detail assigned to clean up after the horses.

When the Caddy drove south on Tenth, then took the ramp onto Highway 40, Nudger figured Rand was on his way to his golf date with Horace Walling, so he settled back in the seat and listened to blues on KDHX, letting the Caddy run far ahead so Rand wouldn't notice him in the rearview mirror. Chadwood Country Club was fifteen minutes away.

He was almost caught daydreaming with Dr. John in New Orleans when the Cadillac veered onto an exit ramp and drove north on Hanley Road. Nudger almost lost his life cutting in front of a madly speeding trash truck as he switched lanes in order to follow.

Here was something interesting. Rand was driving toward Clayton, where Fred McMahon had his office.

Rand made a left onto Bonhomme and steered the Caddy into the tiny lot of a luxury hotel. He eased the big car into the lot's only remaining parking slot. Parking spaces were even rarer in Clayton than downtown.

Nudger pulled the Granada to the curb and sat alongside a Bus Stop sign. He watched as Rand got out of the Caddy, shrugged into his suit jacket, then skirted the swimming pool and entered the hotel's restaurant.

There was a growl and a hiss behind Nudger. His startled glance darted to his rearview mirror and found it full of bus. He raised both hands helplessly, then meekly waved what he hoped was an "I'm sorry" and pulled back into the stream of traffic on Bonhomme. Didn't even look.

Brakes squealed, tires *Eeeeeped*. A guy in a shiny BMW convertible shook the receiver of a cellular phone at Nudger as if he might hurl it in anger. Nudger waved another "I'm sorry" and made a right turn at the next intersection.

There was a parking space! A florist's van was angling out into traffic. Nudger double-parked and waited patiently until the van had left, then he tapped the accelerator and zoomed forward before anyone else could swoop into the space. Once the Granada was safely tucked against the curb, he fed the meter and hurried back to the hotel.

He was walking past the pool when he glanced over and saw that he didn't have to go inside to keep tabs on Rand. The restaurant's wall of windows looked out on the pool, and there was Rand at a window-side table with another man, having lunch.

Nudger casually wandered into the pool area, then over

to a white plastic chair and sat down, as if he were a guest, maybe with a kid or wife in the pool. He sat at an angle, his hand raised as if shielding his eyes from the sun, as if watching the half dozen people in the water splash around. But he could also keep an eye on the back of Rand's neck and would know when he got up to leave.

Right now Rand showed no inclination to get up. He gestured as he talked to the man across the table, whose features Nudger couldn't make out through the reflections on the glass, then raised a goblet of wine.

The plastic chair heated up, and sunlight glancing off the glittering water was making Nudger uncomfortable. He continued to sit calmly, as if there were nowhere else he'd rather be, hoping no one would notice the sweat rolling down his face and neck, dampening his collar. Within fifteen minutes the back of his shirt and the backs of his pants legs were molded by heat and perspiration to the plastic chair. He was learning how it felt to be sculpture.

An obese woman in a remarkably skimpy swimsuit climbed laboriously out of the pool and walked toward the hotel entrance, dripping a trail of water and carrying a towel. As she passed the area where Rand and his companion were sitting inside the restaurant, her shadow muted the reflecting glass and Nudger got a look at the other man.

He was neither Horace Walling nor Fred McMahon. He was a big man with broad shoulders, a gaunt face with dark hair growing to a sharp widow's peak, extremely arched, thick dark eyebrows, a prognathous jaw. It was a face a mother would describe as strong rather than ugly, actually knowing better. Also a face vaguely familiar to Nudger, though he couldn't place it.

He figured if he might have seen the man somewhere before, it might be vice versa, so he stood up casually, peeling the chair off his back and buttocks, then ambled out of the pool area.

That worked out very well. He found a seat in a soft leather chair in the air-conditioned lobby, where he could relax with an open magazine in his lap and see Rand's car in the small parking lot out front. He was sure Rand would drive to his golf date after lunch. Maybe the big man with the skull-like features would play, too. Nudger wondered if he thought the guy looked familiar because he resembled the actor, Jack Palance, but rejected the idea. He didn't really look like a young Palance; his eyebrows were bushier and peaked in those sharp V's over what appeared to be pale eyes, and his hairline was different and had receded farther than Palance's, even in the actor's old age.

About one o'clock Rand appeared outside, standing in the bright sun next to his Cadillac along with the other man. The guy was taller than Palance; he was maybe six and a half feet. Despite the width of his shoulders he was lean; his expensive gray suit was draped elegantly on a rangy frame. He was wearing a white shirt, silky blue-and-gray striped tie, flashing gold jewelry in the summer sun. Nudger almost had who he was, when the man reached in his suit's coat pocket and put on a pair of darkly tinted glasses.

After Rand and the man shook hands and Rand had climbed into the Caddy, the tall fashion plate stood with a hand raised to touch the frames of his glasses and watched the car glide out of the lot. Then he strode out of sight, moving with the liquid ease of an athlete. Maybe he'd played pro basketball, and that was where Nudger had seen him.

Nudger got up from his chair and went over to look out one of the hotel doors. He was just in time to see the tall man drive away in a late-model silver Mercedes sedan. Also in time to catch a look at the car's license plate number, which he jotted down in the margin of one of the pages of the magazine he was carrying.

He tore the corner with the license number from the page, set the magazine on a table, and found the phones in the lobby.

Hammersmith would be happy to run the number through the system and give him the Mercedes owner's name. Well, not exactly happy. But he'd do it.

After the ensuing telephone argument with Hammersmith, Nudger decided he didn't want to go near the golf course this afternoon. It was too hot to sit in his parked car and watch people in loose clothes whack and chase small balls, and what would he learn? Also, the guy with the gun and the earring might be out there.

That wasn't the reason why Nudger wasn't going there, the guy with the gun. And the earring. The reason was . . . well, he was hired to see if Rand was going to make contact with Fred McMahon, so why not follow McMahon? It made just as much sense, in a way.

He drove over to McMahon's office on Forsyth, but discovered McMahon wasn't there. A smashing blond receptionist told him Mr. McMahon wasn't due in today, eyeing him as if he might be the police. Which he might have been, considering McMahon's problems.

From a public phone he called McMahon's house. When a woman answered and asked who was calling, he used a name he'd noticed on one of the office doors where McMahon worked. McMahon wasn't home, the woman said. She didn't know when to expect him. Any message? "Naw, I'll catch Fred later," Nudger assured her, and hung up.

This was hard work, staying away from the golf course. He drove back to his office and spent the afternoon doing paperwork and waiting for Hammersmith to call about the Mercedes license number.

Actually he did little work. Mostly he paced impatiently. Time and guilt hung heavy in the air.

When his back began to ache, he sat down and played the tape he'd picked up last night from the trunk of the blue Chevy. This time when it reached the bedroom part, he listened all the way through, to everything. The moans, the headboard banging against the wall, and something he hadn't noticed before in the middle of that section of tape, a soft female voice, pleading, perhaps with passion. Perhaps. Nudger couldn't make out her words.

He switched off the recorder and raised his arms to stretch. The swivel chair squealed as if in pain as he leaned farther back and meshed his fingers behind his neck and massaged stiff muscles with his thumbs.

He replayed the pleading and moans in his mind and thought they sounded like Sydney's, but he couldn't be sure. He didn't want what Claudia had suggested to be true. Couldn't Rand be a simple coconspirator with Mc-Mahon, a swindler as Norva suspected, without molesting his daughter?

Life under the rock, Nudger thought, where I work.

Claudia had been right about one thing. Nowhere on the tape was love mentioned.

The phone's jangle startled him, making him tip even farther backward. The chair screamed and Nudger's frantic, clawing hand found the corner of the desk. He managed to steady himself and sit upright. Realizing he'd bent back a fingernail on the desk, he lifted the receiver and identified himself.

Hammersmith's voice said, "Mirabelle Rogers."

Nudger said, "You can't fool me, Jack. I recognize your voice."

"She lives at 4360 Waterman," Hammersmith said, not acknowledging Nudger's stab at humor. "She's the owner of a 1993 Mercedes 560 SL sedan, color silver. You already know the license plate number."

"The driver I saw this afternoon didn't look like a Mirabelle," Nudger said.

"Mr. Mirabelle, maybe. Some kinda foreign name, huh?"

"Could be," Nudger said, trying without success to envision a country where a man would be named Mirabelle Rogers.

"Those Mercedes sedans are very expensive machines," Hammersmith said.

"I can imagine." Nudger asked for the address again, and wrote it down on a past-due phone bill. "Possibly you could find out," he said to Hammersmith, "if this Mirabelle has any sort of arrest record."

"Possibly," Hammersmith said, and hung up, perhaps made even more abrupt by the heat that plagued the city.

Nudger replaced the receiver, then went into the tiny half-bath and drank a glass of cool tap water. He let the water run for a while over his wrists, staring at himself in the mirror and wondering which of him was real. St. Louis summers could do that to people's minds.

Feeling better, he returned to sit behind his desk. He played the tape again, listening even more closely to the soft pleas and moans.

He still couldn't be positive that the woman was—or wasn't—Sydney Rand.

He ran the tape again.

He wondered if Claudia was home.

CHAPTER ELEVEN

Nudger slipped the recorder into his pocket, then locked the office behind him and went downstairs to Danny's Donuts. He'd gotten tired of calling Claudia's number and getting no answer.

Danny was behind the stainless-steel counter, draining black sludge from the bowels of the huge coffee urn. "Got plans for tonight, Nudge?"

"Gotta work," Nudger said. Which was true. Not that he wasn't going to take time for supper, or at least a snack. MunchaBunches, maybe. Not what Danny was sure to offer.

Danny absently polished the steel urn with the grayish towel he kept tucked in his belt. He nodded toward the display case where Dunker Delites lay on white napkins like casualties after a major battle. "Help yourself if you want," he said.

Nudger thought he would help himself by not eating a Dunker Delite. "No thanks, Danny. I'm supposed to meet Claudia for dinner."

"Thought you was gonna work." Danny's basset-hound features revealed no suspicion. His somber dark eyes remained trusting and innocent.

"Afterward," Nudger said. "You know how it is, lots of my work's done at night."

"Like a real-estate agent," Danny said.

"Something like that. What I came in for was to see if you were done with this morning's *Post-Dispatch*."

"Sure. Take it with you if you want. I'm gonna be here another half hour before I close up."

Nudger watched the last of the day's dark brew ooze from the urn's spigot. "What if somebody comes in and orders coffee?" It was always possible.

"I got some in a pot just in case. Shame you're having dinner with Claudia tonight. I was gonna see if you wanted to have supper with me and Ray."

Ray was Danny's incredibly lazy nephew who lived down on Manchester in the St. James Apartments, surviving on various disability pensions, government handouts, and interest from a generous out-of-court settlement after faking (Nudger was sure) an injured back after a bus he was on five years ago had a minor accident.

"Ray gonna cook?" Nudger's delicate stomach twitched at the mere suggestion.

"Naw. I'm picking up some White Castle hamburgers on the way over there. We're gonna sit around and watch the ball game outa Chicago on WGN."

"Sorry to miss it," Nudger said. Ray was a Chicago Cubs fan. Another reason to despise him.

After leaving the doughnut shop, Nudger sat in his car for a few minutes, leafing through the grease-stained newspaper until he found the Jack in the Box coupons he knew were in there. After creasing the paper with his thumbnail, he tore out the coupons with reasonable neatness, then studied them. He decided on the grilled chicken sandwich, french fries, and a chocolate milk shake, then drove down Manchester through the heart of Maplewood and went through the drive-thru. He was glad he no longer had to speak to a clown.

After he ate supper his stomach felt a little tender, so he bought some MunchaBunch doughnuts and had them for dessert as he drove toward the address Hammersmith had given him for Mirabelle Rogers.

It was a brick apartment building that looked as if it had gone condo. This was a good block of Waterman, a fairly expensive neighborhood in the Central West End. Mirabelle's building was old but in excellent condition and looked as if it contained eight or ten units. There was a fancy black-iron fence, and an iron-barred gate between two brick pillars topped by what looked like stone wolfhounds resting on their haunches. Beyond the gate were some well-tended yews, a carpetlike green lawn, and a stone-arch entrance with an intercom box mounted by the door. All of the windows had identical rust-colored canvas awnings for eyebrows, and there was a similar awning over the entrance.

Nudger parked across the street and wiped grease and sugar from his fingers with his napkin, then stuffed the napkin into the white paper sack the doughnuts had been in, wadded the sack tight so the "MunchaBunch" lettering wouldn't show, and dropped it on the floor on the passenger side. He looked around but didn't see the silver Mercedes parked anywhere.

That figured. There was probably an alley and garage behind the building. The Mercedes wasn't the kind of car to leave parked overnight at the curb.

He drove down the block and made a left turn, then

another left into a narrow alley lined with the little gray dumpsters that the city provided for trash.

There was a garage, all right. Brick, like the main building. All of its metal overhead doors were closed, and all had locks. Each door was marked with the owner's unit number.

Nudger decided to park down the street on Waterman, then walk into the building's vestibule, if that was possible without using the intercom, and find out which unit belonged to Mirabelle Rogers.

He didn't get the chance. As he turned the corner he saw the big silver Mercedes parked in front of the building. A petite blond in a yellow summer dress was climbing into the passenger side. The tall man who didn't quite look like Jack Palance was walking around the back of the car. He was wearing gray slacks and a navy-blue blazer tonight, still flashing gold rings, watch, and cuff links, using them like a neon sign that blinked M-O-N-E-Y.

Out of sight of the woman, he broke stride for a moment and used the nail of a little finger to dislodge something stuck between his teeth. Then he climbed into the car, steered it away from the curb, and headed slowly down the street, away from Nudger.

Heaven-sent, Nudger thought, slipping the Granada into Drive and following.

Or maybe hell-sent.

He wasn't sure which and didn't want to think about it.

CHAPTER TWELVE

They drove west on the Forest Park Expressway, then north on the Inner Belt. Near the airport, the Mercedes crowded out some lesser vehicles and exited on Interstate 70. A few minutes later it left the highway and wound through a maze of side streets.

Nudger followed at a distance, getting uneasy. This was a rough neighborhood. The streets were lined with small houses that hadn't seen fresh paint in years and yards that were bare earth, which contained either piles of trash or old cars up on blocks and in various stages of repair. Now and then someone on the sidewalk or in one of the yards stared after the Mercedes with curiosity and hostility. Nudger was glad he was driving the rusty old Granada, which seldom drew second looks. Homeboy Nudger.

The houses got farther apart and were somewhat better maintained. Then the Mercedes turned onto a narrow street, which wound around trees, past a cemetery. A sign identified it as Latimer Lane. It curved sharply and became a badly paved road in an area behind the cemetery.

The Mercedes's brake lights flared. It came to a stop in the middle of the desolate strip of pocked pavement.

Nudger eased the Granada to the shoulder and watched as the tall man climbed out and stood in the road while the blond woman scooted over behind the wheel and adjusted the seat. The man leaned low to kiss her, then stood with his hands on his hips, watching as she drove away.

When the Mercedes was out of sight, he strode across the road and into the yard of a small, flat-roofed house isolated on a large lot overgrown with weeds. It had a flat porch roof, which was angled sharply to one side, as if half of it might be missing. A medium-sized maple tree grew from the wheel cavity of a truck tire that had been painted white and laid flat in the front yard years ago when the tree was a sapling. Nudger thought it must have been a real conversation piece in its day, when flowers were planted inside the tire.

The nearest neighbor was about a hundred yards away, on the opposite side of the road, near where Nudger was parked. On the far side of the house was what looked like a drainage ditch and a grove of locust trees, with thicker woods beyond. The house itself was surrounded by out-of-control shrubbery trying to act like trees, some of it entwined with vines bearing beautiful red roses. Here and there were the broken remains of wooden trellises, which had once disciplined and displayed the magnificent roses.

Nudger began to sweat. His stomach growled. The sun was low, but at least an hour away from setting. He knew that what he must do would be safer under cover of darkness, yet he couldn't afford to wait.

Something like duty called. Or identity. If he couldn't do this, what was he? What was his future? This wasn't like refusing to drive out to the golf course to spy on Rand;

there was no self-serving rationale available for him to cower behind with mock dignity.

Thunder roared overhead as an airliner passed low enough for him to glimpse faces in the windows. Apparently he was in the flight pattern of planes landing at Lambert International Airport. The car seemed to rock with the airliner's violent passage.

He drove down the street and parked on the other side of the crumbling concrete bridge that crossed the drainage creek. Since St. Louis was suffering one of its summer droughts, he was sure the creek would be dry.

With a glance in both directions to make sure he wasn't being observed, he got out of the car and walked into the shade of the trees.

Another aircraft racketed overhead, seeming to shake the leaves. It left a low, shrieking whistle hanging in the disturbed air, like a futile protest of its passing.

Moving through the brown carpet of last year's leaves, Nudger made his way down the slope to the creek bed—dry, as he'd assumed—then up the other side, into low underbrush. It was still hot in the dappled shade of the woods, and mosquitoes found him and feasted. A squirrel gave him a horrified look and skittered up a tree. Nudger crept forward and was shocked to find himself only twenty feet from the side of the house.

All of the windows were open and had rusty, torn, and patched-up screens. Except for the end one, where a window fan was humming and rattling loud enough to cover his stealthy advance to the rose-strewn shrubbery near the house. Fine. He wouldn't have to wait for airliners to blast overhead so he could make his moves.

Ignoring the urging of his stomach to emulate the squirrel and run in the opposite direction, he made his way to one of the windows and peered inside.

A bathroom, with an old pedestal washbasin and a sagging shower curtain. Unoccupied, thank God. Nudger didn't want the embarrassment of being mistaken for a peeping Tom added to the agony of being beaten or killed if he were discovered. He knew thinking that way didn't make much sense, but some priorities you couldn't choose. He remembered the time someone had tried to run him down with a truck, and his deep regret as he became resigned to impending death was that he happened to be wearing the ripped underwear he'd long intended to replace, while just the day before, he'd had on jockey shorts so current that they still had the label firmly attached at both ends.

He could hear voices as he crept along the side of the house to the next window. *Ouch!* He almost yelped as a thorn from the climbing roses bit the back of his hand like a snake. Sucking on the puncture to numb its pain, he leaned forward and looked in the window.

It was dim on the other side of the screen, and it took his eyes a moment to adjust. He stayed very still, holding his breath.

There was the Mercedes driver, talking to another man. Nudger's stomach tightened as the listener turned slightly and his face became visible. He was the black man with the gun and earring.

" . . . thought it'd be a good idea for you to see this," the tall man from the Mercedes was saying. Now, though, he wasn't talking to the gunman from the golf course, but to someone off to the side.

Nudger brushed a mosquito from his cheek and quietly shifted position to gain a better angle of vision. His body grew rigid and still.

The third man was Dale Rand.

"We wanted you convinced that it was serious," the tall man said.

His head bowed, Rand said, "I was convinced of that from the beginning."

"Not convinced enough," said the gunman. He glanced at the floor as he spoke, and Nudger realized they'd been discussing some object at their feet.

"Can I count on you?" the tall man asked Rand.

"I told you at lunch you didn't need to worry about me."

"And I wanted to believe you, but you weren't very persuasive. So I'm asking again, can I count on—"

"—Of course you can. Do I really have a choice? I mean, what'll happen to me if I say no."

"Well," the gunman said, "it's one of the two things you have to do for sure in this world, and it isn't taxes."

"You never had a choice from the beginning," the tall man said. "Guys like you always figure that out too late. But somehow you got lucky. With you, it doesn't have to be too late for the big choice. I just wanna make sure you understand that."

"You'll get it all, I promise."

"Getting it isn't enough. Don't we have that straight yet?"

Rand pressed his cupped hand to the side of his neck and looked down at the floor. "It's straight, all right." He jerked his head to the side to look away. "Oh, Jesus!"

"He's found religion," the gunman said. "I've seen that before. And how soon it can be lost."

A plane roared overhead, shaking the house.

"You park where I told you?" the tall man asked, when the noise had faded.

Both Rand and the gunman nodded.

"Let's leave the back way, then," he said, "so we can

lock up behind us. There's a lotta crime in this neighbor-hood."

They moved out of sight, toward the rear of the house.

Nudger backed away into the foliage, then moved paral-lel to the creek until he could see the backyard. Even over the hum and vibration of the window fan, he heard Rand say, "Oh, Jesus!" again inside the house. A moment later the three men emerged and trudged down the three rickety wooden steps to the walk that was overgrown with weeds. Rand was staring hard at the ground, clutching the back of his head now, as if trying to contain pain. The gunman was smiling. The big man looked unconcerned.

"Take him to his car, Aaron," he said.

Aaron the gunman nodded and gripped Rand's elbow, as if Rand might be weak or ill. Rand glared at him but walked beside him toward an open wooden gate in the back of the yard.

Nudger saw two cars parked on a narrow gravel road that ran along the back of the property. One was Rand's black Cadillac. The other was a low-slung red sports car, a convertible with its top raised. A Porsche, Nudger thought, but wasn't sure. They weren't parked directly behind the house, but instead were near the remains of a shack, which looked as if it had been gutted by fire years ago.

The big man followed Rand and Aaron to the cars. Aaron got in the sports car, Rand in his Caddy. The big man leaned on the roof of the Caddy for a few minutes, talking to Rand, then walked to the sports car and lowered himself into the passenger's seat. Both cars drove away slowly.

Nudger's heartbeat evened out as the dust they'd raised settled in a bright haze to the ground.

It was time to enter the house. His stomach knew what he might find there.

The front door was unlocked. Odd, since the big man had mentioned locking up when he'd suggested leaving the back way.

Nudger pushed tentatively on the door, expecting its hinges to squeal to match his mood. But it swung open quietly and smoothly and bumped against the wall. His stomach growled, "Waaaaait!" but he gulped down his fear and stepped inside.

He was in the living room. It was surprisingly dim in there, gloomy. He looked around and saw a brown couch with sagging cushions, an old console TV with a cable box and a ceramic panther lamp on it, a coffee table and end tables equipped with angled wood holders on each side for magazines, but with no magazines in them. On the wall behind the sofa hung a large, dime-store print of the crucifixion, which according to the artist had occurred during a brilliant sunset.

Feeling braver now that he was inside, Nudger crossed the threadbare carpet to the dining room. He stopped cold and his stomach churned as he saw on the floor what the three men had been discussing. A large dog with its throat slashed lay on its side beneath the chandelier, which was glowing as if to display the grisly object on the carpet. A table with steel legs and mismatched chairs had been shoved aside so this was possible.

Nudger quickly looked away as Rand had, and swallowed. Swallowed again. The bitter taste remained thick at the base of his tongue.

Okay, he knew now. The tall man and the gunman had gotten Rand into the house to give him an object lesson, show him what might happen if he didn't cooperate with them, if he didn't do more than simply come across with "it." Nudger figured "it" would be inside information that could earn a fortune in the stock market.

He stepped around the dead dog and the oval of blood soaked into the carpet and wandered toward the kitchen, checking out the rest of the house while he was inside. It was furnished much like the living and dining rooms. Nothing suggested the decorator touch.

He went numb and heard himself gasp. Bile rose bitterly in his throat and he gulped it back down, shuddering.

A man was seated at the small wooden table, staring at Nudger but not seeing him or anything else with his wide, fixed gaze. He was a skinny guy in a black T-shirt with an American flag printed on the chest and the words "America First." His arms hung limply at his sides, and there was an amazing amount of crusted and coagulating blood on the tile floor. Nudger saw an open straight razor on the floor, near the chair. Without moving his feet, he stooped and peered beneath table level and saw gaping slashes in the man's wrists. "My God!" he said softly. He remembered Rand's second "Oh, Jesus!" as the three men were leaving the house by the back way.

Something else caught Nudger's eye as he straightened up. What had appeared to be spilled sugar or salt from a row of canisters on the table seemed to be spread in a deliberate pattern. Sugar, he decided, seeing the lid was off the round ceramic canister.

Careful not to step in blood, he edged forward for a closer look.

The dead man had trailed sugar over the table to spell out "Enough." A suicide note of sorts, though Nudger doubted its source. Rand's associates had to have known the corpse was in the house, and were probably responsible for it. Probably they'd set it up so it appeared that the man had put his dog to death, maybe for a trial run, then killed himself.

Nudger backed out of the hot kitchen that held the

coppery smell of spilled blood. It was a stench he could taste. He remembered the dog and skirted the wall as he hurried into the living room, eyes straight ahead.

He paused then, staring at the phone. He had an obligation to notify the police. To identify himself and explain how he'd found the body, how he'd come to be here.

Or did he?

Certainly it would be better for him not to have been here. In his line of work, sometimes half the secret of success was not showing up.

After taking a moment to compose himself, he left the house and walked as casually as possible back to his car, though he didn't think anyone was watching.

But then, the three men in the house hadn't thought Nudger was watching.

Not a comforting thought.

He climbed into the Granada and drove around until he found a major thoroughfare. From one of those drive-up phone booths at the corner of a service station, he made an anonymous phone call to the county police. Let them examine the house on Latimer Lane. Let them draw their own conclusions.

After all, it *might* have been suicide.

CHAPTER THIRTEEN

It was dusk when Nudger reached his office and climbed out of the Granada. He felt better, calmer. The vision of the dead man at the kitchen table was less vivid and more avoidable in his mind.

Still, death and dusk could change a person's perspective on the world. The office buildings and stores along Manchester took on an almost ethereal look. A white pigeon settled like a dove on the roof of the K-mart parking garage. A bus without passengers rumbled past Nudger toward McCausland Avenue, leaving diesel exhaust shimmering like wild spirits in the hazy, shadowed evening. He felt like a figure in a surreal landscape as he crossed the street to Danny's Donuts, and the door alongside of it that lead to his office.

He checked his answering machine but there was nothing on it of interest. A reminder that his payment was past due on the small loan he'd taken out on the Granada. (It was good that the finance company didn't know how he'd decided to utilize the money, along with the recent signature loans he'd arranged at criminally high interest rates so he could finance his stock purchases.) Some invective from Eileen, who hadn't even waited for the beep before berating him for not keeping up with his alimony payments. (His stocks' impending appreciation would take care of that.) She'd run out of time on the tape, too. The last words of her message were, "My lawyer will skin your—" Henry Mercato was probably sitting or lying next to her, smoking one of his skinny brown cigars and smiling with sharklike cunning, possibly after practicing safe sex, if such a thing was possible with Eileen. Nudger's stomach did its Eileen maneuver, as if something with sharp claws had taken some turns on an internal treadmill.

He erased his messages and phoned Hammersmith at the Third District, but was told the lieutenant had left. Nudger tried Hammersmith's home number. His son Jed answered the phone and told Nudger to wait just a minute, his dad was out spreading fertilizer before it got completely dark in the yard. Taking his work home with him, Nudger thought, but didn't mention that when Hammersmith came to the phone.

"I heard," Nudger said, "that the county police got a call tonight about a dead man in a house on Latimer Lane."

Hammersmith didn't answer for a moment, knowing it was one of those times when it was best to know only so much. "What else did you hear, Nudge?" Not "Where did you hear it?" Wily Hammersmith.

Nudger told him about "someone" seeing Rand and the two other men in the house *after* the man's death, all observed through a window. "It will be considered a suicide," he said.

"And if it isn't?" Hammersmith said.

"If it isn't, then I'll play it a different way." It would be withholding information in a homicide if the county po-

lice catalogued the man's death as murder, something neither he nor Hammersmith could afford to do if they didn't
want to explore the world of unemployment. "After all,
the guy really might have slit his own wrists."

"And I might go back outside and have a lawn. I was
gonna call you anyway, Nudge. I talked to some people in
Narcotics and found out some things. The Mirabelle Rogers
who owns the Mercedes is herself owned by King Chambers, who fits the description of the tall man you saw
lunching with Rand."

"And who was in the Latimer Lane house with Rand and
the guy with the gun and earring, whose name, by the
way, is Aaron. At least that's what I heard Chambers call
him."

"Aaron I still can't tell you a thing about," Hammersmith said, "except if he's associated with King Chambers
he's plenty dangerous. But you knew that."

"Yeah. He left me with that impression after pointing a
gun at me and saying he was going to kill me."

"The thing you should know is that Aaron of the earring
is probably soft as a baby duck compared to Chambers."

"I never heard of King Chambers before all of this,"
Nudger admitted.

"Then you've been associating with the right people.
Chambers is a major drug dealer who's been outsmarting
us and the DEA for years. He's also principal owner of three
escort services that are fronts for prostitution, though you
won't find his name on the corporate records. Having his
car registered to one of his girls is in character, insofar as
he has character. He's rumored to have ordered folks killed
as part of doing business, and he does a lot of business."

"I don't understand what a whitebread type like Rand is
doing with those two," Nudger said.

"Maybe he's into drugs. Or into women more accommodating than his wife. Both those things are always possible."

"Well, he doesn't have a marriage that'd lend itself to surprises from Frederick's of Hollywood."

"How do you know that, Nudge?"

"A guess. When the information comes in on the dead guy on Latimer Lane, will you clue me in?"

"Didn't you bother to look around and get his identity when you weren't in the house you never entered?"

"I would have been too anxious to get outa there, if I'd been in there."

"Yeah . . . your tummy problem. Anything else not to know?"

"Nothing I know of, or don't."

"Okay. I think. I'm going back out to kill some weeds, feed some grass. Put one over on mother nature through chemistry." Click!

Just like that, Hammersmith was gone. Irritating. Nudger hung up the phone.

He scratched viciously and futilely at a mosquito bite on his forearm, until finally he made it bleed and it felt better. He glanced at his watch. It wasn't even nine o'clock. Not too late to call Claudia.

She didn't answer her phone. Maybe she was still mad at him for buying stocks. Mad because he was into something she didn't understand, and she only remembered all those stories about the collapse of the market on Black Tuesday. Or was it Black Monday? Whatever. That was in the past. If she would take a few minutes to thumb through *Money* magazine, she'd realize he wasn't being foolish. There was this couple in Connecticut who just by giving up their car and riding bicycles to work had—

The phone rang and interrupted his thoughts. He decided not to answer; he'd wait for the message and pick up if it was anyone he wanted to talk to.

Beep!

"You bastard, Nudger!" Eileen.

He covered his ears as her message continued. She did this sometimes for amusement. She'd confided to him once that Mercato had told her it was good for her to let off tension this way. As long as she didn't say anything that might hurt her in court when she and Henry converged on him for the kill.

When the machine's recording light had blinked off, Nudger uncovered his ears. Then he called Claudia again with the same unsatisfactory result.

When he got tired of listening to her phone ringing, he hung up and sat staring at the wood grain of his desk, as if the patterns weren't random and might mean something profound. He thought it was possible Claudia was out with another man. Not likely, but possible. When she got disgusted with him she sometimes saw Biff Archway, who coached the girls' soccer team and taught sex education out at Harriet Beecher Stowe girls school. He was a barrel-chested, handsome guy who'd been a college football star and dressed like an L.L. Bean model. Nudger hated Biff Archway.

It wouldn't hurt, he decided, if he drove over to Claudia's apartment and made sure she wasn't home. Or that Archway's car wasn't parked on the block. Nudger's relationship with Claudia sometimes caused stomach pains.

You'd think I'd be lucky at cards, he thought, as he went out the door.

But he hardly ever was.

CHAPTER FOURTEEN

He'd stopped at MunchaBunch first, so it was dark when he got to Wilmington and drove past Claudia's apartment. Her car was nowhere on the block. She didn't have a usual parking space. A slot at the curb was precious in that part of South St. Louis, and residents often had to park some distance from their homes. It wasn't unusual to see trash cans or lawn chairs in empty parking spaces to keep them unoccupied while people were away on brief errands.

So it wouldn't be unusual if the red Mustang convertible parked two blocks down from Claudia's building was Biff Archway's. He might have parked, then walked to Claudia's apartment, and they'd gone out in her car rather than walk all the way to Archway's.

Nudger swallowed the bite of doughnut he'd been chewing and slowed down as he passed the convertible for the third time. It seemed to be exactly like Archway's car, if it wasn't actually his. Same year, same model—everything. There was a lacy white garter hanging from the rearview mirror, though. Nudger didn't remember it from the last time he'd seen Archway's car, but it had been quite a while. A white garter, huh? It would be just like Archway to dangle such a trophy from his mirror. Maybe he'd raped a bride. No, he'd probably been able to seduce her fair and square before the honeymoon. Nudger memorized the car's license plate number; someday he'd compare it to Archway's convertible.

He drove around the block a final time and saw that Claudia's windows were still dark. For a second he considered parking and going inside to knock on her door, make sure she and Archway weren't . . . No, that was too sick and cynical even for him. Unthinkable!

He poked another tiny doughnut into his mouth and stomped on the accelerator. The Granada's tires almost squealed as it rocked and rattled up to forty miles an hour before he braked for the stop sign at the corner.

Driving more sensibly, he took Grand Avenue north to Highway 40 and set course for Ladue to collect the day's taping from the trunk of the blue Chevy.

After cranking down the window to let in the warm but pleasant breeze, he switched on the radio and tuned to the ball game Danny and Ray would be watching on TV in Ray's apartment. The Cubs were ahead ten to one in the eighth inning. Nudger was doubly glad he hadn't taken Danny up on his invitation. Cub fan Ray would be unbearable.

An hour later Nudger was in his apartment, feeling bloated with miniature doughnuts, sipping decaf, and listening to the Rand tape.

6:45 P.M., real time:

SYDNEY: "I wouldn't know where Luanne is. She seems to pay more attention to you than to anyone else these days."

RAND: "I told her to be here for dinner. She doesn't do anything I say."

SYDNEY: "She doesn't do anything anybody says. You suppose that's healthy?"

RAND: "It's normal behavior for a teenage girl, but I still don't like it. Did she come home from school at the regular time?"

SYDNEY: "Hasn't been home at all. Hasn't been to school, if you ask me. Her counselor says she's absent more than she's there. She's gonna flunk if she doesn't—"

RAND: "—I'm not worried about her grades, I'm worried about her."

SYDNEY: "Maybe with good reason."

RAND: "Don't try to be cryptic. It bores. You got anything to say directly?"

SYDNEY: "No."

A door slamming.

7:32 P.M., real time:

"Eberhardt's Liquors."

SYDNEY: "This is Mrs. Rand, Eb. Can you have your boy bring over a fifth . . . "

(Nudger fast-forwarded through the carryout order and its delivery fifteen minutes later.)

10:08 P.M., real time:

RAND: "Luanne? Luanne? Ah! Where the fuck have you been?"

LUANNE: "Out's where."

RAND: "It's past ten and your mother says this is the first time you've touched base since leaving the house this morning."

LUANNE: "Old Mom's not much anymore on how time

passes. Or anything else that goes on under her nose, if you catch my meaning."

RAND: "Don't smart-ass me. And don't insult your mother. Who've you been with?"

LUANNE: "I thought you liked me smart-assed."

RAND: "Don't press. Who were you with tonight?"

LUANNE: "You mean in the biblical sense?"

RAND: "Luanne, damnit!"

LUANNE: "Okay, okay. I was with Nan and some other kids. Over at her house."

RAND: "Nan Grant?"

LUANNE: "Not Nan Reagan."

RAND: "Jesus Christ! Nan Grant. Watch what you say to that one."

LUANNE: "I watch what I say to everyone, just like I was a comic-strip character and my words were in little white balloons. God, I'm thirsty!"

Silence.

Footsteps.

LUANNE: "We outa real-life soda? God, I hate that diet shit!"

RAND: "I had a talk about you today. Until Labor Day—"

SYDNEY: "So, you're finally home."

LUANNE: "And you're finally drunk. Big fucking surprise."

SYDNEY: "Watch your mouth. Dale, tell her to watch her mouth, why don't you?"

RAND: "That's just what I've been telling her."

LUANNE: "You two are real prizes."

SYDNEY: "We try, anyway."

LUANNE: "Try what?"

RAND: "To keep you out of permanent trouble."

SYDNEY: "You'll understand and appreciate it someday. Won't she, Dale?"

RAND (his voice sad): "I doubt it."

LUANNE: "Screw this! I'm going up to bed. Gonna lock my door and forget all about you dorky people till morning."

RAND: "I'm going to bed too."

SYDNEY: "I'm staying up a while. Gonna watch television. Maybe 'Love Connection' is on, even if it's a rerun." After a pause: "I'll be up in fifteen minutes, Dale. Maybe sooner."

10:27 P.M., real time:

CHUCK WOOLERY: "Welcome to—"

Nudger switched off the recorder.

Then he fast-forwarded it to make sure there was nothing more on the tape.

Only silence.

He sat sipping his cooled decaf and letting his mind roam.

At 11:00 P.M. he pulled the phone over to him and punched out Claudia's number.

He was surprised when she picked up.

"Where you been this evening?" he asked.

"Spaghetti dinner out at the school. I was just about to go to bed, Nudger."

"Were you by yourself?"

"No, and it's a good thing—there were acres of spaghetti. The PTA and the kids ate most of it."

"I mean, did you go there alone?"

"Of course. Well, I didn't drive there alone. Biff Archway delivered some papers to my place, then I drove both of us out to the school because he's been having car trouble."

Car trouble! Oh, Nudger just bet! "Did his car start okay so he could drive home?"

A long, exasperated sigh. "Nudger?"

"I mean, it's a reasonable question. Isn't it a reasonable question? Or am I being unreasonable?"

"Nudger?"

"You said he was having car trouble. So maybe he'd have to spend the night someplace else other than at home, if one of his fuel injectors got clogged or something."

"Nudger?"

"What?"

"Come over here. Right now. And stop on your way and buy some of those delicious little doughnuts. After all that pasta, I'm in the mood for something sweet."

He decided he could probably force down a few more MunchaBunches.

CHAPTER FIFTEEN

By morning Nudger was convinced that Claudia's evening with Biff Archway and spaghetti had been innocent. She lay beside him in her bed, listening to National Public Radio on the clock radio that had awakened them. A man was being interviewed about unnecessary cruelty practiced by exterminators on insects.

Nudger was stretched out on his back with his hands behind his head. Like Claudia, he was nude and on top of the sheets. The morning was already warm and the air conditioner had been overworked last night until the condenser had frozen, so it wasn't running at peak efficiency. Nudger liked to think he'd had something to do with its inability to cool the room.

Traffic noises were building up outside, a steadily increasing hum from over on busy Grand Avenue, and the occasional swish of cars passing below on Wilmington. Satiated with lovemaking and sleep, Nudger was thinking of other matters. Such as Dale Rand and the stock market. Rand might be trading on inside information to make himself richer, but there was nothing to suggest it had anything to do with Norva Beane's bad investments.

He said, "I don't think there's any connection."

Claudia said, "Who knows what insects feel?"

"No, I mean I don't think there's any connection between Dale Rand and Fred McMahon."

"They have families too," the man on the radio said.

"What's that supposed to mean?" Claudia asked.

"It means I'm probably finished with the case. Whatever Rand's into, it apparently doesn't have anything to do with my client."

"I mean, about families."

"I don't know. But I can't take her money on false pretenses. She's already lost too much of it where Rand's concerned."

"Social insects, I suppose he meant. Like ants and bees."

"She probably made some bad investments and took a loss when the market went down. It'd be natural for her to blame somebody else."

"Like you will."

"What?"

"Ants and bees. I guess you could say they have families."

"I guess," Nudger said.

Claudia switched off the radio and kissed his forehead, then swiveled on the mattress so she could stand up and go into the bathroom to shower. Nudger turned his head to watch her walk. Every movement was a wonderful mystery. He pondered whether other men derived the same pleasure from observing Claudia walk. Archway, probably, but what did that matter?

When he heard the shower running, he climbed out of bed and trudged into the bathroom to try to talk his way under the water with Claudia. She'd be in a no-nonsense frame of mind, hurrying to leave for work on time, but it was worth a try.

She didn't see things his way in the steamy bathroom. Not at all.

By the time he was finished showering, she was already dressed. Still damp, he slipped into yesterday's clothes. They were only slightly wrinkled, he decided. He could make do with them instead of driving over to his apartment to change. And he'd shaved with one of Claudia's disposable razors. He saw himself as presentable even if a little mussed and damp.

When he joined Claudia in the kitchen for breakfast, she looked him over and said nothing.

"I look neat enough?" he asked.

"Did you ever see any of those modern sculptures of everyday solid objects made soft and melting?"

"No. How do I look?"

"You'll do." She poured coffee for both of them and set the cups on the table. She was wearing a navy-blue dress with white trim, white high heels. The simpler she dressed, the more elegant she became. She glanced again at him. "Have you put on a few pounds?"

"No. Why do you ask?"

"I noticed last night, when you weren't wearing any clothes, you looked as if you might be gaining weight."

"I don't know why I should be," he said, more gruffly than he'd intended.

She said nothing as she sat down across from him at the table.

They finished the remaining MunchaBunch doughnuts for breakfast, and Nudger poured himself a second cup of coffee.

"I better get out of here if I'm going to get to work on time." She kissed him on the lips, and he slipped an arm around her and held her fast, pulling her down on his lap. She said, "I told you, I might be late. Be fair, Nudger."

He released his grip on her, knowing she was right, he was going too far. Fair was his middle name. Fair was what often got him into trouble. Fair was a curse. For instance, without fair, Claudia would still be in his lap.

She reminded him to lock up when he left, then *tap-tapped* on her high heels across tile, then silent carpet, then wood, to the front door. The door opened and closed and he heard her descend the stairs to the street.

He carried his coffee into the living room and saw that she'd brought in the morning newspaper from the hall and had tossed it on the sofa for him to read. After settling into the soft cushions, he leisurely finished his coffee and caught up on the greater misery beyond his own life.

Well, it wasn't all misery. Not on the financial page, anyway. Synpac was up a quarter, and Fortune Fashions was up a half. Nudger smiled, visions of feather boas dancing through his mind. He turned to the sports page and saw that the Cardinals had scored eight runs in the last of the ninth and defeated the Cubs nine to eight. He wished now he'd gone to dinner with Danny and watched the game on Ray's TV.

Still smiling, he decided things were breaking right and the day held bright promise. Why spoil it by reading his horoscope. It might tell him he was out of tomorrows. After all, if those readings were accurate, everybody had to get that prediction eventually, yet you seldom if ever saw it in the paper. He moved to toss the section of paper containing daily horoscopes aside, spilling a dribble of hot coffee in his lap and staining his pants.

It was ten o'clock by the time he'd driven to his apartment, showered again, and changed clothes. His bathroom scale did indicate that he'd gained three or four pounds, depending on how he shifted his weight from toes to heels. But when he stepped off the scale, he noticed the needle didn't return quite all the way to zero. He was pretty sure the scale was registering slightly on the high side.

Feeling better about himself, he called Norva Beane to tell her they needed to talk.

She offered him lemonade again, but this time he refused. While she poured some for herself in the kitchen, he sat on the sofa in her cheap but clean living room and stared at the row of stuffed bears on the shelf above the stereo. They seemed to be staring back at him as if they knew something he didn't and it amused them immensely.

Norva came back into the living room with her lemonade and sat in a chair opposite Nudger. She was wearing slacks with a Mickey Mouse pattern on them, and she was barefoot again. Maybe she never wore shoes when she was home, because of her country origins. She raised her cheese glass of lemonade out toward him and looked at him questioningly. "You sure?"

"Thanks, but I'm really not thirsty." He scratched a mosquito bite on the side of his neck and watched her sip. A lemon rind was floating among the ice cubes, and she deftly moved it out of the way with the tip of her tongue as she tilted the glass toward her lips. Lemonade seemed to be an art with her, the making and the drinking.

She carefully placed the wet glass on a cork coaster on the coffee table and sat back, clasping her hands over one raised knee. "So, you went and learned something?"

"Yes and no. Dale Rand's into some nasty business, but it's got nothing to do with Fred McMahon, and there's no evidence it has anything to do with your investments."

Norva said, "If you'll pardon my French, that's bull-shit."

"Maybe," Nudger admitted, "but it would be impossible to prove. You're throwing good money after—"

"So tell me what you learned," Norva interrupted. "About everything."

"Everything?"

"It's why I went and hired you, to get my money's worth. The good money I'm throwing after—"

He got her point. "I followed Rand, listened in on conversations with business associates, eavesdropped on family conversations."

Norva lowered her leg and rocked forward, her elbows on her knees. "However did you do that?"

"It doesn't matter. Thing is, there was no conversation with McMahon about junk-bond or stock swindles, no conversation with McMahon at all. Nothing to indicate the two men ever so much as met."

"So what did him and his wife talk about?"

"They didn't talk much, but they argued a lot. Mostly about Luanne, their teenage daughter."

"What about Luanne?"

"She runs around, stays out late, cuts classes. The usual thing."

"Hm. The wife got some kinda problem?"

"Why would you ask?"

"I dunno. I got an extra sense. All us Beanes has got it. If you doubt my word, you can ask anybody down around Possum Run. They'll all tell you."

"The wife drinks too much."

"Well, that's a curse I seen before. What about Rand? You mentioned he was into something nasty."

Nudger sighed. She'd paid him to find out about Rand, so maybe she was entitled to know. Well, definitely she was entitled to know. But not about the inside information on stocks. She wouldn't have any money to invest anyway; that was why she'd hired Nudger, because she'd taken a bath in junk bonds. He said, "I saw him in the company of some known criminals."

"Oh? What kinda criminals?"

"Not white-collar types. People in drugs, prostitution, those kinda things."

"If he's involved in that, how come you don't think he stole my money?"

"I don't know how he's involved with those people, and proving he stole your money would be almost impossible. If I took this investigation any further, I'd be stealing your money." He scratched again at the mosquito bite on his neck. "You know, Norva, a lot of people lost a lot of money on junk bonds."

Norva picked up her glass and sort of nibbled at the lemonade. Then she placed the glass back on the coaster. She didn't seem to have heard him. "What about the daughter?"

"Huh?"

"There's something more about the daughter, Luanne. I can feel it."

Wondering about country wisdom, Nudger said, "I've only got a suspicion, from listening to tapes of what went on inside the house."

"You're working for me, so I got a right to know even your suspicions."

"Well, it wouldn't surprise me if Rand was sleeping with his daughter."

Norva's mouth fell open and she went pale.

"It happens," Nudger said. "But I'm not positive it's happening with Rand and Luanne."

"Drugs, prostitution, incest with a child . . . What kinda

man is he? An animal like that, what else might he be doing?"

Nudger decided not to mention Rand's presence in the house of a man who was almost certainly murdered.

Apparently her sixth sense didn't detect that, because she didn't pursue it.

"This Luanne," she said, "she seem happy at all?"

"Not that I could tell," Nudger said.

"Gotta feel for a kid in that position," Norva said, her voice breaking.

"If she is in that position."

"She surely is. I can sense it."

"I'm not so sure. In any event, there's not enough evidence for me to notify the police. Also, the way I came by the information. Well . . . "

"It wasn't legal?"

"Let's call it a gray area. Anyway, none of it has anything to do with junk bonds or mismanaged funds."

"What's the wife say about Rand and their daughter?"

She certainly seemed hung up on that. Maybe she was an incest survivor herself. "She doesn't say much. If it is true, which isn't positive, I'd say the wife is into denial."

"How could that be, if she can stop what's happening?"

"Admitting that about her husband and daughter would mean the end of her world. And it would mean admitting something about herself, at least in her mind. And she probably has strong suspicions but no actual proof. So, like a lot of other women in that position, she simply denies there's a problem. The way not to have to deal with it is not to believe it's happening in the first place."

Norva ran the tip of her tongue over her teeth. "Maybe that makes sense, if you say so. I s'pect that's why she drinks."

"You're jumping to conclusions," Nudger cautioned.

The way you did about a bond swindle and Fred McMahon. "I told you there might not be anything like that going on between Rand and his daughter."

Norva scrunched up her face, then shook her head from side to side violently, as if tossing away an unpleasant thought. "Yeah, I s'pose you're right. I just can't get it outa my mind Rand's a creepy, untrustworthy sonuvabitch."

"Oh, you're probably right about that. But the world's full of them. They even hold conventions."

"Really?"

"No, no, I was kidding." He stood up. "I'll send you an itemized bill, along with a refund."

She pushed herself up from her chair. "Whatever you think's fair, Mr. Nudger. I sense you're a fair man."

Scary.

She saw him to the door, and they shook hands with an awkward formality.

As he was lowering himself into the Granada, he glanced up and was sure he saw her duck back out of sight from watching him out a window.

He had a sense about her, too, but he wasn't sure what it meant.

CHAPTER SIXTEEN

When Nudger got to his office there was a message on the machine to call Hammersmith at the Third.

Instead of picking up the phone, he went down to the doughnut shop and waited for the air conditioner to make the stifling office habitable before returning Hammersmith's call. Danny was serving coffee to a chunky, middle-aged woman at the end of the counter. Nudger recognized her, thinking she worked down the street at K-mart. She gazed morosely into her cup, as if it might contain hemlock, and didn't look up when Danny walked away from her to where Nudger had taken a stool at the opposite end of the counter. Maybe she was working up the nerve to buy a doughnut.

Danny coaxed another cup of coffee from the complex network of gauges and pipes running down the face of the steel urn and placed it in front of Nudger on the counter. "Doughnut, Nudge?"

"Not this morning."

Danny's sad eyes gazed with concern from their pouches. "Tummy bothering you again?"

"Always."

"Eileen?"

"Among others."

"Oh, yeah! Speaking of others, there was this fella came by to see you early this morning."

"Fella?"

"Yup."

"Say what he wanted?"

"Sure." Danny untucked his gray towel from his belt and moved it in a circular motion on the stainless-steel counter.

"Say what he wanted."

"I said sure."

"I mean *say* what he wanted—to me."

"I was gonna. He said he needed to talk to you about your golf game. I didn't know you played golf, Nudge. Some game that is. Looks like a kinda useless exercise to me. Heck, you might as well walk up to the hole with the ball in your hand and—"

"What did this fella look like?" Nudger asked. Or maybe it was his stomach that asked.

"Black guy, real well dressed in a casual sorta way. Wearing a fancy earring, like a Nazi trinket dangling on the end of a little gold chain. I told him you'd likely be along soon if he wanted to wait, offered him coffee and a Dunker Delite, but he said no, he had things to do and he'd catch you later. Told me to make sure you knew he was here, and to tell you he was looking forward to him and you teeing off together again real soon. I asked his name, but he just smiled and walked on out."

Nudger stared into his coffee like the woman down the counter. He felt sick.

"He's a fella you golf with, I guess."

Nudger continued to stare silently, trying with will-power to keep his stomach in delicate balance.

"Sure you don't want a doughnut, Nudge?"

"Argh!"

"You okay?"

"Yeah. 'Course. I better get back up to the office. If that guy comes around again, Danny, tell him I never did come in. Then phone up to me right away, okay?"

"You betcha." He tucked the gray towel back in his belt. "If you're not feeling up to par, Nudge, you best go see a doctor instead of even thinking about going golfing."

Nudger stared at him, then decided it was true, Danny wasn't joking. Danny often amazed him that way.

He lifted his hand in a brief wave to Danny, then swiveled off his stool and went outside, where he made a U-turn and went through the adjacent door and upstairs.

The office had become reasonably cool. Nudger got a fresh roll of antacid tablets from a desk drawer and chewed and swallowed three of the chalky disks in quick succession. He wished he owned a gun, but he was afraid of them. He always had been, really. They killed people, and often the wrong party.

He assured himself that if Aaron of the earring did show up again, he could swear to him he was off the case, no longer following Dale Rand, and Aaron would believe him and leave him alone. It was possible, anyway.

So was a perpetual motion machine.

He phoned the Third and asked for Hammersmith. The lieutenant picked up his phone on the first ring. Nudger told him about Aaron coming around.

"I doubt he wants to kill you, Nudge, seeing as he walked right into the doughnut shop and let Danny see him."

Nudger quickly embraced that line of reasoning. "You've got a point."

"More terror tactics is all it is," Hammersmith said jovially, "not to be taken seriously."

"You're right, Jack. I know you're right."

"What I called about was that guy whose wrists Aaron mighta slit."

Nudger's stomach sped through roller-coaster maneuvers.

"Nudge? Still there?"

"Yeah."

"His name was Clark Morris, and he was a small-time drug pusher. He sold to college kids, mostly."

"Did he have a connection with King Chambers?"

"Wouldn't be surprising if he did. Chambers is the guy to know in that line. Morris had a long list of prior convictions for possession and dealing."

"Jack, you think he was small-time enough to be dispensable? To use as an example?"

"Him and his dog, Nudge. That's how I see it, too. An object lesson for Dale Rand."

"But why?"

"There could be a thousand reasons, but right now the official finding is that Morris's death was a suicide. Nobody's much interested when a guy like him leaves the world, Nudge. NHI, far as Narcotics is concerned." Nudger knew what the letters stood for in police slang: No Humans Involved. It was sometimes used to describe crimes when the perpetrator and victim were both known criminals of the lowest sort. "Nobody wants another crime they can't solve. I'd leave it a suicide if I were you, Nudge."

"That's exactly what I intend to do," Nudger said. "Believe me, I—"

Click! Hammersmith had terminated the conversation.

Nudger stayed at his desk and busied himself with paper-work, trying not to think about Aaron of the earring or King Chambers or Norva Beane. Dale Rand he thought about. And the stock market. He wondered if maybe he should get some graph paper and start charting his holdings.

It was late afternoon before he remembered the recorder in the blue Chevy. Aaron hadn't yet shown up near the Rand house, so driving out there wouldn't be so risky. Besides, Nudger thought, what am I, a coward?

Well, how much of a coward?

Driving to Ladue seemed no less dangerous than sitting and waiting in his office. He decided he might as well pick up the tape, then leave the second recorder in the trunk for the bug man to retrieve along with the car and the rest of his equipment. Nudger would find out what he owed the bug man for his services, then figure what would be left after his payment from Norva Beane. And that would be it. End of investigation.

Another day, another inadequate dollar.

CHAPTER SEVENTEEN

Nudger parked the Granada across the street from the blue Chevy and figured, why waste time?

He peeled his sweat-soaked shirt away from the car's vinyl upholstery and got out. The shirt was plastered to his back now. He reached around, pinched the material between thumb and forefinger, and stretched it out away from his flesh. That felt cool for about two seconds.

Nothing seemed to be happening at the moment down at the little strip shopping center. There were a couple of cars parked there, but no one in sight. After looking up and down the deserted street, he jogged over to the Chevy, fishing in his pocket for the key the bug man had given him.

He'd opened the Chevy's trunk and was bent over staring at the recorder's tiny red power light, when he paused. A subtle something kept his hand from switching off the recorder and removing the cassette.

His mind was ahead of his hand. His stomach was ahead of his mind. It growled in worried protest. Rand would probably arrive home soon, so why not wait a few more hours? Maybe Horace Walling would phone him and stocks would be discussed. Nudger might very easily hear about another investment opportunity. This was probably the way fortunes were made, he thought. Inside information, overheard by someone bold enough to act. And if it was a crime, it was victimless. Nudger had always thought that was an oxymoron, "victimless crime." And some of the worlds great fortunes had grown from injustices, legal and illegal, which were far from victimless. That was undeniably so.

An hour. He'd give Rand precisely one hour after he went in the house, then he'd get the cassette from the Chevy's trunk, and the clock would stop running on what he would owe the bug man. And that way he wouldn't have wasted the drive out here. He could park down the street where he could see the Rand property, risking for the final time another run-in with Aaron of the earring, then when he had the cassette he'd play it on his office recorder, see if there was any valuable investment information on it. That would be the finish to this mess. It wouldn't take much time for Aaron to learn that Nudger was no longer a player or a problem. Word got around, and always to people like Aaron. They had a network the police envied.

He closed the trunk, glanced around, and crossed the street to climb back in the Granada.

Bracing himself to endure apprehension for the next hour, he found a shady spot to park near the corner of the Rand property and settled back in the car. The heat settled in with him. His shirt quickly molded to the vinyl upholstery again. He kept looking around, periodically checking the rearview mirror. The car's windows were down, and the mosquitoes that had feasted on him out near Latimer Lane must have somehow contacted the Ladue mosquitoes.

They found their way into the car and gave him the option of cranking up the windows and sitting in a sauna or being devoured by mini-vampires.

Nudger was determined to stick to his plan of waiting one hour. It was a test now, the machismo thing, a determination of his worth as a man. Biff Archway would never make it through the next—he looked at his watch—oh, God, forty minutes!

He pressed the watch to his ear, noticing that moisture was beaded beneath its crystal. But it was ticking lustily, and it was a cheap windup model, so it couldn't have a weak battery. Well, thirty-nine minutes to go now. Only.

After twenty minutes had passed like eons, fear, or maybe loss of blood, got the better of him and he leaned forward to start the engine. He was going to drive fast away from where he was parked, letting the rush of wind flush the pesky little insects, and his trepidation, from the car's interior. Then he'd get the final cassette from the Chevy and be gone and done with everything except cashing in on his investments when the time was right.

But as his fingers touched the ignition key, something on the Rand property caught his eye. Movement in the bushes near the back corner of the house, next to the garage. He was sure of it. His stomach bucked and groaned. It had endured more than enough and was letting him know it wanted no more strain.

But there was the movement again. Unmistakable.

And Nudger, sitting very quietly now and ignoring the heat and mosquitoes, saw what it was.

Norva Beane.

Cradling a long object in her arms.

A rifle or shotgun!

His stomach didn't like that at all. It was in a race with

his heart to see which part of his torso could be made to pulsate fastest.

Both organs went into overdrive when Nudger saw Dale Rand's black Cadillac turn the corner and glide sedately down the street toward the driveway, as if already practicing for the funeral procession.

He looked back at Norva and saw her settle down into shooting position, seated on the ground at an angle, with the rifle barrel leveled and an elbow resting on her knee for support. The way she was set up made it clear she'd handled plenty of guns.

She obviously intended to open fire on Dale Rand, and he'd soon be a target no one from a place called Possum Run could miss even in a dream.

CHAPTER EIGHTEEN

Nudger hated the sight of blood, hated what he knew was about to occur. He was out of the car and running without thinking about it, realizing what was happening only when he felt the spring of grassy earth beneath his soles and sensed the scenery flying past. Instinctively, he'd stayed on the grass so Norva wouldn't hear him approaching.

Blurred in the corner of his vision, the long black form of Rand's Cadillac was slowing to make its turn into the driveway, affording an easy shot through the windshield.

Somehow Nudger ran even faster, stretching his stride so he felt it in his groin. He was aware of weight around his middle jiggling with each step. The Dunker Delites he'd had to eat and the MunchaBunches he couldn't resist had burdened him with a spare tire in a remarkably short time. He was gasping for oxygen now and his knees felt rubbery. Sharp pain stitched his right side.

Norva's body shifted slightly and he knew she sensed his approach. Yet she ignored him, her concentration beamed along the rifle barrel, the imagined trajectory of the bullet.

The rifle made a loud smacking sound, like a hand slapping hard on a flat surface.

No, no, no! . . .

Norva was sighting down the barrel for a second shot.

Nudger closed his eyes as he launched himself at her.

Pain jolted through his left shoulder. He struck her leg, he thought, as he hit the hard grassy ground and skidded on his side. He could feel his shirt and pants scraping and catching on small things in the earth, twisting and wadding against his flesh.

He sat up in the bushes. He'd knocked Norva back about six feet. She looked angry and she was scrambling to her feet, still gripping the rifle. Nudger grabbed a thick, leafy branch and levered himself to standing position. He staggered out away from the shrubbery at the corner of the garage. He could hear himself rasping, sucking air deep into his lungs with each desperate heave of his chest. Someone seemed to have set his left shoulder on fire.

Norva said, "Darn it, Mr. Nudger," and hopped to the side so she could have a clear shot around him.

He ducked and turned away as she aimed the rifle down the driveway. This time the blast of the gun made his ears ring, and he was sure he'd heard the bullet snap past him like the crack of a whip. A sound within a sound; the reverberation of death.

"Oh, fudge!" Norva said.

She was pointing the rifle at Nudger now. His legs began to tremble.

"Norva, no! . . ."

Sirens were warbling in the warm evening air, and not very far away.

"Don't you move even a gnat's inch now, Mr. Nudger," Norva said. Still with the rifle leveled at him, she backed away. She scissor-stepped over a low hedge into neighboring property, backpedaled facing him until she was several hundred feet away, then turned and ran hard and fast, holding the rifle out to the side, well away from her body.

Nudger stood numbly and watched as she disappeared among some graceful willow trees.

His heart slam-dancing with his ribs, he slowly turned around and looked down the driveway.

Dale Rand was sitting on the concrete next to the Cadillac. The car's windshield had turned milky and there was a huge hole in it, high and to the left of center. Apparently Nudger's approach had thrown off Norva's aim just enough to make her miss her mark.

Nudger hoped.

He didn't see any blood on Rand, who was staring at him with a shocked, stupid expression on his long, usually composed face. Not with any look of pain, though. His hair was mussed, and one leg of his dark, chalk-striped suit had worked its way up and was wadded around his knee, which was scraped in the manner of a child's who'd fallen at play.

Nudger took a few steps toward him. "You okay?"

"Think so," Rand said shakily, starting to stand as he leaned on the side of the car. His pants leg had straightened out, and he looked down to see a long rip in it. "Oh, damn!" he said, as if being shot through the head might have been preferable to a ruined suit.

Nudger realized he'd be smart to make his exit, so he stepped off the driveway and started across the lawn toward where the Granada was parked down the street.

But the warbling police siren grew louder and changed pitch as it rounded the corner. A cruiser with winking red and blue roofbar lights braked hard and angled leaning toward the curb. The driver was enthusiastic. The cruiser skidded and one front tire hopped up onto the sidewalk as its doors flapped open and two uniforms piled out and crouched low with guns drawn.

Rand had turned and was slumped against the Caddy, staring at them. "It's okay!" he shouted. "She's gone. He scared her away." He pointed at Nudger the hero.

Oh, no! This was no way to conduct an unobtrusive stakeout.

"It's safe now!" Rand yelled. He sounded desperate to convince them and probably himself.

One of the uniforms had begun moving up the driveway, his head swiveling, his face pale. His eyes seemed huge. His partner stayed half-concealed behind an open car door, ready to return hostile fire. They weren't completely buying Rand's assessment of the situation.

"We had reports of gunfire," the uniform in the driveway said, when he got near Rand. He caught sight of the Cadillac's shattered windshield. "Brace yourself with both hands on the car, legs spread."

"I live here!" Rand replied. "I was the target, damnit! Look at my car, if you don't believe me. You think I shot the windshield out from the inside? You don't frisk me, goddamnit, I'm a taxpayer. You work for me!"

The uniform didn't reply, but his hard, frightened gaze, and the gun in his hand, were now trained on Nudger. "Over here, you!"

"He saved my life," Rand said. "I saw who shot at me. It was a woman. This man tackled her and knocked her down, frightened her away."

"That right?" the uniform asked, staring with skepticism and with a touch of awe at Nudger.

"More or less," Nudger said.

"Uh-huh. Get a good look at her?"

"Not really."

"I did," Rand said. "Won't ever forget her. She was a skinny redhead, wearing Levi's and I think a black T-shirt. Had a rifle, and she meant business."

"Looks like it," the uniform said, glancing again at the windshield. He told Nudger and Rand to stay where they were, then he hurried back to the patrol car and said something to his partner, who immediately got on the radio. The police of Ladue and neighboring municipalities were on the hunt for Norva Beane.

The uniform had his gun holstered and was armed with a leather-bound notepad as he trudged back up the driveway and confronted Nudger and Rand. Sydney had emerged from the house and was standing close to Rand. Nudger hadn't seen her up close. She was slender, the skin of her face stretched tight over a prominent nose and cheekbones, as if she'd had recent cosmetic surgery that had been overdone. Her eyes had an unnaturally wide, startled look to them. They would wear that expression all the time, Nudger thought, not just now because someone had shot at her husband. She was still attractive but taking on a haggard look, a hardness despite the startled ingenue eyes. Alcohol, working on the inside against whatever beauty fought hard to survive on the outside.

In a low voice, Rand was explaining to her what had happened. She replied unintelligibly in an equally soft voice. Her brittle gaze fixed on Nudger for a moment, and he might have caught a whiff of gin. Rand straightened up and was silent.

The uniform had his black notepad flipped open, a pen in his hand, and Nudger waited for the question he knew he'd have to answer. There was no choice now. He was in the middle of an attempted murder in tranquil and moneyed Ladue.

"Anybody recognize the woman?" the uniform asked.

"Of course not," Rand said. "She was a total stranger. A crazy woman."

Sydney said, "I never even saw her." More gin fumes. Unmistakable.

Nudger sighed and said, "I know who she is."

Everyone turned toward him and stared.

CHAPTER NINETEEN

The Ladue police interrogated Nudger for three hard hours. A lieutenant from the county department sat in, along with a representative from the Major Case Squad, the team of city and municipality cops assigned to particularly serious crimes so that various departments in the quiltwork of the metropolitan area could be coordinated in a single effort. The right hand being able to trust the left. To an extent.

The St. Louis County and Major Case Squad guys were only acting as observers. Mere *attempted* murder wasn't enough to activate all forces. But this incident had occurred in Ladue. That someone had disturbed the peace by firing a rifle was bad enough; that she had actually aimed the weapon at someone of substance and standing was intolerable.

A captain named Massinger did most of the asking, politely, insistently, laying subtle conversational traps. He was a portly little man with mint-scented cologne, squarish eyes, and a slow smile that revealed overlapping stained teeth. Nudger admired his skill. He told Massinger almost everything. He did not tell him about seeing the dead man on Latimer Lane, or about Rand's bugged house, or about secret investment knowledge and the imminent return of the feather boa.

When finally he walked out into the syrupy warm night, he was reasonably sure he'd acted within the law and his livelihood wasn't threatened. In fact, he was still being regarded as something of a hero. That was a new and not unpleasant sensation.

As he approached the parked Granada, he was surprised to see the corpulent figure of Hammersmith leaning against a back fender. Hammersmith was dressed casually in an untucked silky gray shirt, billowing out over blue-jeans he'd somehow found in his size. He was puffing on one of his horrific greenish cigars, and smoke was suspended over him in a noxious pall, as if there'd been an explosion at a poison gas factory.

When Nudger was a few feet away, Hammersmith removed the cigar from his mouth and balanced it delicately on his fingertips as if it were a dart he was about to toss. "I got a call about you at home, Nudge. All about the exciting goings on here in Ladue."

"I've been talking about that with the Ladue law for the last three hours."

"Nevertheless, if you're not too sore from the rubber hoses, maybe we oughta go someplace and chat."

"I'm dog-tired," Nudger said. "And they didn't need rubber hoses. They're good at their work."

"They gotta be, out here in moneyland. Taxpayers with clout are forever on their ass."

"People like Dale Rand?"

"Sure. And they're naturally curious about who shot at him, being the police."

"Well, I told them who squeezed the trigger."

"You're a heroic figure, Nudge. It's gonna be in the morning paper. Get you a big kiss from Claudia, I'll bet."

Nudger couldn't help but feel a thrust of hope. Stirrings of pride. Had Biff Archway ever hurled himself at a loaded gun? "Let's go get some coffee, have that talk."

"Right." Hammersmith nodded toward his unmarked Pontiac. "I'll follow."

Nudger got in the Granada and drove to the Steak 'n' Shake restaurant on Manchester, not far from his apartment. On the way over, it began to rain, so gently it was almost a mist. The Granada's wipers were frustrated by it and screeched on the windshield with impotence, further fraying Nudger's nerves.

When Hammersmith arrived, Nudger was already inside the restaurant, seated in a booth in the No-Smoking section, facing north so he could see traffic out on the slick and reflecting street. A Maplewood police car sped by, siren off but roofbar lights blazing, casting beautiful red and blue hues that danced over drab wet pavement and the used-car lot across the street.

Hammersmith paused just inside the door and glared at him for being in the No-Smoking section, then snubbed out his cigar in an ashtray and headed for the booth with that graceful, gliding walk of his that gave the impression he might be inflated with helium.

When the waitress appeared, Nudger ordered black coffee, resigned to enduring more nervousness in exchange for wakefulness. Hammersmith said he wanted a chocolate milk shake. The waitress, a heavyset black woman with sad eyes, wrote down their order dutifully on a notepad and said she'd be right back. Because of how long it took to concoct the milk shake, it was several minutes before she returned. Neither man spoke until she'd gone back behind the counter.

"I'm sorta walking the line, knowing what you told me about that suicide on Latimer Lane," Hammersmith said. He sampled the milk shake and smacked his lips in appreciation.

"There's no reason to think Norva Beane was involved in that," Nudger said.

Hammersmith poked the straw in and out of his milk shake, sinking the maraschino cherry that had been perched on top on a dabble of whipped cream. "You were at the scene because she hired you, Nudge."

True enough. Nudger sampled his coffee and scorched his tongue. *Yeow!* Why did he always do that without thinking?

"I better know everything you told the Ladue police," Hammersmith said.

Nudger told him.

By the time he'd finished, the waitress had refilled his cup, and Hammersmith was on his second milk shake.

"I talked to some people while you were being questioned by the law," Hammersmith said. "I guess you wanna know what I found out."

Nudger nodded. "That's why I'm buying the milk shakes."

"Your client's—"

"Former client," Nudger corrected.

"Okay. Norva Beane's first shot went through the Caddy's windshield, barely missing Rand. There's no doubt she wanted to kill him."

"None in my mind," Nudger said, remembering Norva frantically hopping to the side to angle a second shot around him.

"The first bullet deflected off the rearview mirror, went

through the back of the car's front seat, then lodged in one of the door panels. It's too distorted to be used in a ballistics test. The second bullet hasn't been found and probably won't be."

"What about Norva?"

"She's disappeared like the second bullet. Ladue called in, and we sent a squad car to her apartment to pick her up. No surprise when she wasn't home. Ladue's there now with our guys, searching the place to know what there is to know about the lady, what's on her closet shelf, buried in the back of her dresser drawers, in her diary if she keeps one. Figure out her motive and such."

"Motive? She thinks Rand swindled her out of her investment money, so she took a shot at him. Maybe that's how it's done in Possum Run."

Hammersmith dabbed milk shake from his lips with his napkin and stared at Nudger. "Possum Run?"

"Town where she's from."

"If there really is such a place."

"I looked on a map. It's there, down near the Arkansas line."

"Far as is known," Hammersmith said, "Norva Beane's got no connection with Dale Rand. No motive. There's no record of any sorta business transaction between her and Rand."

Nudger took too big a sip of the fresh coffee and scalded his tongue again. "Then why did she hire me?"

"I don't know, Nudge. But then, much of your world is a puzzle to those of us on the outside."

"What about Fred McMahon?"

"I think he's going to prison."

"I mean, Norva thought Rand might be in on some crooked junk-bond deal with McMahon. Maybe McMahon and Norva are connected in some way."

"The Ladue police say not." Hammersmith finished his milk shake with a loud slurping sound that caused several heads to turn. He sat back and kinked the straw as if trying to render it useless for anyone else, any other milk shake. "I've gotta be sure there's nothing you're not telling me, Nudge. Our friendship's put me in a gray area that's almost black, and we might be talking about murder if Norva Beane takes another run at Rand for whatever reason."

Nudger said, "You know it all. Everything. Except for . . ."

Hammersmith leaned forward over his empty glass with its kinked straw.

Nudger told him about the stock information and suggested he should call his broker first thing in the morning.

Hammersmith gazed at him with his neutral blue eyes and said, "You've gone stark raving bonkers. I'm going home to watch Jay Leno."

"It's already higher than when I bought it," Nudger pointed out. "Fortune Fashions is up a half."

Hammersmith huffed and raised his bulk to standing position. "Better lock in your profits and buy tax-free municipals."

He didn't look back at Nudger as he glided to the door and outside.

There would come a time, Nudger vowed, when with pleasure he would lay the financial page of the newspaper in front of Hammersmith with certain stocks circled in red.

No, circled in black.

Still exhausted, but on edge from the coffee, he decided he'd go to his apartment and watch some television himself. Maybe get bored enough to doze off.

He paid at the register, then went out into the rain and climbed into the Granada. The old car's interior stayed dry in weather like this, but it sure smelled musty. Like a moldy basement that leaked.

He drove the short distance to his apartment and parked on Sutton. It began raining harder as he was crossing the street. A deluge. He forgot about dignity and ran. When he opened his apartment door, he was breathing hard and he was soaked. Also more wide awake than ever and possibly catching a summer cold. When you got exhausted like he was, then got jacked up on caffeine so you couldn't sleep, it lowered your resistance. Bacteria loved that. It was their reason for living. He'd look in the medicine cabinet; maybe there was something he could take.

He forgot about all that when he switched on the light and saw Norva Beane seated on the sofa.

CHAPTER TWENTY

Norva looked concerned and said, "It appears to have rained hard on you, Mr. Nudger."

"All my life." He smoothed wet hair back from his forehead and came the rest of the way into his apartment, closing the door behind him. Only one lamp was on, one of the matching set on either side of the sofa. In the soft, yellow sidelighting, Norva looked schoolgirl young and vulnerable. It was difficult to imagine her with a rifle, aiming to kill. "How did you get in here, Norva?"

"You left the door unlocked, so I just walked on in."

He knew that wasn't true. "The police are doing their best to find you."

"I 'spect they are."

"Maybe you should help them and yourself. Get a good lawyer and give yourself up."

"Good Lord, no! I'd never do that. Anyways, there's no such thing as a good lawyer."

"I know a few, Norva, believe me."

"Well, giving myself up at this time is purely out of the

question." She didn't move from where she sat on the sofa with her legs crossed. She seemed so calm and sweet in her bucktoothed, country way, this fugitive deemed armed and dangerous.

Nudger crossed the room and sat slumped in an armchair, facing the sofa. It was warm and humid in the apartment, but that didn't seem to bother Norva. "You haven't been on your honor with me," he said.

"Well, that's so, Mr. Nudger. I've told you some untruths."

"Lies, you mean."

"If you care to say it in so coarse a way. But I had my reasons."

"I'd like to hear them, since I'm still alive after this evening."

"It's why I came here, Mr. Nudger, to square things between us. To tell you the whole story."

Nudger leaned back in the soft chair, resting his head against the swell of upholstery. He closed his eyes, but not quite all the way. He'd know it if Norva rose from the sofa. He said, "Are you really Norva Beane from Possum Run?"

"That part is certainly true. The rest mostly isn't."

"What else is true, Norva? What's the pure truth?"

"I gotta go back a ways for that, Mr. Nudger. When I was just a freshman in high school, a boy got me pregnant, then off he went and joined the Marines. I went away to Little Rock and carried to term, then gave up my baby for adoption and come back home. Everybody there acted like nothing had happened, like I'd just been away to visit an aunt like my ma said. Only word gets around in a place like Possum Run. Everybody knew what had really happened. That didn't bother me none. What did bother me was I gave up my own baby. I been tortured by remorse ever since, even though I knew I'd made the right decision for the child at the time. A fifteen-year-old mother with neither dime nor dollar, in a place like I was from, what else could I do?"

She'd asked the question as if she didn't want to hear an honest answer. Hurried on with her story:

"My own family was so poor they was barely feeding themselves. Another soul to keep alive would have broken Ma and Pa's backs. My way was clear. But sometimes the heart won't listen to what the head knows is right."

Nudger told her he understood, it was the source of many of his problems.

"Not very long ago, Billy Halliman reappeared in Possum Run."

She made it seem he'd taken form like a magician's illusion. "The father?"

"Yep. He'd been a career military man, a mechanic working on big jets, then some defense cuts forced him to resign. Least that's what he said. He told me he was on his way to some kinda civilian job in the Middle East, and he wanted to talk to me before he left."

"Seems odd he'd want to see you, after so many years."

"Billy wasn't without his own remorse, Mr. Nudger. He told me he'd taken the trouble to find out what happened to our daughter, even though the adoption service tried to keep such information confidential. He thought I deserved to know what he'd learned, that she'd been raised by a family here in St. Louis. I was determined to find out what I could about her, maybe to put my mind at ease. But what I discovered from Billy and my own inquiries was that she grew up and was living in an environment even worse than any I coulda gave her. A twisted and evil environment, Mr. Nudger. I feel even more guilt and remorse about giving her up now, and I'm in a frightful rage at the adoptive parents—'specially the father—who ruined my little girl's life."

Something cold moved through Nudger. He leaned forward and stared at Norva.

"What happened, Mr. Nudger, is my daughter Luanne grew up the adopted child of a drug trafficker and molester. I did truly come to you under false pretenses, and for that I apologize. I read about Fred McMahon in the newspaper, and I decided to link together him and Dale Rand so I'd have a good story when I tried to hire you. Dale Rand never had a thing to do with Fred McMahon nor any junk-bond deal—I barely know what a junk bond is—but I had good reason to kill him and still do."

Nudger was still trying to absorb this. "You're saying Luanne Rand is your daughter?"

"Yes, that's how fate worked it out."

Nudger was quiet for a while, listening to night sounds off in the distance. The whir of traffic on Manchester and over on Highway 44. A distant siren. Dogs barking frantically, very far away. "You hired me to find out about Rand, but it was Luanne you were most interested in."

"I'd heard things about Dale Rand, and I wanted to find out more. I thought a professional like you could get the information. And you surely did a fine job of that, Mr. Nudger. What I heard was true. Now the only way I can make things up to Luanne is to kill Dale Rand."

She spoke as if they might be discussing killing a chicken for dinner.

Nudger ran his fingers through his damp hair again. "I don't think it's that simple, Norva."

She stared guilelessly at him. "I do believe it is."

"I have to tell the police you're here," he said.

"Well, of course. I figured that. One thing I know you got is professional ethics. Lots of personal ones, too. But I felt I owed it to you to explain anyways, regardless of where your sense of duty was to lead you."

"Murdering Dale Rand won't change anything for Luanne that can't be changed some other way," he said. "And your getting imprisoned for life or executed won't do her any good."

"Hardly matters now what happens to me. Best thing I can do is remove Rand from my daughter's life, as I was the one put her in his. The man deserves to die, and I'm the instrument of justice, no matter what the law says or does."

"God's justice, huh?"

"It's got nothing to do with God. It's got to do with what I did to my own daughter long ago, and what I can do to save her now."

The flesh at the corners of her mouth twitched when she said this. Her eyes were hard and red-rimmed, not as if she'd been crying, but as if she hadn't slept for a long time. She was exhausted, Nudger knew, and running on raw nerve. She might do anything.

"Tell you what," he said, "I want you to talk to a friend of mine. Guy named Hammersmith." He reached for the phone on a nearby table.

She said, "I think I won't do that, Mr. Nudger."

A subtle change in her eyes should have warned him.

An arm clamped around his neck from behind. Thick, powerful. He dug his fingernails into it, trying to pull it away, but it had iron invincibility. All he'd accomplished was bending back his fingernails and possibly inflicting a few scratches. He lashed backward with both fists but made only light contact when he wasn't thrashing air. The shoulder he'd banged on the ground tackling Norva near Rand's driveway exploded with pain. The arm around his neck tightened and he fought to breathe. Felt and heard cartilage crackling in his throat. He got panicky then, but only for a brief moment. Then he was outside himself.

His vision blurred, his head felt weightless, as if his brain had become detached and was hurtling madly among the stars like a faintly aware comet.

The room tilted in light-speckled blackness and whirled him away into nothingness.

CHAPTER TWENTY-ONE

There went a cockroach. A small one, but he was sure it was a cockroach. It stopped. It waved its antennae as if taunting anything or anyone watching.

Nudger hated roaches almost as vehemently as he hated pigeons. Usually his apartment was free of them—roaches and pigeons. But the damned things got in now and then—roaches, not pigeons—in boxes or grocery bags, carried in sometimes in the clothes of other people. Nasty little invaders—the roaches, not people. And there one was, only a few inches from his face, staring at him. Not a person, but a small cockroach. It occurred to him that it was odd, being on eye level with an insect.

Hey, what was he doing on the floor? Nudger, not the insect.

Then he remembered last night, Norva Beane, the iron arm that had choked him into unconsciousness. The man must have been hiding in the apartment all the time Norva was telling her tale about her illegitimate daughter.

Luanne. Dale Rand's adopted daughter and maybe his victim. Good Lord, what a world!

Nudger was stretched out on his stomach on the carpet, in front of the armchair he'd been sitting in when he was choked. His cheek was pressed flat against coarse fibers. Wet fibers. He'd drooled during the night.

This was unpleasant. He raised himself up on his elbows, watched the alarmed cockroach scurry away, and thought: Enjoy life while you can, you little bastard, before I call the exterminator.

When he rolled onto his side to start to get up, pain struck his shoulder like lightning. He swallowed the terrible taste in his mouth and realized his throat was dry and as sore as if he'd been . . . well, choked almost to death.

He sat all the way up, leaning his back against the lumpy front of the armchair, and moved his left arm experimentally. The shoulder burned with pain, but he had mobility. He swallowed again. His throat still hurt. He wondered if he could speak. Said, "Testing, one, two, three." Heard, "Traagh, un, tooo, thray."

Maybe a shower, then some hot coffee would help. He aggravated his shoulder again by lifting his arm to look at his watch. 9:35. He'd been unconscious for over nine hours. That was a lot of rest. Aside from the pain, he should feel refreshed. Hah!

With great effort, he managed to get to his feet and lurch into the bathroom. Now his head was throbbing as if he had the mother of all hangovers, and any extended family. He sat on the toilet seat and worked out of his clothes, then ran some water and climbed into the shower, almost pulling down the plastic curtain with the fish design in the process. He stood for a long time letting the hot needles of water roar against his sore shoulder.

While he was toweling dry, he heard the phone ring. He

hurried, nude and leaving a trail of wet spots, into the bedroom and picked up.

Danny, from the doughnut shop.

"That guy with the fancy earring was back by here this morning, Nudge. I thought you oughta know before you came in to the office."

"He gone?" Nudger croaked.

"You catching cold, Nudge?"

"Kinda. Got a sore shoulder, too."

"Bursitis? Like that?"

"Not exactly."

"You still got some of that Mother's Extra Care liniment I gave you?"

Nudger remembered the tube of off-brand liniment Danny had brought him last time he'd suffered muscle soreness. It smelled like gasoline but it was effective. "I think the tube's still around, Danny. What about the guy with the earring?"

"Oh, yeah. He's been gone about ten minutes, is all. I phoned you earlier but didn't get an answer."

"I was in the shower. What'd he say?"

"Never said a thing. Never even got outa his car, a big white Lincoln with one of them padded roofs that looks like a mattress. But he drove by real slow a couple of times, then he stopped and parked right in front of the shop. Sat there a few minutes just staring in through the window, like he wanted to make sure I'd see him and tell you about it. So, it worked, right? Here I am telling you."

"Thanks, Danny."

"S'okay, hero."

"What?"

"Ain't you seen the morning paper, Nudge? It tells how you saved that rich guy's life out in Ladue. Got your picture and everything."

138

Nudger understood then what Aaron might want this time. He and King Chambers would be curious as to what Nudger had told the police.

"Nudge?"

"I'm still here, Danny. Thinking."

"Well, I guess you got a lot to think about."

"And not much to do it with this morning. I had visitors late last night so I overslept. My head feels the size and shape of a watermelon."

"C'mon over and have some breakfast, you'll feel better."

Nudger's stomach grumbled. "I don't have time this morning, Danny. That guy comes back, give me another call."

"Sure. You think he knows where you live?"

Yike! There was a thought! "Maybe, Danny. I gotta hang up."

"Okay, Nu—"

Nudger was already jogging into the living room, aware again of his midsection jiggling. He promised his new paunchy self he'd diet, if he survived. That was the condition.

Not only was the door to the hall unlocked, it was ajar several inches. He closed it quickly and threw the deadbolt, then fastened the chain lock.

Then he rubbed some of Danny's liniment into his shoulder and the back of his neck and got dressed. For a few minutes he thought he smelled too much like fuel to go out, but soon the gasoline scent subsided.

He phoned Hammersmith and told him about last night. Then he called Captain Massinger. Massinger wanted to talk to him immediately. Big surprise.

Nudger's head didn't hurt so bad now, and he was hungry. He went into the kitchen and fried up an egg and three strips of bacon, and ate that along with toast, strawberry preserves, and coffee.

Then he drove out to Ladue.

Massinger wrinkled his nose and said, "You stop on the way here to buy gas?"

"No," Nudger said, puzzled.

"Okay, never mind." Massinger settled down behind his desk and sat with his hands folded over his ample but firm stomach. He'd been in good shape once and was probably still tough. He studied Nudger with his square little eyes and said, "Quite a piece about you in the paper this morning. Nice photograph, too. You seldom see leisure suits these days."

"I haven't read the paper yet."

"How characteristically modest."

Knowing sarcasm when he heard it, Nudger said, "You wanted to hear about what happened in my apartment last night."

"Yes, do fill me in."

Nudger did.

Massinger looked more and more stricken as he sat and listened. When Nudger was finished, the portly little lieutenant said, "Incest, child molestation, drug dealing. For Christsakes, Nudger, this is Ladue!"

Nudger said, "Think Palm Beach."

Massinger glared at him with horror. "You're an ex-cop, and you never so much as got a glance at the guy who choked you?"

"No, it all happened too fast. I was unconscious before I could follow the rulebook."

"Well," Massinger said with a sneer, "you sure put up one hell of a struggle."

"I was a hero yesterday," Nudger said. "Whaddya want?"

"A partial description. What about Norva Beane? She give any hint of where she might be hiding out or running to?"

"No. She's not that stupid, Lieutenant."

"Was she armed?"

"Not that I could see. She didn't have her rifle with her, but she might have had a concealed handgun. She's from a part of southwest Missouri where there are more guns than personal computers, so it'd seem natural to her to be carrying."

"Thanks at least for that information."

"Does Rand have any record at all on drugs?"

Massinger rubbed his chin, considering whether he should confide in Nudger. He must know Nudger could find out. "No," he said after a while, "he's clean as vanilla ice cream. What he is, Nudger, is a goddamn civic leader. Gives to charities, attends highfalutin' social functions. Even goes to the Veiled Prophet Ball, where all the debutantes come out."

"Speaking of which," Nudger said, "what about Luanne Rand?"

"She was never a debutante." Massinger's features tightened. His eyes became even more square.

Nudger knew there was something here. "I mean, does she have any kind of record?"

Massinger placed both hands over his stomach again and sighed. "Couple of arrests for possession. Marijuana once, cocaine the other time. No convictions. In fact, neither case even made it to court."

"Why not?"

"Grease."

"The musical?"

"No, the influence, the money. You know what I mean. The social lubricant. People here got grease, Nudger. Their sons and daughters get outa scrapes that'd put other kids behind bars." Massinger chewed his lower lip, as if debating whether to say more. "The times Luanne Rand got herself in trouble were no big deal. She's not alone among rich Ladue kids who get tangled up with narcotics."

He paused. "She's got another thing on her record here. But no charges were ever brought. She was arrested in the lounge of a hotel in Clayton on a soliciting-for-prostitution charge. She tried to pick up an undercover Narc. Turned out, though, she hadn't actually requested money, at least not in so many words. So maybe it was just boy-girl stuff. A misunderstanding. And she was only fifteen, even though she looked older, so the whole matter dissolved the way that kinda thing does sometimes, and everybody went their own way not quite sure what it was all about except it was something they'd all laugh about in twenty years when they were sitting around the pool. Part of growing up, like in a Disney movie. One of the new Disney movies, anyway."

"Anything else?" Nudger asked. "Any homicide charges?"

"She had no way to buy that poison," Massinger said. "Huh?"

Massinger smiled, looking like an improbable pixie. "Only kidding, Nudger. No homicide charges against you or Luanne Rand." He stood up. Obviously, the interview was over.

Nudger stood also.

"One more thing," Massinger said. "The business about incest, drug dealing, Norva Beane's story and everything in it, none of it might be true, so let's you and I not talk about it to the news media."

142

"Fine by me," Nudger said. "They'd get it all mixed up anyway."

"Pick up a paper on your way to wherever you're going," Massinger said, "if you want to read about how they get things wrong."

Nudger thought his leg was being pulled again, so he didn't reply. He started to leave the office.

"You sure you didn't stop on the way here and buy gas?" Massinger asked again behind him.

"Sure," Nudger said, and went out, wondering about Massinger's persistence with the gas thing. The cop in him, he decided.

CHAPTER TWENTY-TWO

Nudger stopped at a vending machine, fed it two quarters, wrestled with it to see who'd keep the quarters, and managed to come away with a scratched wrist and a morning *Post-Dispatch*.

He sat in the car and crinkled the paper open between his chest and the steering wheel, his gaze roving over the newsprint made dazzlingly translucent by the sun streaming through the windshield. He found himself on page three of the front section. A shooting in Ladue was always front-section news, even if no one had been hurt.

Yep, there he was in his leisure suit. The photo had been taken years ago, when he'd been working as Coppy the Clown at various schools and social functions. It was the role the department had assigned him after learning that his nervous stomach simply wouldn't allow for regular police work. But a new chief had decided a clown didn't suit the department's desired public image, so Nudger had found himself all dressed up in polka dots and a red nose with no place to go other than into the private-investigation business. He remembered the reporter who'd asked him a few questions about his talk at a grade school, along with the photographer who'd taken the leisure-suit shot. Nudger had felt fairly important that long-ago day. It was probably the only photograph of him not wearing his clown suit that the paper had on file. He looked a little dated, he had to admit, with the Fu Manchu mustache and the long side-burns, but he was younger and actually not a bad-looking guy. It was all in the eye of the beholder, he knew, but he wasn't embarrassed by the photograph.

He wasn't so sure the news article treated him as a heroic figure. It merely mentioned that he'd scuffled with the gunwoman (in a nod to political correctness) and spoiled her aim. Then the gunwoman had overpowered him and escaped. He'd later revealed (said the article) that the gun-woman was his client.

Nudger folded the paper and laid it on the seat. He thought the news item made him seem like a boob and wouldn't do his business a bit of good. Maybe that would change if the press gave him better treatment in any later news reports.

He pinched the bridge of his nose between his thumb and forefinger, hoping his headache wasn't coming back to plague him along with his nervous stomach. He was begin-ning to understand why he stayed in the detective business rather than enter sales or manual labor. Gastronomically unsuited though he might be for the work, he had his pride as well as his curiosity. The result was a stomach-churning compulsion to locate Norva Beane and to find answers to questions. That was what he was about, really, not giving up, getting answers. If only he had enough answers, maybe he'd understand his life and be able to do something about it.

He sat there in the Granada for a while with the engine

idling roughly, threatening to quit as it always did, bluffing. He figured it was possible the city police were watching Norva's apartment, but the manpower shortage being what it was, that was doubtful. She was running from the Ladue police, wanted for a crime committed in the county. If the Major Case Squad wasn't involved, usually there wasn't much coordination among the crazy-quilt patchwork of police departments clustered around the city of St. Louis.

Also, Nudger figured, slipping the car into Drive and heading toward South St. Louis, if anybody was watching the building, they probably wouldn't know who he was, so he could walk right in. He'd be just another tenant or visitor. He could make sure he wouldn't be seen actually entering Norva's apartment.

But as he turned the corner near her building, he saw a white Lincoln with a padded roof half a block in front of him. He slowed the Granada to a gradual halt, like a prey animal not wanting to do anything sudden and attract predators.

The Lincoln was parked, but he could make out someone, a man, sitting behind the steering wheel. This wasn't the kind of neighborhood that was crawling with new luxury cars. And Danny had said Aaron was driving a white Lincoln with a padded roof this morning.

Nudger's stomach twitched out a caution signal. He didn't think he'd been seen, so he put the Granada in reverse and backed up to where he could turn around in a driveway. He accomplished the maneuver slowly and with precision. Then he drove back up the street and around the corner.

He hit the accelerator then, winding down narrow side streets, watching his rearview mirror.

When he was sure he wasn't being followed, he drove

back to Grand Avenue, then headed west on Highway 40 toward Ladue. Rand would no doubt have police protection, but Nudger figured it still wouldn't be too much of a risk to retrieve the last tape from the parked Chevy in the block behind the Rand house. Besides, he was paying the bug man for as long as real time was being registered on the recorder.

He didn't go past Rand's house. The law was sure to be keeping an eye on things there. At the very least, no matter where Rand was, they'd be running frequent patrols past the house.

After parking the Granada behind the Chevy, he briskly but casually got out and collected the last tape. Then he closed the trunk, climbed back in the Granada and drove away.

Simple.

No reason for his knees to feel weak and his heart to be beating so fast.

When he got back to his office, he phoned the bug man and left a message on his answering machine that the job was ended. He mentioned the time, too, the *real* time, so the bug man wouldn't succumb to the impulse to overcharge him.

Then he settled in behind his desk to listen to the last tape.

8:07 P.M. Last night, just after the police had gone, Nudger figured.

Rand and Sydney were talking, not arguing for a change.

RAND: "I never heard of Norva Beane, and I never met Fred McMahon. I got no idea what the fuck's going on."

SYDNEY: "I never heard of her either." A beat. "You telling me the truth, Dale?"

RAND: "Of course I am! I never did any business with any such woman, never saw her before, and she goddamn tried to kill me. Can you imagine?"

SYDNEY: "You think she'll be back? I mean, you think the police can really protect us?"

RAND: "They'll catch her. They've got her description. Her address. Everything. Oh, Jesus!"

SYDNEY: "That's your third Scotch, Dale. You're drinking too much."

RAND: "You should know."

Oh-oh, Nudger thought.

SYDNEY: "Neither of us is perfect, *sweetheart*. It's not that kinda world. Not for anybody. But at least I'm not regularly sneaking into—"

RAND: "Into where?"

SYNDEY: "Never mind."

RAND: "I know just as well as you do what kind of world it is. So do me a favor and don't become a philosophical drunk. You're difficult enough as it is."

SYDNEY: "I'm difficult? Why are *you* wound so tight lately? What kinda shitty deal are you into? Your mysterious phone conversations, your mention of—"

RAND: "I use the phone for business. There's nothing mysterious at all about it. What's mysterious is why this Beane woman thinks I cheated her and why she's trying to blow my head off."

That jolted Nudger until he remembered that Massinger hadn't yet learned Luanne was Norva's daughter when the recording was made. Massinger still might not have relayed that information to the Rands. Norva's story was, after all, nothing more than allegations made by a woman on the run from the law.

SYDNEY: "You think Luanne might know who she is? I mean, about some connection between you two?"

RAND: "No! I asked her. She said no and I believe her. I can tell when she's lying."

SYDNEY: "Where is she?"

RAND: "Nan's probably. That's where she spends too much of her time."

SYDNEY: "Well, I don't blame her for not wanting to spend time here, with you. Any more time than you force her to spend, that is."

RAND: "Piss on you! And on that idiot private detective."

SYDNEY: "Yeah, piss on the people who save your life."

RAND: "That's right, take a drink. A tall one."

SYDNEY: "Gotta catch up with you, lover."

Silence.

9:16 P.M.

Sydney, apparently alone in the house, phones Eberhardt's Liquor for a delivery.

9:30 A.M.

This morning. Sydney phones Kearn-Wisdom and asks to speak to Rand. A woman informs her that he won't be in today. Sydney says something that sounds like "Uhhumph!" As if she's not surprised.

End of sound on the tape.

Nudger punched Rewind. His chair *eeped* as he swiveled this way and that, listening to the smooth whir of the recorder until it clicked off. Apparently Rand hadn't come home last night. Neither had Luanne. No chance for family values here. The Rands seemed to be coming unglued under pressure from within and without.

He got the rest of the cassettes from a drawer and inserted one in the recorder. Listened patiently, rewinding and fast-forwarding a few times, then inserted another. He played with the cassettes until he found what he wanted.

Nan's last name. He thought he remembered Rand mentioning it when he was grilling Luanne. Nan Grant. Nudger wrote it down on a piece of scratch paper, then stared at it.

A thread, he thought. That's what it was called sometimes in his profession.

Who knew what it might unravel?

CHAPTER TWENTY-THREE

"I need this," Nudger had said to Claudia, but she'd refused to regard him as a hero. She noted that he might easily have been shot last night.

"I was simply doing my job," he replied.

"Then there's hardly anything heroic about it."

"I need this," he told her again, two hours later, when the Mets were changing pitchers in the seventh inning of the Businessman's Special. She had only morning classes today, so Nudger had visited her apartment, and after striking out there, he suggested they go to the ballpark, lunch on hot dogs and nachos, and watch the rest of the afternoon game, the Businessman's Special. He didn't figure he had to worry much about King Chamberlain or Aaron or being mugged again by Norva's friend here in bright sunlight among forty thousand people.

Claudia said, "I really don't understand it."

"There are certain responsiblities that go with the profession," Nudger said. "Things you owe any client. It was a matter of honor, I guess." Honor. He was surprised by how easily the word had slid from his lips.

"I mean, I don't understand why the Mets don't put in a left-hander." Claudia was knowledgeable about baseball. She and several other teachers had combined resources to buy season tickets. It was her turn to use the seats, which was another reason Nudger had suggested lunch and a ball game. He wondered if Biff Archway had ever sat where he was sitting.

Nudger said, "There are over two hundred 'Grants' in the phone book."

"That has nothing to do with a right-hander being brought in to pitch to a left-handed hitter late in a tie game. The percentage is with the Cardinals."

"Good. Nan Grant is a student, probably at the same school where Luanne Rand is enrolled. It should be easy for you to call the right people and come up with her address." Cheering began on the other side of the stadium, and section by section, fans stood briefly and raised their arms, so that the undulating movement swept sequentially around the circular ballpark. The wave. Nudger loved baseball but not the wave. Not furry or feathered mascots, either, nor ball players who refused to slide headfirst in the last year of their contracts, or owners more interested in the bottom line than in winning games. But especially not the wave.

Instead of answering him, Claudia stood up and yelled, raising and lowering her arms. She was wearing a red Cardinals T-shirt, and Nudger liked the way her small breasts protruded when she stretched and raised her arms, but that was the best he could say for the wave.

He said, "The Mets' manager knows that if he brings in a left-hander, the Cardinals will counter with a right-handed pinch hitter who's a threat to hit a home run."

Settling back into her seat, she stared at him. "Why didn't you say that in the first place?"

"I was asking if you'd use your connections to try to get Nan Grant's address for me, waiting for your answer."

The bearded giant in a tank top behind Nudger suddenly screamed, "C'mon! Let's plaaaay baaaaaall!" Nudger jumped, spilling most of the beer from his paper cup.

Claudia made a face and said, "God, that uniform."

Confused, Nudger said, "You've seen the Mets' uniforms before."

"I meant that outfit you had on in your newspaper photograph this morning."

"Leisure suits were the style when the photo was taken."

"It's not a very flattering style, even though you were a lot thinner then."

The giant kicked the back of Nudger's seat in frustration. Nudger sensibly directed his anger at Claudia. "Damn it! I try to hold a conversation with you and you won't give me an answer. You jump the rails! You—"

She grinned. "Relax, Nudger, I was only giving you the needle. Tell you what, you go buy us some more nachos, and when the game's over I'll try to get Nan Grant's address."

It sounded like a bargain to Nudger. He needed another beer anyway. He stood up and wedged his way between seat backs and knees to the aisle and descended into the shade of the tunnel beneath the stands.

He was reaching into his pocket to pay for the nachos at the concession stand when he heard the crowd roar.

It was still roaring when he got back to his section. He squinted to see better in the sunlight. Claudia and the giant were both standing, giving each other high fives. "Three run homer!" the giant was booming over and over, as

153

Nudger edged back toward his seat, balancing the nachos and beer. Some of the beer spilled over the side of the cup and ran down his arm. "Three run homer! Terrific shot to right field. Longest I ever seen! You missed it, buddy!" The giant gave Claudia a hug as if they'd known each other for years. They slapped each other's hands some more.

It must have been quite a home run, all right. Even the players in the Mets dugout were buzzing about it.

Gradually the crowd settled back down in their seats, but they were still excited. Nudger sat and watched Fredbird, the mascot, strut arrogantly back and forth on the roof of the Cardinals dugout. He wished the absurd maroon bird would trip and fall.

He loved baseball.

Downtown traffic was brutal after the game, so it was almost three-thirty when they got back to Claudia's apartment. Nudger sat on the sofa, listening to blues on the radio and enjoying the air conditioning, while Claudia went into the bedroom to use the phone there for her queries about Nan Grant.

Fifteen minutes passed before he heard her call him, and turned to see her standing in the bedroom doorway wearing only panties and bra.

She smiled and said, "I've got the air conditioner on high in here, hero."

He stood up and went to her, tried to grab her and kiss her, but she spun out of reach, then snatched his hand and led him to the bed. The air was cool in the bedroom. The sheets were cool. Everything other than Nudger and Claudia was cool.

He was supported on his elbows and knees, poised over her in the play of cool air, and she was breathing heavily into his ear, when the phone rang.

"Probably about Nan Grant," she breathed.

"Maybe not. Might be your landlord. Better not answer it."

"My landlord doesn't phone me."

The phone seemed to be getting louder with each ring. Nudger lowered the length of his body an inch. "Claudia . . ."

"No, no, I can't stay in the mood if I don't answer." She wriggled halfway out from beneath him and snaked out an arm to lift the receiver. She pressed plastic to her ear and said hello in a way that might melt some microchips. Nudger waited.

"For you," she said.

Supported on his knees and one elbow now, he held the receiver to his ear. Hammersmith said, "Nudge?"

"Yeah."

"I calling at a bad time?"

"Well, yeah."

"She's disappeared."

"Who?"

"Luanne."

"She's done it before."

"But this time Sydney Rand went to the police and reported her missing."

"Luanne hasn't been gone long enough for that."

"How would you know?"

"I know."

"This is Ladue we're talking about, Nudge. The rules are different out there. The kid left the house yesterday morning and didn't come home last night. There's the possibility Norva Beane abducted her. Luanne's not in school, and nobody seems to know where she is. Considering her father was shot at last night, that's good enough for

Massinger. Truth is, it might be good enough for me, too. Believe me, she's missing."

"Well, I don't know where she is."

"Just be sure you don't, Nudge. I thought you oughta hear about this for when the Ladue police contact you. Massinger already called here. He told me he'd informed Dale Rand that Norva Beane says she's Luanne's natural mother. If that's true, it's hard to believe Norva didn't have anything to do with the girl's disappearance."

"Massinger say that?"

"That, and he asked if I'd seen you. He said he tried your office and your apartment all afternoon."

"I was at the ball game."

"Lucky you. Some game. Historic home run, huh? The radio said the ball went over four hundred fifty feet, hit high enough to bring rain. Musta been something to see."

"Musta been."

"I reminded Massinger you weren't involved in this case anymore, now that you've lost your client. You're not involved, right?"

"Only in a very limited way."

"Okay. I'm not gonna ask how limited. I'll let you get back to whatever it was you were doing, Nudge. I expect it was important." Hammersmith's voice was perfectly neutral. You could never tell with him.

He hung up.

Nudger handed Claudia the receiver and she replaced it. "What was that about?" she asked.

"Luanne Rand is gone."

She looked down at him and smiled. "So are you."

Nudger said, "Damn!" and rolled onto his back.

"Don't worry about it, lover. Relax." She kissed him gently on the lips. "Relax," she repeated.

No sooner had he relaxed when the phone rang again.

This time it was for Claudia, someone returning her call to tell her Nan Grant's address.

Though Claudia's Board of Education informant told her Nan Grant was indeed a classmate of Luanne, she lived nowhere near Luanne. She was attending the expensive private high school on a scholarship, and resided in a tough, gang-infested, and impoverished area of North Saint Louis.

Nudger didn't know how to feel about that.

Certainly not relaxed.

CHAPTER TWENTY-FOUR

The slim, neatly dressed black girl who emerged from the decrepit brick apartment building the next morning didn't look as if she belonged in such a ruinous neighborhood. She was wearing brown slacks, a yellow blouse with a white collar, white cuffs on the short sleeves, and white jogging shoes with a multicolored design on the sides, which made each shoe look like a miniature *Grand Prix* race car. Nudger assumed she was Nan Grant. Herbert Hoover High School summer classes began in less than an hour, so the timing was right, along with the approximate age of the girl and the fact that she had books slung under one arm.

Nudger sat in the parked Granada and watched her. Two hulking street-corner loungers watched him. He was getting uneasy. Nan Grant wasn't walking toward the bus stop two blocks away as he'd assumed she would. Instead she was standing at the base of the apartment's cracked concrete stoop and staring at a paper in her left hand. She seemed completely unaware of the graffiti on the boarded-up windows behind her, of the trash in the gutter, of a wino or homeless man curled sleeping, unconscious, or dead in the doorway of the next apartment building.

A rusty white Toyota pickup truck with oversized tires and little in the way of a muffler rumbled past the Granada. The young black guy driving gave him a gunfighter glance. Nudger watched as the truck pulled to the curb. The driver opened the passenger-side door and extended a hand to help Nan Grant climb up and into the cab.

Nudger started the Granada and followed as the truck made its noisy way up the street. One of the loungers, a skinny guy with a shirt that looked to be made of fish net, grinned at him and began leaping around as if trying to get out of the way of something that wasn't there. His companion stared at Nudger in the same deadpan way as the kid who'd picked up Nan Grant. A gangly boy about twelve, walking down the opposite side of the street, scowled at Nudger, went into the moonwalk, and made an obscene gesture. Maybe it all meant something. Nudger couldn't figure it out.

The truck didn't lead him to Luanne Rand, as he'd hoped. It clanked and roared out to Ladue, where it was the odd fish among sleek and sharklike newer model cars, and stopped in front of Herbert Hoover High. Nan Grant climbed out of it without a word to the driver and strode along the hedge-lined walk to the school's entrance.

Nudger watched the truck deliberately cut off a Mercedes as it pulled back out into the stream of traffic, then disappear down the street. He drove to a public phone he'd noticed near a big drugstore, where he called Nan Grant's home and asked to speak to her. The woman who answered said Nan would be home from school at two-thirty, could he call back then. Nudger said he could, it was nothing important.

* * *

At two o'clock he was parked outside the high school, feeling heavy and guilty about the MunchaBunch doughnuts he'd had for lunch, watching a parade of BMWs, Mercedes Benzes, and Volvo station wagons queue at the curb to pick up students. He didn't see the beat-up Toyota truck.

Still with books slung beneath her arm, Nan Grant emerged from the school with two preppy-looking blond girls. They piled into a late-model blue BMW driven by a teenage girl with dark hair, cut almost military short on one side and arranged in a kind of rooster comb on the other. As the BMW passed Nudger, he could hear music blasting from it even though its air conditioner was on and its windows were closed. He fell in behind it, amazed at the way all its occupants seemed to be talking and gesticulating at once, all of them waving lighted cigarettes. They seemed to understand what they were saying to each other, despite the multiple-track conversations and the music roaring from the stereo, and somehow they did not set each other on fire. In some ways, God looked after kids the way He did for drunks.

The girl with the rooster hairdo drove to a vast shopping mall on Clayton Road and cruised around the airport-sized parking lot until she found a space. Nudger had to park farther away near the edge of the lot and jog to the mall entrance to catch up with the four girls.

They were having a fine time ambling around the mall, now and then entering a clothing or specialty store and trying things on. They seemed never to stop talking and finding each other vastly amusing.

They had more energy than Nudger. Within an hour his feet felt as heavy as diver's boots. He didn't want to wait outside one more shop, sit on one more hard bench near one more small tree near one more pool or fountain. It was past three o'clock. Apparently Nan Grant was no more predictable than Luanne about arriving home when expected.

Finally Nudger got a break. When it was nearly four o'clock, the other three girls giggled their goodbyes and left Nan standing near a shop that sold records, tapes, and compact discs. Nudger wasn't surprised; he couldn't imagine three preppy teenage girls in a BMW penetrating Nan's neighborhood to drop off a friend.

What now? Nudger wondered, wriggling his toes to keep his sore feet from cramping. Would she go to a bus stop? Would the kid in the Toyota truck make an appearance?

She began walking with a sense of purpose. Breathing heavily, Nudger kept pace. All the way to the food court.

She got some kind of massive creation with a hamburger at its center, french fries, and a gallon of soda, then sat alone at one of the small, phony marble tables. Nudger bought a Busch beer at one of the food counters and sat several tables away, grateful to be motionless for an extended period of time even if the tiny chair was causing permanent spine damage.

He watched Nan sit and slowly, solemnly now that she was alone, work on her food and soda. She didn't seem to be in any rush. Didn't seem to be waiting for anyone. She seemed oblivious to the people streaming past on their way to and from nearby escalators, or crowded around some of the food counters. Music was being piped in, an old Rolling Stones hit that had been neutered.

After a while, Nudger walked over and sat down opposite her. "Can we talk a minute, Nan?"

She stared blankly at him, unafraid in such a public place, trying to figure out if she knew him. She looked much younger close up. Round cheeks, small features, interesting eyes with crescents of white showing beneath the dark pupils. Too much red lipstick and violet eye shadow. She would have looked cheap if she weren't so young. What she looked like was a child who hadn't learned how to apply makeup. About half a minute passed before she said, "You're the guy tackled that woman who shot at Mr. Rand. I saw your picture in the paper, in that leisure suit."

"That's right. Can I ask you some questions about Luanne?"

Nan sipped some Coke and stared at him over the straw. Her eyes were alert now, intelligent. She straightened up and licked her lips. Lipstick rimmed the top of the straw. "I dunno. Can I trust you?"

"Can I trust *you*?"

"To do what?"

"To tell me the truth."

She took him in with her eyes and her mind. Somewhere inside her was the wisdom of her pain, of what it took even to try to transcend her circumstances. It was something her girlfriends at Herbert Hoover High wouldn't understand. He'd seldom felt so scrutinized. It only lasted a few seconds, then she was a naive teenage girl again. "Yeah, I guess so. I mean, why should I lie?"

"Why should either of us? First question is, do you know where Luanne can be found?"

"First answer's no. She missing or something?"

"Yes." He'd carried his beer over. He took a pull of it and set the glass down next to the bottle. "I'm worried about her."

Nan didn't ask him why. She said, "You oughta be."

Nudger went fishing. "You mean because of her father?"

"Uh-hm. Man's a real dork."

"Because of how he treats her?"

Nan looked unblinkingly at him, the older Nan again. "You know he's balling her?"

"Yeah." Nudger tried to keep his expression neutral but knew he hadn't.

"Don't look so mad and shocked. I got other friends with the same complaint. Maybe you shoulda let that crazy woman go ahead and shoot a hole in Mr. Rand. Shoot his lousy dingus right off."

"Maybe," Nudger said, thinking about it. "That why you figure Luanne might be missing? She ran away because of what her father was doing?"

"No, she got used to that years ago. Used to it as anybody could get, anyway. I think she's gone because of what else he's got her into. He set her up with some guys, and more'n once."

"Set her up?" It took a few seconds for Nudger to grasp what this kid with the paint-splotch eye shadow was telling him. "Wait a minute, you mean he's pimping for her?"

"Sure. Luanne said he got himself in a position where he didn't have any choice, but she still hated him for it."

Nudger stared out at the shoppers passing by, at customers carrying trays of food among the tables. They all seemed the type to lead quiet, normal lives. He knew better. It was a world of facades. His work had taught him that. It was teaching him again. He said, "Did he get her into drugs, Nan?"

"No, she did that on her own. But when he found out about it, he sure never did anything to help." She shoved away the rest of her hamburger and looked sick. "He watched while she sucked more and more of that stuff up her nose. While she went to smoking crack and then to the needle. A habit like Luanne's, it can make people do anything. Lie, fuck, steal. It can get them to put up with anything."

"Should I ask if you do drugs?"

She said, "You shouldn't ask that."

"Know a man named King Chambers?"

"No."

"A black guy named Aaron? Wears a swastika on a gold chain for an earring."

"No."

"What if Luanne reported Rand to the authorities? Would you testify and help the charges stick to him?"

"If I did that, I'd be in trouble with him. Trouble beyond what he did to Luanne. He's got these associates who are bad people. You understand?"

"I think so. But I hate to let him keep messing up Luanne's life."

"If Luanne's gone, maybe she did something about it on her own."

"You're good friends, right?"

Nan nodded.

"It makes sense she'd get in touch with you."

"But she hasn't," Nan said. "That's why I'm talking to you. I care about Luanne. We care about each other."

Nudger considered, then said, "Does Luanne know she's adopted?"

For the first time, Nan looked shocked. Her lower jaw dropped like a trap door. The violet disappeared as the whites of her eyes showed all the way around her pupils. "Adopted? No. I'm sure she doesn't know."

"If you see her, I think you should tell her. Tell her that her real mother loves her, maybe too much, and she's worried about her."

Nan had regained her composure and was staring at

Nudger. She was quick as well as bright. "Wow! The woman with the gun! You gotta be kidding!"

"Not," Nudger said. "Luanne needs to know people care about her and want to help her. Her mother—both her mothers, actually. You, she knows about. And tell her I want to help."

"Why should you wanna help Luanne?"

"It's my job."

Nan gave him a wicked, violet glance. Old eyes again. "You wanna help her the way her father did? That your interest?"

Nudger didn't understand.

Then he did. He had to fight to keep from reaching out and slapping Nan Grant. He told himself she was a kid and couldn't help it, that her life must have driven her to a distrust of all men. He told himself that, but he wasn't very convincing.

Nan smiled. "We done talking?"

He breathed out hard. "We can be."

"Good. I'm meeting somebody here any minute. A friend from my English class. We gotta do some studying together for a big test that's coming up."

Nudger finished his beer in a couple of gulps and stood up. He pinched foam from his mouth with his thumb and forefinger. "Thanks for talking with me, Nan. And when I said I wanted to help Luanne, that's exactly what I meant."

She nodded but didn't look up.

He walked away, glancing back once to see her watching him, munching on her giant hamburger again.

He went out the mall entrance and walked outside, along the side of a white, cast-concrete building to a department store entrance. Then he cut back through the store to the mall and approached the food court from another direction. He sat on yet another hard bench near yet another small potted tree and watched Nan Grant from a distance.

Watched her for almost half an hour until her friend showed up.

It wasn't a friend from school. Unless Aaron of the earring was taking remedial courses.

CHAPTER TWENTY-FIVE

At work and at home, Dale Rand had constant police protection. But a bullet was a small object that could travel a great distance accurately and at an astonishing rate of speed. The protection might make it more difficult for Norva Beane to kill Rand on her second try, but it couldn't prevent it. Nudger figured she'd wait until police protection slacked off, and time worked on Rand so that he felt more secure, before closing in on her quarry again. She was a country girl with a hunter's patience as well as a marksman's eye. Nudger was glad he wasn't Rand, whose destiny lay in the cross hairs of the woman from Possum Run.

Nudger was still determined to find Norva, and Luanne. Rand might be a help, but he refused to return Nudger's calls. Following Nan Grant had led Nudger nowhere. She behaved like an ordinary high-school girl. She didn't meet Aaron again, and Nudger was sure she didn't know Luanne's whereabouts. He knew it would be useless to ask her about Aaron, who was probably simply her drug contact, anyway. Or possibly Nan herself was dealing to the other high-school girls. An interesting possibility. Even alarming. But not surprising, really, and most likely irrelevant as far as Nudger was concerned.

After a week of frustration, he decided to approach the one other player who might have some insight into where Norva or Luanne might be, and if they might be together.

He waited until Rand had left for work in his black Caddy, watching as the police tail fell in behind the big car at the corner. It was possible the house was still being watched, even after a week, but Nudger knew he had to take the chance. He wasn't going to break a law; the worst that could happen was that he'd be apprehended and taken in for an intense and unpleasant conversation with Massinger.

He got out of the Granada, crossed the sunbaked street, and cut across the Rand's front lawn. After leaning hard on a fancy brass button, listening to chimes sound like tolling bells deep inside the house, he waited and stared out at sunlight and shadow lying in soft patterns on the manicured grass. Something about grass and summer and sunlight. He'd played a lot of baseball as a kid, and staring at the level green lawn made him remember the smell of grass stains and oiled leather, the sting of his knuckles from pounding them into his glove in anticipation. The solid clonk of bat against ball, and the feel of lofting the tiny round mass from the sweet spot on the bat. He'd been able to hit pretty well, but he—

The door opened. "Mr. Nudger. Hello."

Sydney was wearing a lacy pink robe with the hem of a pale blue nightgown showing around her knees. She was barefoot, reminding him of Norva Beane. She wore no makeup and he smelled no gin on her breath. She seemed sober.

Nudger gave her the old sweet smile. She did seem to melt a bit. "I thought we oughta talk," he said.

She gave him back his smile, fainter, but he was sure more genuine. "My husband said for me not to talk to you. He sees you more as part of the problem than as part of the solution."

"That sounds Reaganesque."

"Well, my husband's Reaganesque, some might say."

"Are you?"

"No, I'm a lifelong Democrat."

"I mean, are you going to talk with me?"

She studied him. Her eyes were puffy. Had she been crying? "Well, you *did* save Dale's life." She stepped back to admit him into the flow of cool air that was pressing out from the house. "We owe you, whether or not he thinks so. Anyway, a woman shouldn't always do what her husband says."

"Sets a dangerous precedent," Nudger agreed.

He moved beyond Sydney, catching a whiff of lilac-scented perfume. Nice. Despite the ravages of Dale Rand and alcohol, she seemed a woman hanging onto her femininity and onto hope. But there was a brittleness about her, a subtle scent of desperation that the perfume couldn't conceal.

She led him through a short entry hall and into a large living room with a green carpet and ornate, flawless Victorian furniture that had obviously been manufactured within the past decade. Chairs and drapes had a matching flower design. In a corner stood a tall, burled walnut cabinet, which was probably an entertainment center containing video and stereo equipment. There were clear plastic covers on the fancy sofa and on one of the chairs.

Sydney apparently noticed Nudger staring at them. She said, "This isn't the room we relax in. That's in back, overlooking the pool." She walked over and perched on the edge of the chair with the plastic cover. "Have you any idea where Luanne is, Mr. Nudger?"

He found her pathetic. Plastic woman on plastic chair in plastic community asking about a daughter who wasn't her own, to whom she apparently was plastic. "I'm trying to find Luanne and Norva Beane, Mrs. Rand."

"Of course. We all are."

If she thought the search for Luanne was none of his business she gave no indication. Why should she? The more people looking for Luanne, the more likely it was that she'd be found. He said, "I don't think Norva abducted her or that they're necessarily together."

"If she's with that woman," Sydney said, "I doubt she's in any danger."

"Why do you say that?"

Weariness, maybe resignation, crossed her features like a play of dim light. "Just a feeling." Hammersmith had said that Massinger had told Dale Rand about Norva's claim that she was Luanne's biological mother, but had Rand told his wife?

"Have you searched for Luanne?" Nudger asked.

"I've called everyone I could think of who might help, but they know nothing. I'd go out looking for her personally, but my car . . . hasn't moved in months. A misunderstanding led to my license being suspended."

Nudger thought about sitting on the sofa but decided he'd be more comfortable standing. "I thought you might be able to tell me something that would help me locate her," he said. "You're her mother."

She looked down at her feet, then back up at him with a brave smile. "Luanne's adopted, you know."

"I don't see how that makes much difference. You must know her better than anyone."

Sydney took a deep breath. Pain moved like something alive in her eyes. "That woman Norva Beane is Luanne's biological mother, isn't she?"

"Why do you think that?"

"A feeling I got the night of the shooting, and stronger after reading her description in the paper. Of course, Dale and I, we were never told the identify of Luanne's true mother, but we did learn she was from the Ozarks. So it's certainly possible. Besides, I always had this fear in me she'd enter our lives someday. But then, maybe all mothers who adopt feel that."

Nudger said nothing, musing on how impossible it was for him to understand what adoptive mothers felt.

"And it would explain why she tried to kill Dale."

"I don't see the connection," he lied.

"There is one."

"Did Massinger tell you Norva Beane claimed to be Luanne's natural mother?"

"No. Is she? Is my suspicion correct?"

"That's what she says."

"And you believe her?"

"Yes."

Sydney nodded, weakly, as if she were an old woman whose head had become too heavy for her spindly neck. "Somehow she must have found out about Dale."

"Found out what?"

"He hasn't been quite the father he should be, that's all."

"In what way?"

Sydney had stopped nodding and sat with her head bowed. "He ignored her. All her life, he ignored her. Treated her like a ghost."

Sydney was still dancing around what she knew in her heart, around her guilt at not having stopped what was happening. Nudger wasn't going to stab her with the truth.

"My husband's requested that the police drop their protection of him," she said. "Demanded it, actually. He doesn't realize the potency of Norva Beane's desire to see him dead."

Nudger wondered if she knew the rest of it, the drugs, the pimping, and whatever might be going on with Horace Walling and illegal inside stock information. He could understand why Dale Rand didn't want the police lurking about. They might afford some protection, but he also had something to fear from them. "I think he takes her seriously enough now," he said.

"Maybe."

"Have you talked to Nan Grant? I understand she and Luanne are good friends."

"I've talked to her," Sydney said. "She doesn't know where Luanne is. She doesn't know anything about this."

"What about Labor Day?" Nudger asked.

She jerked her head up and looked at him curiously. "I don't know. What about it?"

"I just heard it mentioned, I think. I forget where. But it seemed to be in connection with whatever's going on here. Was the family planning something for Labor Day?"

"No. I think my husband has some sort of business deal that has something to do with it. That's all I know about Labor Day. Other than it's the week when Luanne will go back to school full time."

"Do you know Dr. Horace Walling?"

"No. Dale's been having mysterious conversations with someone he's called *Doctor*. I suppose that could be him. Is Dale secretly ill? I've heard him refer to an illness."

"What kind of illness?"

"Nothing serious. A cold or the flu. That's all it is, right? He isn't ill and keeping it from me?"

"Not that I know of. Walling isn't a medical doctor, he's a business associate of your husband."

"Well, I wouldn't know about any of that. Or a lot of other matters." Her voice was rising in pitch and vibrancy. "Dale doesn't tell me things, Mr. Nudger. I don't know certain things! Do you understand that? Do you?" She suddenly slammed her palms to each side of her face, covering her eyes. She began to weep. Not sob, but weep. Wail.

Nudger had no idea how to react to this. He uneasily shifted his weight from leg to leg, then he lumbered over and gently laid a hand on her trembling shoulder. She gave no indication that he was there. His throat tightened with sympathy. Her troubled daughter was missing and someone was trying to kill her husband. Dale Rand might be a bastard, but she loved him. That was her big problem. Nudger hated feeling so ineffectual. Hated the moistness that came to his own eyes and threatened to spill over into tears.

He swallowed. "You gonna be all right, Mrs. Rand?"

He thought she nodded, but he still wasn't there. Not for her. She was as alone as a woman could be.

After a while, he showed himself out.

That evening Hammersmith called him at Claudia's and told him death had caught up with the Rand family.

Not Dale, though. Luanne.

She'd been found in a vacant lot, her hands wired behind her, and a bullet in her head.

CHAPTER TWENTY-SIX

Two blocks from the scene, Nudger saw bright lights in a haze among the stark outlines of two- and four-story buildings. A block away, he slowed the Granada and told a uniform that Hammersmith had sent for him. Nudger was scowled at and waved on. He parked near a yellow Crime Scene ribbon, which had become twisted like festive decoration in the warm breeze.

An ambulance was at the scene, along with four patrol cars and several unmarked police vehicles parked at various angles. The crime scene unit's white van was parked near the corner of the vacant lot that was flanked by condemned and obviously abandoned brick apartment buildings.

Nudger climbed out of the car into the hot night and pushed his way through a crowd of onlookers, some of them somber, some of them jocular, and ducked beneath the yellow ribbon. He walked toward a knot of uniformed and plainclothes cops standing on the sidewalk. Several vehicles were parked with engines idling; exhaust fumes hung suspended in the humid air. When he got nearer, a white-haired detective named Smatherwell recognized him and nodded. Nudger asked where Hammersmith was, and Smatherwell jerked his snow-capped head in the direction of several men, including a couple of uniformed paramedics, standing in a bright circle of light in the middle of the dark lot.

One of the detectives said something, and everybody laughed, as Nudger waded into the knee-high weeds that grew determinedly from the lot's meager soil. Rocks and broken glass crunched beneath his soles as he walked, and the weeds snatched at his ankles as if trying to trip him. There was a lot of moonlight as well as illumination from the bright lights that had been set up at the crime scene, yet darkness lay at Nudger's feet, and now and then an odor like that of garbage drifted up to him. He didn't like to think about what he might step on.

He untangled his ankles from a snarl of rusty wire, almost falling, drawing the notice of Hammersmith. When he was free, he walked slowly toward the pool of bright light and the object of everyone's attention on the ground. Hammersmith broke away from the knot of cops and technicians and joined him.

"Lonely place to die, hey, Nudge?"

"Everyplace is, I guess." Nudger glanced at the bundle of dark clothing and pale flesh on the ground. Two men were bending intently over what was left of Luanne Rand, expert interpreters in the language of violence, reading her body for instructions as to how to solve the riddle of her death. A camera flashed, for a moment casting the scene in silhouette as if lightning had struck behind it. "You sure it's her?"

" 'Fraid so, Nudge. No ID on the body, but she matches Luanne's photographs. We'll get a positive on her when we compare prints, and we'll have the mother or father come down and identify her when they get to the morgue. You've seen the girl before, right?''

Oh-oh. Nudger nodded reluctantly.

"Take a look, why doncha? Verify what we think we know. It's not bad. She's not messed up, and there doesn't seem to have been any sex stuff.''

Nudger's stomach moved. "How long's the ME think she's been dead?''

"Two days, maybe.''

"Jesus, Jack!''

"You know how to hold your breath, Nudge. C'mon.'' Hammersmith was already walking toward the body. He turned and said again, "C'mon, Nudge!'' As if summoning a recalcitrant dog at obedience school.

Nudger knew he had to do it. Breathing through his mouth, he approached the illuminated scene in a dreadful dream. People not quite real made way for him. There was no sound in his dream. He held his breath. He held his courage. He looked.

At first it didn't seem so bad, one of those experiences that was a relief after the anxiety of anticipation. Hammersmith was right. She wasn't messed up. She was lying on her stomach as if sleeping, her head twisted to the side. Her wrists were wired behind her with what looked like brown electrical cord. Both hands were clenched into fists. There was no sign of blood, and her hair was barely mussed. It was the chalky paleness of her decomposing flesh that suddenly caught Nudger's stomach and heart. It was obvious she'd died sobbing, even though her lips were purplish and slack in the lurid light and her closed eyes were sunken in her head. A fat black roach crawled across the whiteness of her neck and disappeared inside her collar. She should have shrieked, this ghastly parody of a young girl, and jumped up and tugged wildly at her blouse, trying to shake the insect out. But she didn't. She wouldn't. Not ever again.

Nudger gulped in a sob, swallowing the corrupt odor, and reeled away. His stomach was bucking violently. He leaned over and spat several times, but he didn't vomit. He refused to do that.

Hammersmith was beside him. "Her?"

"Her," Nudger said, straightening, breathing deeply. Several of the people around the body were staring at him. No one was smiling.

"Sorry, Nudge. Tummy okay?"

"Hell no!"

"Let's walk over here." Hammersmith touched his arm with an odd gentleness and guided him to a small clearing in the weeds, about twenty feet from the corpse. He fired up one of his huge greenish cigars, knowing Nudger wouldn't mind under the circumstances. He knew what Nudger was still smelling, tasting. Cigar smoke would be preferable. "Sho," Hammersmith said, puffing to get the thing lit, "how do you shee thish?" He removed the cigar from his mouth and blew a cloud of pungent green smoke, black against the night sky.

Nudger put his hands on his hips and stared straight up at the bright stars; the distance between them was so great it could be measured in time. Stared straight up from the squalor and death and crushed dreams all around him. It was clean and clear and forever up there. A vacuum that tugged at him, way down here on earth.

He said, "What was she doing in such a hell hole of a neighborhood? Half the buildings down here are condemned, along with most of the people."

"I thought you might have some idea, Nudge. She was killed where she is; the body hasn't been moved. Hands wired behind her back with ordinary electrical cord that's crimped like it was cut with a wire cutters. Marks on her ankles where there'd been been more wire. Looks like she was driven here, had her legs untied so she could be walked into the lot, then shot. Single small-caliber bullet through the temple, still in her."

"Execution style," Nudger said.

"Uh-huh." Hammersmith drew on the cigar and exhaled a cloud of smoke that blocked out some stars. "Captain Springer's gonna want to talk to you, get everything you know about Norva Beane."

"I told Massinger out in Ladue all of that," Nudger said, covering himself. Springer could be nasty. In fact, couldn't be any other way. It was in his genes.

"Well, Springer won't mind if you repeat yourself. He figures Norva's good for this one."

"She might abduct her own daughter," Nudger said, "but she wouldn't kill her."

Hammersmith puffed out his jowls and blew more smoke. "You know better, Nudge. Things get out of hand. Norva might not have planned it this way, but she still might be responsible for the girl's death."

Thinking like a cop, Nudger thought. Well, Hammersmith *was* a cop, then a friend. It had to be that way when murder was involved. "I talked to Sydney Rand earlier today," Nudger said. "She loved Luanne a lot. This is gonna rip her up."

Hammersmith looked at the ground for a moment, then licked at the tooth-marked damp end of his cigar where it was beginning to peel. "I'm glad somebody out in Ladue's gonna tell her about this," he said.

Nudger said, "You really think Norva shot the kid, Jack?"

"I got no opinion on it at this point. I wrestle with facts, not hunches. I do know Springer's got Norva Beane down as the chief suspect. She took a shot at the girl's father and she might have abducted her. Norva hasn't exhibited what you'd call mental stability. Maybe this thing about her being Luanne's mother is only a delusion."

"I believe it," Nudger said. "And it'll be easy enough to prove. Adoption records, DNA. Sydney told me Luanne was adopted. Though I will say Nan Grant seemed surprised when I told her."

"Nan Grant?"

"Luanne's best friend at school. Somebody you definitely oughta talk to."

"Oh, we will." Hammersmith glanced over at the dead girl, for a second giving up his professional's hard-ass act and looking furious. He started to toss away his half-smoked cigar, then remembered he was standing in the middle of a murder scene and crammed it back in his mouth. "We'll talk to lotsh of people now."

Captain Springer, a pinch-faced, unscrupulous, and ambitious bureaucrat, didn't want to talk to Nudger tomorrow. He wanted to talk to him tonight, down at headquarters at Tucker and Clark.

In Springer's office, Nudger told almost everything to Springer, another officer acting as witness, and to a recorder. Springer folded his arms tightly across his chest and paced—no, strutted—back and forth across the office as he interrogated Nudger, putting on a show for the other cop, trying to sound like Walter Cronkite for the recorder. He made no secret of the fact that he considered Nudger probably in some way involved in Luanne's murder, the theft of the Hope diamond, and the Brink's robbery. He didn't mention either of the Kennedy assassinations.

Nudger's statement was then transcribed and he signed it. He was exhausted. Springer looked sprightly and eager to interrogate six more evildoers.

It was past midnight when Nudger staggered wearily from the mausoleumlike headquarters building and over to City Hall where his car was parked. He hadn't told Springer about Rand's house and phone being bugged; he didn't like not telling him about it, but his silence was part of the deal with the bug man. If anyone ever did find out about the sound job, Nudger would simply have to take his lumps. That was the agreement and it ran in both directions. The bug man, being among the few creditors who promptly received payment from Nudger, had by now destroyed all evidence that the bugging had occurred and would himself be silent unless tortured to an extent that would have long since broken Nudger.

Nudger also hadn't mentioned the stock-market information to the ferret-faced and despicable Springer. It seemed irrelevant. Besides, there was no way to reveal some of it without admitting to Rand's phone conversations being recorded. None of it figured to be any more pertinent than Sydney's frequent liquor deliveries.

Anyway, Nudger studied the stock quotations daily, and neither Synpac nor Fortune Fashions had moved more than half a point in either direction. How important could they be? Luanne's murder was about drugs and youth and prostitution by a minor, not about the Dow Jones Industrials. About double lives and bad company where you might least expect to find them.

So why had Springer merely sneered and continued to focus on Norva when Nudger suggested a prostitution or narcotics connection, possibly even a family friend or neighbor, might have murdered Luanne? Even Massinger would admit that some of the rich and respected in Ladue stole. So why wouldn't some of them copulate illegally? Or sniff, smoke, or shoot up dope?

Why wouldn't some of them kill?

CHAPTER TWENTY-SEVEN

The man sitting in Nudger's apartment, in the armchair where Nudger usually sat, said, "I don't think you need to turn on the light. There's enough glow from the streetlamp outside so I can see you."

Nudger recognized the voice. Imagined the gun. He stepped the rest of the way into the apartment and closed the door. The instant the latch clicked, fear got a grip on him, deep in his bowels. He told himself that if Aaron planned to kill him, it would have been done by now. Hammersmith's objective reasoning. Nudger still found it a logical argument. His stomach still didn't buy it.

"Move over by the window so I can see you better," Aaron said. He motioned with his head. Dim light glanced off his dangling swastika earring.

Nudger's rubbery legs propelled him over to stand by the window. He stared out at Sutton Avenue, washed in the sickly glow of the streetlamp, deserted at 12:45 A.M. Not many people had places to go in this area after midnight.

Oh, people who killed people. And the people who were afraid of being killed.

"Look over here, Nudger," Aaron said. "We're gonna have a face-to-face chat."

When Nudger did look, he was surprised to see another form in the room, standing near the black rectangle of the door to the kitchen. A tall, broad-shouldered figure who could only be King Chambers. Chambers was well back in the shadows, his face invisible. These guys used light and shadow like Orson Wells directing old black-and-white movies.

"I see you noticed my friend. He's interested in our conversation. Can you guess the subject?"

"What I told the police about Luanne Rand's murder?" Nudger said.

"Right. And what they told little old you."

Nudger's mind was darting and diving along with his stomach, trying to figure his strengths and weaknesses in this confrontation. Weaknesses were easy.

Then, out of a desperation near panic, he thought of one great strength. The truth. If Chambers knew he'd mentioned seeing him lunching with Rand, and had told the police about Aaron accosting him out by the golf course, Nudger's death or even disappearance would trigger an investigation of Chambers and Aaron. The truth, Nudger thought with some irony, was what might set him free. Bold front, he urged himself. Time for a bold front. His stomach said, huh? Nudger said, "Hello, Mr. Chambers."

The figure in the shadows didn't move for a long time, but something in the atmosphere changed. The dynamics of the midnight meeting were in a state of flux. Somewhere in the dimness of the quiet apartment a fly was droning. Nudger envied its freedom and invisibility. The possibility that he knew more than was originally supposed, and maybe had said more, had tilted the balance in the room. Not much, but enough. Nudger hoped.

Chambers eased forward so the dim light struck his face at a severe angle, making his bony countenance a death's head. Wells would have loved it.

"Maybe I oughta introduce you two formally," Aaron said, "since you seem to know each other in a casual way."

"No need," Chambers snapped, boss to uppity flunky. The death's-head turned to face Nudger. "Nudger. That's what everybody calls you. That's how you're listed in the phone book. You got a first name?"

"I'm just Nudger." He noticed Chambers wore a peculiar kind of cologne or aftershave. Smelled like nutmeg.

"One name," Chambers said in an amused voice, "like that rock star Sting."

"Like that dwarf Dopey," Aaron said, "if we're comparing him to show-business types."

Chambers said, "Mr. Nudger's no dope, even if he's not Mensa material. Tell us what we want to know, Nudger. Tell us all of it."

Nudger described the statement he'd given the police, how it contained reference to Aaron warning him not to follow Rand, how Nudger had seen Rand having lunch in Clayton with Chambers. That should be enough to protect him somewhat. Best not to mention seeing Rand, Chambers, and Aaron in the dead man's house on Latimer Lane. That might make it worth the risk for Chambers to see that Nudger disappeared. Anyway, Nudger hadn't told Springer about that one. There was no need, unless the suicide was recategorized as a homicide. Such a fine and indistinct line Nudger had to walk. He said, "Right now, the police like Norva Beane for Luanne's murder. They think she abducted her, then Luanne gave her trouble, and she killed her."

"Kinda thing that happens," Aaron said.

"What do you think?" Chambers asked Nudger.

Nudger hesitated.

"He's afraid to answer," Aaron said.

"You think Aaron did the girl, Nudger?" Chambers asked.

"I see it as a possibility."

"It's a distinct possibility," Chambers said. "It's more than a distinct possibility that if you continue playing in my backyard, you're gonna die much slower than that girl, but just as certainly. We clear on that, Nudger?"

"Sure. Clear." Nudger was ashamed how his voice had risen several octaves. In a firmer tone, he said, "I don't have a client anymore. Why should I care how it all plays out?"

"He's the kinda guy who'd care," Aaron said. "He whistles while he works."

"No, I think Nudger grasps the situation and he'll stop mucking around where he doesn't belong. Right, Nudger?"

"Yep."

Aaron stood up. "Shall I underline for him why we came here?" he asked Chambers. "Make sure he keeps his keen grasp of the issues?"

"Maybe. What do you think, Nudger? You need any underlining to guarantee you won't need undertaking?"

"No," Nudger said, "I promise not to muck anymore."

The death's-head emitted a nasty chuckle. "That's how I like you," Chambers said. "Meek. Stay that way and you'll stay alive. You don't strike me as a particularly brave man."

"Oh, I'm not."

"Sometimes he substitutes stupidity," Aaron said. "I'd like to knock that notion out of him before it takes hold."

"I don't think Mr. Meek will entertain any such notion. You don't plan on being difficult, do you, Mr. Meek?"

"Nope. I'd rather stay alive and inherit the earth."

Aaron said, "I'd rather put you under it."

"The police got any leads on Norva Beane?" Chambers asked.

"Nobody does," Nudger said. "Nobody has the slightest idea where she is."

"If you find out, Mr. Meek, you call Happy Nights Escort Service and ask for Alice. Then tell Alice you've got a message for me. She'll page me and I'll call you wherever you are. You be glued to the phone waiting for my call like its the night before the prom and you need a date. Understood?"

"Happy Nights. Alice. No problem."

"Well, I hope not."

"Guy like him," Aaron said to Chambers, "there'll always be a problem. He's fuckin' problematical."

"But he hasn't really told the law anything important about us, and he can't prove we were here. Maybe he's Mensa smart after all. What he did tell them is enough to tie us neatly together, so if anything happens to him, the cops come after us like killer bees. You that smart, Mr. Meek?"

"Naw!"

Aaron said, "Let me just shoot out one of his eyes."

"Maybe later," Chambers said. He walked to the door and stood very still. "Ciao, Mr. Meek."

"Take care," Aaron said, moving to the door and opening it for Chambers. The two men slid noiselessly into the hall.

"Have a good one," Nudger said.

He didn't think they heard him. That was okay, he didn't mean it.

CHAPTER TWENTY-EIGHT

My God, they're back!

That's what a sleep-fogged Nudger thought when a slight sound and the sensation he wasn't alone jarred him awake and caused him to sit up in bed. His heart and stomach collided when he saw the two figures standing in the dimness of his bedroom.

"I agreed!" he moaned. "I promised I'd stay out of the Luanne Rand case!" He didn't remember actually having promised, but he was doing that now.

"We sure didn't mean to startle you, Mr. Nudger." The ceiling fixture winked on, washing the room in light that hurt Nudger's eyes. He squinted. Peered.

Norva Beane stood near the door, her hand still on the light switch. A huge redheaded man with thick arms, a bull neck, and a stomach that sagged over his belt like an overfilled sack, stood near the foot of the bed. He was about forty but his thinning, slicked-back hair would probably have him looking fifty in a few years. Despite his bearlike build, he appeared amiable. His even, florid features were arranged in a smile that seemed used to being on his face. He was wearing jeans and a red muscle shirt lettered "Say No to Drugs." His leg-sized arms were decorated with faded tattoos. A U.S. Marines insignia was on one bulging bicep. Nudger figured it was one of those formidable arms that had choked him unconscious the last time Norva had appeared in his apartment.

"This here's my own cousin Bobber Beane," Norva said. "When he heard about my troubles, he right away found his way here to help me."

"Here from where?" Nudger asked. "Possum Run?"

"Thereabouts," Bobber said. He had a deep, lazy voice that suggested white lightning and slowly flowing rivers at their widest points.

"This is a dream," Nudger said.

"Nope," Bobber said.

Norva said, "I been hearing about Luanne on the news." And suddenly neither of the Beanes looked amiable. Bobber's tiny blue eyes glinted steel, and Norva's haggard features became set in a way that somehow reminded Nudger of King Chambers. "I do dearly need to talk to you, Mr. Nudger."

"The police are looking for you," Nudger said inanely. Why would she be here at—he glanced at his watch—4 A.M. if she didn't know that.

"Lookin' for her and nobody else," Bobber said. "Tha's exactly the problem." One of his tattoos, Nudger saw, was a Confederate flag flying over crossed sabers. Good Lord!

Norva's earnestness carried her a few steps toward the bed. "They say I killed my own sweet daughter, Mr. Nudger, but I didn't! I swear it!"

"I never thought you killed her," Nudger said. Which was true.

"My Luanne was mixed up with some bad types. Drug addicts, dealers . . . them kinda people."

"Them folks would as soon kill you as take a piss," Bobber said.

Nudger had found that to be true.

"Mr. Nudger and me, we trust each other," Norva said to her giant cousin. "He's a man with a good heart and he speaks the truth."

Bobber gazed down at Nudger. "That more or less the case?"

"It is right now," Nudger said.

Bobber said, "So tell us somethin' that's surely true."

Nudger thought that one over. He knew Bobber wouldn't be interested in philosophical edict; this was something of a test. "When you two leave here," he said, "I've got no choice but to call the police."

Bobber smiled.

Norva said, "We know that. You got your professional obligations and all. We talked it over and decided to come here anyways, 'cause you're the one I want."

Bobber was still smiling. "Norva says there ain't no one like you, Nudger. I told her that was true of everybody and fingerprints and DWI prove it."

"That's DNA."

"What counts is if you ain't just different, but if you're special."

"Oh, he's special," Norva said.

"Thought he might be when I seen his picture in the paper. Somethin' unique about that man, I said to myself. His manner of carriage and dress, like. So yeah, he'd be the one we want."

"Want for what?" Nudger asked, just beginning to get an inkling, to feel the draw of the whirlpool.

"We wanna hire you to find Luanne's killer," Norva said.

"We'll pay good," Bobber assured him

Norva said, "Bobber's got him a special interest in this matter. I mean, even beyond us being cousins."

"Norva, there's a murder warrant out on you. I can't—"

"I told Norva you'd most likely cooperate," Bobber said, "knowing the score as I thought you did, just lookin' at your picture. Shit, I could tell by your eyes."

"We know you gotta level with the police every step of the way," Norva said. "We don't mind that. It might even help convince them I didn't have nothing to do with Luanne's death."

"You wouldn't be breakin' no laws by helping us," Bobber said. He reached inside his untucked shirt and pulled out a white envelope. "This here's a thousand dollar retainer." He tossed the envelope on the mattress near Nudger's feet. "We ain't even gonna ask for a receipt. We'll call you now and again, find out what you learned." He moved around the side of the bed, very near to Nudger.

Norva said, "Bobber! Mr. Nudger's reasonable as well as trustworthy."

"Well, I expect he'll work for us, then. Help us out."

"It ain't like you got no choice," Norva said.

"No," Bobber said, "just not much of one."

Nudger's throat was dry. His tongue was thick and foul. His throat and stomach felt as if he'd gulped down drain cleaner. With Bobber looming over him, the threat of King Chambers and Aaron didn't seem so ominous. He did feel reasonable. Besides, he believed in Norva's innocence. If she were guilty, she wouldn't have come here. He was sure of it.

"You're my client again," he said to her.

"Now, didn't I tell you he'd help?" she said to Bobber.

She hopped over and snaked her arms around Nudger's neck. Kissed him on the cheek. Bobber looked on with seeming disinterest.

When Norva had straightened up and was standing next to him, Bobber said, "You got your duty, so you go right ahead and call the cops soon as we walk out the door. We'll be gone every way but Sunday by the time they get here."

"Fair enough," Nudger said.

Norva grinned toothily and said, "I do thank you, Mr. Nudger. We both do."

Nudger shrugged. "I felt compelled."

The Beanes moved to the bedroom door. Bobber switched off the light. Just before blackness closed in, Norva raised a hand in a shy wave.

"What I think I liked about that picture," Bobber said, "was that suit."

Nudger sat in darkness, listening to them blunder through his dark apartment, then down the stairs to the street door. A few minutes later, he barely heard a car engine start.

Then silence.

He gave his clients another five minutes before he switched on the lamp by the bed and dragged the phone over to him.

Hammersmith, he decided, sitting with the phone in his lap. If I'm going to wake someone at four in the morning, it's going to be Hammersmith.

The Maplewood police came immediately, in a fury of light and sound. Then came the Major Case Squad. Then Springer and Hammersmith. Nudger drank coffee and told it all to Springer, exactly as he had to Hammersmith on the phone.

190

"So who the fuck is this Bobber Beane again?" Springer asked.

"Norva's cousin. From Possum Run. Or around Possum Run."

"So why's he here sharing her problems?"

"They're kin," Nudger said.

Springer rolled his eyes, shook his head. "If he cares so much about her, he oughta convince her to get an attorney, turn herself in."

"I told him that," Nudger said. He hadn't actually. He should have, he knew. But damnit, he'd been awakened from an uneasy dream about Aaron and King Chambers. Norva and Bobber Beane were too much for him at 4:00 A.M. in the real world. He hadn't been jolted out of sleep to sit straight up in bed with his heart pumping pure fear, and then calmly mulled over his options. Any cop would understand that. Any cop other than Springer.

"You can't have those people as clients," Springer said. "You'll be interfering with an official homicide investigation."

"The law's not exactly clear on that."

Hammersmith made a face at Nudger over Springer's shoulder.

Springer said, "You call your lawyer or something?"

"Sure," Nudger said. "Wouldn't you, if you were going to have to deal with you?"

"No. Why would I call your lawyer? You stop trying to wise off, trying to fuck with me, Nudger. It'll only get you in the deepest shit."

Behind Springer, Hammersmith was stonefaced.

"This Bobber Beane touch anything?" Springer asked.

"Nothing. He only stood near the bed and talked. I don't think you need his prints anyway. Norva said he was her cousin, and he probably is. You can check with whatever law there is in Possum Run."

"Uh-huh. Sheriff Andy or some such." Springer scrunched up his rodent features as if he smelled something foul. "I don't take for granted this guy is her cousin, or even that his name's Bobber Beane. How can you take for granted anybody's got a name like that? The Beane woman's a mental case who thought Luanne Rand was her daughter, so she kidnapped her and things went sour, so she killed her. That's how it looks, and most likely how it was. Why would she come barging in here in the middle of the night and tell you the truth, of all things?"

"Because she's innocent. She wouldn't kill her own daughter."

"I told you it's probably not her daughter. She's just some dumb-ass yokel with a mental fixation. Like the guy that shot Lenin."

"He didn't think John Lennon was his son."

"Not John. The other Lenin. In Russia."

"That Lenin wasn't shot to death."

"You say. I guess you believe the Russians, too, just because they split up. Like they're not still holding something back."

Nudger decided Springer resented having to climb out of bed and drive over here and was taking it out on him. If Nudger mentioned that King Chambers and Aaron had also called on him, Springer wouldn't at all mind the inconvenience. But then, Springer probably wouldn't believe him.

"The Rands are plenty pissed, Nudger." Springer sprayed Nudger's bare arm with spittle. "They want Norva Beane found and they want you arrested as her accomplice."

That doesn't make sense," Hammersmith said, finally

unable to keep quiet. "Nudger's the guy that stopped her from shooting Rand."

"That don't keep him from aiding and abetting her in kidnapping and murdering Luanne."

"Or shooting Lenin," Hammersmith said under his breath.

"Whazzat?"

"Nothing. What was Norva Beane wearing?" Hammersmith asked, changing the subject.

"Levi's, white sleeveless blouse, sandals."

Hammersmith made a show of writing that down.

"We already got all that shit," Springer snapped at him. "Got all we need from this jerkoff." There was only one uniform in the apartment, Springer's driver, a young cop named Charles. "Let's get down to the car," Springer said to Charles, who'd appeared to be asleep on his feet but snapped instantly awake.

"Grab some sleep, why don't you, Nudge," Hammersmith said, following Springer and the driver to the door.

"It's too late to go back to bed. I'll probably stay up, have some breakfast, listen to some Beatles records."

Hammersmith said, "Do everybody a favor and stop smarting off."

Springer liked that. He was smiling as the door closed behind the three men. *Bourgeois* bastard.

CHAPTER TWENTY-NINE

She was planning on riding the bus to school this morning. Bright girl striding along the littered sidewalk, on her way to the bus stop and her summer classes. She was ignoring the jeers and suggestive remarks of the same two street-corner loungers, who apparently lived curbside at this intersection. The skinny one who danced yelled something to Nan Grant then did a neat spin while giggling and clutching his crotch. The other one glared at Nudger; maybe it was the same glare from last time he was here. They were both staring as he drove the Granada slowly past them to intercept her.

She was on the opposite side of the street but there was no traffic, so, feeling like a child molester, Nudger swerved over next to her and cranked down his window. Warm air rolled in to displace the moderately cool breeze the car's air conditioner was offering. "Want a ride to school?" he asked. Like a cookie, little girl?

She didn't hesitate. Without answering, she stepped down off the curb and walked around the front of the car.

He thought she might be putting on a bit of a show for the loungers. She got in and shut the door, then stared straight ahead with her books in a neat stack on her lap. Still without talking.

"Wha's he got we ain't?" one of the loungers yelled. "Hey, sweet stuff! You hear?"

"Mus' be his caaaar!" the skinny one shouted. Nudger saw him pirouette in the rearview mirror. The guy really did have some great moves.

Nan said, "Ignore them. I do."

Nudger eased down on the accelerator and pulled away from the curb. "What do you think of Luanne being killed?"

Her grip on the books tightened. "It shook me up at first. I've seen people killed before, though. This neighborhood, you know? Gangs are starting to take over. Even older guys like those dorks back on the corner are scared of them."

"The cops think Luanne's real mother kidnapped her then killed her," Nudger said.

Nan didn't answer. They passed the bus stop that had been her destination. An old woman and a very young boy stood side by side near the battered metal bus-stop sign, looking as forlorn as if they were going to a funeral. Maybe they were.

Finally Nan said, "Cops probably got that wrong, like most everything else."

"So who do you think might have killed her?"

From behind her protective veneer, Nan said, "I got my ideas, but I'm keeping them to myself. World the way it is, loose lips can sink the whole damn navy." Was this kid in the strategically torn jeans and high-top joggers actually talking like this?

"Naval warfare aside, will you give me some straight

answers, Nan? I see your point and I won't pry if you say I'm off limits, but I want to find Luanne's killer and I need more than you gave me last time we talked."

"You think what the cops do? About Luanne's real mom killing her?"

"No."

"But that woman really is her mom, right?"

"I think so."

She looked off to the side, at the depressing view of moribund buildings gliding past like a bad dream. She said, "Radio work in this thing?"

He reached out and switched it on. News. Nan punched buttons until she was satisfied with the music, then turned up the volume. Rap music. Nudger hated rap music. He gritted his teeth while deep bass notes and staccato insult pulsated through the car.

Over the noise, Nan said, "Go ahead and ask."

"How deep into drugs was Luanne?"

"Deeper'n people knew. She was a hard-core addict. It pissed off her father, and that pissed her off, 'cause he's a user himself."

The radio screamed, *Got a yearn to burn, got a fit to hit!*

"Has he got a habit as bad as Luanne's was?"

Nan made a little hopeless gesture and let her hands drop back to her books. "Who knows? Maybe. It bothered Luanne, the way he'd now and then advise her to stop using, telling her it was ruining her life. You know, that just-say-no business. People can't even quit smoking cigarettes but they'll try'n cram it down everybody's throats."

"Luanne ever mention Labor Day?" Nudger was shouting like Nan to be heard above the rap. Well, it would have to be that way, or she might decide to hold her silence. It was like having a conversation next to a jet plane.

"The holiday? No. Why?"

"It's come up a couple of times, that's all. Probably it isn't important."

"There's a school orientation the Friday before Labor Day, and Luanne was gonna be a guide. That's the only connection I can think of."

An' the brotherhood gonna spill some blood!

An old man on a corner where Nudger had slowed for a yield sign stared curiously at him. The music must be audible for some distance outside the car.

"What did Luanne really think of her parents?" Nudger asked. "The ones who raised her."

"I don't believe she gave them much thought except as people who got in her way from time to time with their silly rules. I can't even say she really hated her father, you know? She was confused by what was going on. We used to talk about it a lot, and she couldn't understand why he did things."

"Ever hear of a man named King Chambers?"

"No."

"Off limits?"

"Just no."

"We said we were leveling with each other," he told her.

"We are. Far as it goes."

"So I'm gonna be honest with you. I'm not sure about King Chambers, but I think you know the other man I asked you about at the mall. Fella named Aaron, wears a dangling gold swastika earring. I think you're a user and he's your supplier. Maybe he even has you dealing. Am I right?"

She seemed undisturbed by his allegations as she turned to stare at him with her knowing dark eyes, but there was a faint tightness around her lips. "You're prying now."

"Okay. Sorry." He slowed down and rounded a corner.

They were in a better neighborhood now, the world Nan aspired to live in someday on a regular basis. He said, "Tell me something I don't know about Luanne."

She ran her fingers slowly back and forth over the faded purple cover of the top book, as if its rough texture might convey some message in braille. "There's probably lots neither of us knows. She was scared of something."

Nudger glanced over at her calm profile. "What was the something?"

"I don't know. And I'm not saying that 'cause you're prying. I really don't know. She wouldn't tell me or anybody else."

So you better pray, 'cause you be in the fray!

"What did she *say*—what did she say or do that made you think she was afraid?"

"Nothing I could tell you that'd mean anything. But we were good friends. She couldn't hide it from me. When I asked her what was frightening her, she wouldn't tell me, but she didn't deny she was scared."

"The problem with her father, maybe?"

"No, that bothered her but it didn't scare her. It wasn't her father."

"Then what? Got any kind of guess?"

"No. But whatever it was, I think it killed her." She shifted in the seat and adjusted the stack of books in her lap. She looked so small and vulnerable then, so young, that Nudger felt an overwhelming pity and admiration for her. Too much had been loaded on her, more than any child should be asked to bear, asked to accomplish. But here she was, engaged in the the slow war of attrition that gradually devoured the soul. School instead of summer camp, drugs instead of junk food, study instead of childhood. It would wear on her, and maybe the eventual victory wouldn't be worth it. Maybe the only difference between her and her less opportunistic sisters in the ghetto was that someday she'd OD with an MBA.

She glanced over at Nudger and said, "Think you can drive a little faster? I got a test this morning."

He thought, "every morning," and pulled out into the fast lane.

She smiled and turned off the radio. Teenagers.

When they reached the school, Nudger steered the Granada to the curb and left the engine idling. "Thanks for your help, Nan."

"If you wanna learn some more about Luanne," she said suddenly, "you maybe oughta talk to him." She pointed through the windshield at a tall, gangly boy with a bald head. He had on baggy, pleated pants, a multicolored T-shirt, and was lugging a canvas bookbag slung over his shoulder on a long strap.

"What was he to Luanne?" Nudger asked.

"Boyfriend, sorta. For just a short time. But Chuck's the last guy she had anything at all to do with—here at school, anyway."

"Chuck got a last name?"

"He's Chuck Wise. A senior. Or he would be if he could get himself straightened out."

"What's his problem?"

Nan tapped her nose and sniffled, giving Nudger a confidential glance. Then she opened the door and got out, smiled at Nudger, and slammed the door hard enough to make the fillings in his teeth jump.

She was running up the wide concrete steps to the entrance, not looking back, when Nudger climbed out of the car and approached Chuck, who appeared in no hurry to go inside the dread building.

"Chuck Wise?"

The kid with the shaved head stopped and turned

around slowly, as if he couldn't quite believe someone would know his name. There was faint dark stubble over his head that could be seen from up close, as if someone had rubbed soot there. "That's me," he said. He had round, full features for such a skinny kid. Or maybe the hairlessness made him look that way.

"I was a friend of Luanne's," Nudger said

"Yeah, well, so was I."

"I'm looking into her death."

Chuck's red-rimmed blue eyes grew wary. "A cop?"

Nudger laughed. "Not hardly. I'm a private investigator."

"You just dropped Nan Grant off, didn't you?"

"Yep. She was telling me what she knew about Luanne. She said you might be able to add to it."

"Well, I'm kinda late."

"You didn't seem to be in any hurry. All I need's a few minutes."

Chuck thought about it, then shifted the weight of his bookbag to his other shoulder. "So ask me what you want, then I'm outa here."

"How well did you know Luanne?"

"Not as well as I thought. We went out a few times, is all. I thought we was more than just friends, then I kept hearing how she was keeping some mean company outside of school."

"What kind of mean company?"

"Older guys. You know. So I followed her one afternoon and she met some older guy, all right."

"Then what?" Nudger asked, when it appeared Chuck was finished talking.

"They talked, is all. At a bar down in South Saint Louis. I didn't go in, but I could see them through the window. They sat at a table and had this talk, then they left."

"Did you know the man she met?"

"Never seen him before."

"Was he a black man with a fancy gold earring by any chance?"

"Nope. He was a white guy, going bald but with a lot of frizzy gray hair around the sides. Old. 'Bout fifty, maybe even older."

Horace Walling? Nudger wondered.

"Luanne went and met some of her girlfriends after that," Chuck said. "A few nights later, when I asked her about the guy, she told me to mind my own business. We had a big argument, then things cooled off between us and stayed cool. That was about six months ago." For the first time, Chuck's carefully controlled nonchalance slipped a bit. He seemed about to sob, then stiffened his features and said, "I miss her. I hope you find the shithead bastard that killed her."

"Did she ever—"

Nudger had been about to ask Chuck if Luanne ever talked about her father, but the boy wheeled and hurried up the steps toward school, his canvas bag bouncing off his hip. He'd been about to lose his composure completely, Nudger was sure, and didn't want to be observed crying. Nudger didn't blame him.

He turned around and got back in the car. Then he drove away from there before somebody called the police about a suspicious man hanging around outside a high school.

He decided to hang around outside somewhere else.

Mirabelle Rogers' apartment.

CHAPTER THIRTY

Nudger's guess was that King Chambers had something to do with Luanne's death. Following Chambers might bring results, and the logical place to find him and begin doing that was Mirabelle's apartment.

The silver Mercedes was parked in front of the building. That didn't necessarily mean Chambers was inside with his lady love, but it was possible. Nudger drove around the block and parked a prudent distance behind the Mercedes, facing the same direction. He killed the engine, then tuned to a blues station on the radio, and settled in for a long wait. Waiting was a large part of his work, and he'd learned to put himself in a kind of suspended mental state involving half his brain. At least that was how he saw it. He was at rest, his eyes half-closed and his conscious mind at idle speed, but at the same time he was alert.

It was hot in the parked car and getting hotter, but Nudger barely noticed. He was perspiring heavily and he would have been uncomfortable if he'd allowed himself to feel. He told himself that if the heat really began to get to him he'd start the engine and run the air conditioner. That wasn't much of a consolation, really, since the Granada's air conditioner leaked Freon and wasn't much more than a fan, and running it for any length of time while the car was sitting still tended to overheat the engine. Still—

He sat up slightly and peered through the windshield as a man exited Mirabelle's apartment building.

Then he saw that it wasn't King Chambers, so he rested his head again on the warm but soft seatback and began tapping a finger on the steering wheel in time to an old Hoagy Carmichael tune, thinking there really should be a Hoagy Carmichael revival.

When the man who'd exited the building had opened the iron gate and walked between the two stone wolfhounds, Nudger stopped thinking about Hoagie Carmichael and sat up straighter again.

The guy still didn't look like King Chambers, but that was because he was Dale Rand.

Was Rand secretly spending time with Chambers' girl?

No. More likely he'd been seeing Chambers in the apartment, on business.

Rand crossed the street and got into a blue Cadillac. A loaner. His own car was probably in for repairs after Norva Beane had raked it with gunfire. The comprehensive clause in his insurance should cover that. Stockbrokers were fired on all the time.

Nudger bent down and to the side, out of sight, until he heard the Caddy whisper past. Then he straightened up and started the engine.

He sped down the street and made a hard right turn, just in time to see the blue Caddy pass the intersection. He counted to ten at the corner, then made a left turn, and followed half a block behind Rand, leaving five cars between them. Keeping his gaze fixed straight ahead, he cranked down both front windows. Then he contorted his body and lowered the rear side window directly behind him. A breeze rushed and eddied through the car; it was itself warm, but it chased away the worst of the heat.

Rand didn't go far. The Cadillac wended its way through a maze of side streets, some of which were permanently blocked off to make the neighborhood less accessible and presumably safer, then it turned onto Kingshighway. After a few blocks, Rand turned again, east this time, and drove to Euclid Avenue. On Euclid he parked near a restaurant that had tables out on the sidewalk under a green awning. He got out of the Caddy and stuffed coins into the parking meter, then walked toward the restaurant.

Nudger parked a block away and walked back on the other side of the street. He saw Rand seated in the shade of the awning at one of the outdoor tables, sipping a glass of beer. There was a small bookstore almost directly across the street. Nudger ducked inside it and pretended to browse through paperback mysteries while he kept an eye on Rand through the window.

Rand checked his wristwatch now and then between sips of beer, apparently waiting for someone. Nudger thought a good bet would be Horace Walling.

Wrong again.

Gazing over the cover of a Rex Stout reprint, he watched a short, muscular man with dark hair and a dark, full beard sit down opposite Rand. He was wearing neatly pressed slacks and a short-sleeved shirt unbuttoned to reveal glinting gold chains. There was a rolling motion to his walk, as if he were a small trained bear pretending to be a man. He looked familiar but Nudger couldn't quite place him.

The two men talked for about fifteen minutes while Nudger stalled for time, examining one book after another, wondering why so many of them featured cats on their covers. Rand and the man seemed to know each other well. At one point the bearded guy tapped Rand on the chest several times in succession as if to emphasize a point. Neither man was smiling, but the conversation seemed calm enough and in no way hostile.

"I recommend that one," a voice said behind Nudger.

The other customers had made their purchases and left, and the attractive blond woman behind the counter had walked over to help Nudger. She was wearing gray slacks, white socks, and Birkenstocks.

"Have you read it?" Nudger asked, still watching across the street. The waitress was standing at Rand's table now. Were the two men ordering brunch, or a drink for the bearded guy, or was Rand paying so they could leave?

" . . . everything written by Kaminsky," the bookstore woman was saying.

Rand and the bearded guy were standing up.

"Your word's good enough for me," Nudger said.

He quickly paid for the book he'd been holding, stuck it in his back pocket, and left the bookstore as Rand and the other man were leaving the restaurant.

"You'll be hooked," the woman said with a smile, as Nudger closed the door behind him.

Nudger was worried about that. About being scaled and filleted, too. He leaned his back against the store's brick wall, trying to be small, as Rand and the other man stood near Rand's parked car and talked.

That was when Nudger recognized the man with the beard.

Al Martinelli.

Nudger had seen his photograph dozens of times in the newspapers and on TV, during a murder trial last year when Martinelli had been called as a key witness. He should have been a suspect, according to the news and

Hammersmith. Martinelli was the city's most notorious and affluent illicit drug dealer. He also owned a restaurant, which he used as a front, and did his own advertising on late-night television while wearing a chef's cap. An ego thing, apparently. Hammersmith said Martinelli hadn't been inside the restaurant in years. Hammersmith said he himself had gone there once and found the toasted ravioli abominable and had never returned.

The two men parted without shaking hands. Martinelli strolled with his rolling gait down the sidewalk on the other side of the street. He had his hands in his pockets and appeared to be whistling. Rand wore a grim expression as he climbed into his rented ride and drove away.

Nudger, unable to talk himself into following Martinelli, jogged to the Granada and tried to catch up with Rand.

He did, on Kingshighway. Rand drove the Caddy south, then east on Highway 40.

It wasn't long before Nudger realized where they were headed: the Chadwood Country Club.

Nudger relaxed and hung far behind the blue Cadillac. He stayed with Rand just long enough to watch him pull into the country club parking lot and meet Horace Walling. Both men hoisted golf bags out of the trunks of their cars, then disappeared into a low, tile-roofed wing of the main building.

No point in staying around here, Nudger figured. Or it might have been his persistent fear doing his reasoning. A kind of reverse Pavlovian response: He got near this golf course and his mouth went dry.

After making a U-turn, he drove back to his office to phone Hammersmith to tell him about seeing Dale Rand with both King Chambers and Al Martinelli. Rand was possibly a major player in the area's drug trafficking.

* * *

The office was so hot and humid that at any moment it might break out in toadstools, but Nudger didn't plan on staying there long, so he left the window unit off.

There was one message on his machine. Hammersmith had called.

Convenient, Nudger thought, and punched out the Third District number. When he asked for Hammersmith he was put through immediately.

"I've got some information for you," he said, when Hammersmith came on the line.

"Good," Hammersmith said. "You can tell me about it when you get here."

"When I get there?"

"The Third District station house. My office."

"I know where 'here' is," Nudger said. "Remember, I just called you on the phone. But get there why?"

"To go with me to identify a body."

Nudger realized he was holding his breath, and not a lot of it. He began to feel light-headed.

"Nudge?"

"Yeah?" he wheezed.

"Somebody cut the throat of our friend Aaron. Prints confirm ID, but we'd still like an eyeball witness to say it's him. You have to look at a morgue photo is all, considering your delicate stomach."

"Thanks, Jack."

"Is right now convenient for you?"

"I guess."

"Good. Afterward maybe we can go out and get some lunch. I'll buy."

Nudger's stomach flipped. "Jack?"

But Hammersmith had hung up.

CHAPTER THIRTY-ONE

There was the gold swastika earring.

There was the pencil-line mustache.

There was the smug smile. Only now it was below rather than above the chin.

"That's Aaron," Nudger said, and handed the black-and-white morgue photo back to Hammersmith.

They were in Hammersmith's office at the Third. Hammersmith had ordered the photograph delivered there to spare Nudger a trip to the morgue. He was thoughtful sometimes, when he allowed himself to act on what lay beneath the protective sarcastic exterior so necessary in police work. He knew how Nudger felt about going to the morgue, how it bothered him for days afterward.

"Fingerprints show his full name was Aaron Burr Washington Smith—no lie. Some kids found the body behind some trash cans in an alley down by Laclede's Landing, near the river." Hammersmith slid the photograph back into its yellow envelope. "The ME report says Aaron died about four o'clock this morning. I figure anybody running around at that time is gonna be dead the rest of the day anyway, so the murder seems kinda redundant."

"Are you tying it in with the Luanne Rand murder?" Nudger asked, ignoring Hammersmith's stab at dark humor.

"The Major Case Squad's leaning in that direction."

"I lean in the direction of King Chambers."

"He doesn't usually kill direct, Nudge."

"I know. But didn't he usually send Aaron?"

"Yeah. That was why he kept him around, to scare people, then do what was necessary if they weren't scared enough. But I still don't see Chambers hitting Aaron, especially in such a messy manner. The late Aaron was useful, maybe even indispensable. Why would Chambers do away with his naughty right hand?"

"Aaron became a loose end that had to be snipped. Be realistic, Jack; Chambers or Aaron were never suspected of killing anybody living in a respectable neighborhood, much less Ladue. There's plenty of heat over the Luanne Rand killing, so if Aaron did murder her on Chambers' orders, Chambers would play it safe and make sure Aaron couldn't talk."

Hammersmith leaned back in his chair and folded his hands on his protruding stomach. His nails were neatly clipped and appeared to have been buffed, as if he'd recently had a manicure. "Chambers used to do that kinda thing, I'm sure, but he's way beyond wet work now. He sees himself as a kinda chief executive. Slitting throats is menial labor. Temporary work. Even if it lasts for years, like Aaron's job did before he got terminated."

"So you think Chambers called a Kelly girl?"

"Sorta the equivalent."

"That would only create another dangerous loose end,"

Nudger said. "Some things a guy like Chambers has to do himself. He's perfectly capable of slitting a throat."

"Oh, sure. We all are, under the right circumstances."

Nudger didn't know about that. His mind flashed again on the grisly photograph of Aaron stretched out on the morgue examining table. Those tables were equipped with drains. His stomach moved.

"We'll no doubt get around to Chambers anyway, Nudge. He doesn't have the kinda juice to stay out of a murder case when the victim was his employee."

"Speaking of Chambers," Nudger said. And he told Hammersmith about seeing Dale Rand leaving Mirabelle Rogers' apartment, then meeting Al Martinelli at the Central West End restaurant on Euclid.

Hammersmith fondled the greenish cigar protruding from his shirt pocket, but he didn't take it out and remove the cellophane wrapper. Maybe he remembered Aaron's photograph, and he didn't want to pollute the air and have Nudger make a mess in his office. "That'll put Rand in a different light with Captain Massinger," he said. "That guy thinks Ladue residents are only capable of bloodless white-collar crimes involving the funds of blue-chip corporations."

"It puts Chambers next to Martinelli, too."

"There was never any doubt about that, Nudge. You do or sell drugs in any major way in this town, and you work for, or you're a customer of, Al Martinelli."

"Then Martinelli might be Chambers' boss."

"It's probably safe to say that. He's certainly above him in the pecking order."

"It's like one of those Chinese puzzle boxes," Nudger said. "Open one and you find another."

"Like life itself. And if you think King Chambers is a badass, just get mixed up with Martinelli. He's got people working for him that barely qualify as human. Some of them probably still have tails, and long ones."

Nudger thought that one over. "You think feather boas will ever come back in style in a serious way?" he asked.

"Huh? That some kinda snake?"

"No, it's a long, thin item you wear around your neck. They have feathers on them."

Hammersmith looked at him in the way Nudger had seen him stare at perpetrators guilty of inexplicable violence. "Your neck, not mine."

"For women, I mean. As a fashion statement."

Hammersmith narrowed an eye at him. "Why?"

"For the reason women wear lotsa things—to make them more attractive?"

"I mean, why do you care?"

Nudger suddenly feared the SEC. A number of insiders had gone to prison in recent years as the result of Stock Exchange Commission investigations into trades based on confidential information. Just how legal were those overheard conversations that formed the basis for Nudger's stock purchases? Nudger knew they'd stay legal if no one ever found out about them. Why drag Hammersmith into this? He was a friend. "I dunno," Nudger said. "Claudia and I were talking about it a few nights ago."

"Claudia doesn't need a feather boa in her wardrobe to be attractive, Nudge."

"I'll tell her you said so." Nudger stood up. He knew he'd better not mention guided missile systems. Hammersmith wouldn't know anything about those, either, except that Claudia didn't need one. "Thanks for skipping that visit to the morgue, Jack." He edged toward the door.

"Where you going, Nudge?"

"Work to do. I've got other cases to worry about."

"Your biggest worry is that some other investigator's working them. Some guy who's competent."

"I'm going someplace where I don't have to hear insults," Nudger said, a little nettled, even though he knew Hammersmith and was used to his remarks.

Hammersmith unclasped his hands, then sighed and leaned forward in his chair. It was as if a mountain had shifted. "Okay, Nudge. Thanks for coming in on short notice."

Nudger nodded and went to the door.

As he was going out, he heard Hammersmith say, "I think the feather boa as a serious fashion statement is as dead as Aaron Smith."

Nudger knew what he had to do. Where he might find some indication as to what was really going on. With Aaron dead, he wasn't so afraid, and if King Chambers had killed Aaron, as Nudger suspected, Chambers would be making himself hard to find.

At a drive-up public phone in the corner of a service-station parking lot, Nudger tried to look up the number of Mirabelle Rogers. But the R's were among the many pages ripped from the weather-faded directory dangling on a chain. He called Information and asked for the number, and was told it was unlisted.

That made sense, Nudger thought, for a woman who looked like Mirabelle. Her kind of beauty was a magnet for ugliness.

He decided to take a chance.

When he reached Mirabelle's apartment, the silver Mercedes was parked in the same spot on Waterman. He didn't think that was significant.

He parked across the street, chewed two antacid tablets,

then climbed out of the car and strode over the sun-warmed pavement to the opposite sidewalk.

His strategy was simple. He'd ring Mirabelle's apartment from the vestibule, and if anyone answered on the intercom he'd leave fast.

If there was no answer, he'd go upstairs and force his way into the apartment. Guilty or innocent, King Chambers was sure to know the law would be looking for him after Aaron's murder, so it was unlikely he'd be here, at the home of his lover. And wherever Chambers was, Mirabelle was almost sure to be with him.

Nudger held that thought as he stood in the quiet tile vestibule and pressed the button over Mirabelle's brass mailbox.

No voice came over the intercom.

He pressed the button three more times, waiting a full minute between buzzes.

No answer.

Good! He hoped.

The building wasn't equipped with a security door, so he simply climbed the stairs to Mirabelle's apartment door. He glanced around to make sure he was alone in the hall, then got his honed Visa card from his wallet. He might be able to slip the lock easily, if it was one of the cheap brands on so many apartment doors.

Apparently it wasn't. It ate his Visa card. He bent over and picked up the shattered plastic so his account number wouldn't be lying on the hall carpet. The problem was that the other half of the card, with his name on it, had dropped on the other side of the door, inside the apartment.

In a gesture of futility, he twisted the doorknob and cursed silently. He was surprised to find the door was unlocked. Either it had been unlocked from the beginning, or the Visa card had done its job.

He opened it a few inches and peered inside.

Cool air flowed out against his perspiring face. The apartment looked unoccupied from his perspective. All he could see were a white leather sofa, a matching chair, and a glass-topped table with slick and colorful magazines fanned out on it like a hand of face cards.

He swallowed the fear that kept trying to crawl up his throat, opened the door the rest of the way, and stepped inside.

His stomach and his heart lurched at the same time and seemed to collide.

Mirabelle Rogers was lying on the floor, looking up at him, surprised.

For an instant Nudger thought he'd interrupted her while she was exercising, stretched out loosely on her back and cooling down from a strenuous aerobics routine. Then he saw that no, she wasn't actually surprised, or even looking at him.

She was cooling down, though.

Because she was dead.

CHAPTER THIRTY-TWO

Nudger didn't have to examine the body to be sure Mirabelle Rogers was dead. She'd been brutally beaten. Her nose was incredibly crooked and her jaw wasn't hinged quite right. The worm of black blood trailing from her left nostril joined a congealed pool of blood beneath her head. Nudger was sure the back of her skull had been crushed, but he didn't want to lift her head to verify that. His imagination was having a violent enough effect on his stomach without bringing reality into the picture.

His next move, he knew, should be to phone Hammersmith. That would be proper and legal, even though it might be like the first step into quicksand. Or maybe he should get out of the apartment and make an anonymous phone call to the police, thus remaining as uninvolved as possible. That would be the safe thing, the Nudger thing to do.

But he didn't have to make up his mind immediately. He could look around the apartment and try to learn something. It was a good time for the detective to detect. Thinking that way, he knew for sure that he'd leave and make the anonymous phone call—at least a part of him already knew it.

What he was doing now was staring at Mirabelle's feet. One of her sequined, open-toed shoes was missing. He glanced around and saw it near the wall on the other side of the room, where it must have been flung during her struggle with her attacker.

It hadn't been much of a struggle, Nudger decided. A throw pillow had been knocked off the sofa, and one of the white leather chairs was propped sideways against a small glass-topped table. There was a sprung, empty leather attaché case on the floor alongside the table. Mirabelle, the petite beauty, hadn't lasted long once the attack began. There was no blood visible anywhere other than beneath the body. He imagined she'd run about the room trying to elude her assailant, and when he'd caught up with her, he'd killed her quickly near the spot where she'd fallen. Nudger found himself glad she probably hadn't suffered. He wasn't sure why; he hadn't known the woman, and she'd slept with scum like King Chambers.

A faint sound made the back of his neck feel as if a carpet of ants were moving across it. He rubbed his hand over it and tried to quell the creepy sensation, all the time backing toward the door.

The sound came again.

A low moan. One of pain, of helplessness.

Feeling less threatened, Nudger edged forward. Again he heard the sound. He crept to an archway leading to a short hall and stood listening. When the moan came again, he was sure it was from the nearest room on his left.

The room's door was open. Wishing he weren't afraid of guns and had one with him, he moved into the hall and peered inside.

It was a large bathroom, mostly pink and gray tile. The fixtures were gray marble, the plumbing gold. Everything was bathed in pale fluorescent light. On the floor was a torn plastic shower curtain, white with a pattern of gray and dark brown.

No, not brown actually, but a red so deep that it looked brown. The color was the result of blood smeared over the curtain.

Nudger looked in the medicine cabinet mirror and saw King Chambers nude and lying in the bathtub. Chambers was smeared with the same color that was on the shower curtain. One of his legs was draped over the side of the tub, as if he'd tried to climb out but hadn't been able to muster the strength. The leg was smeared with blood like the rest of him. He opened his eyes halfway and saw Nudger in the mirror.

"Well, don't you have some balls," he said admiringly. His head didn't move but his gaze flicked downward. "I wonder if I still got mine."

Nudger stepped forward. He saw that the bottom of the tub was a soup of blood and water. Fresh blood was seeping slowly from the slash wounds on Chambers' body. He understood why Chambers hadn't the strength to work his way out of the tub.

"I was taking a shower when the bastard came at me," he said in a whisper.

Nudger said, "Mirabelle's in the other room, on the floor."

Chambers might have shrugged, as if that hardly concerned him. In the gray tub, he looked pale as bleached bone. "It was a big guy. Crazy." Something rattled deep, deep in his throat. "Musta been hired by that double-crossing asshole Rand. He kept saying Luanne's father was getting even, all the time working on me with the blade."

"What do you mean, Rand double-crossed you?"

Chambers actually smiled. "Some detective you are. Rand engineered a major drug deal with a Central American cartel. Deal went sour because Luanne fucked up. Product was stopped at the border. Some people went down hard."

Nudger saw a portable phone on the toilet tank. He got it and dialed 911, gave them Mirabelle's address, and said a man was badly hurt. When the emergency operator asked his identity, he gave King Chambers' name.

"Too late for nine-one-one," Chambers said.

"Maybe. Tell me more about this drug deal that went bad."

"I been laying here a long time, listening to my blood trickle down the drain."

The phone rang. Nudger knew who it was. He lifted it and repeated his information to the 911 operator, who'd phoned back to authenticate his call before dispatching emergency vehicles. Nudger told her he'd stay at the scene. Well, he was pretending to be King Chambers, and the real Chambers would stay at the scene.

Nudger hung up the phone and laid it back on the smooth gray lid of the toilet tank. "The drug deal," he reminded Chambers.

"Never mind that. Too complicated to talk about, and I haven't got that much talk left in me."

"You said the man who did this to you was big. How else did he look?"

"Mean. Outa control mean." Chambers' voice was getting weaker. His paleness and his skeletal bone structure made him appear already gone.

"You never saw him before?"

"Never. He was heavyset but not fat. Thinning red hair. Arms thick as telephone poles."

Nudger didn't want to believe it. The ants were back at the nape of his neck, beneath his skin this time. "Did he have any tattoos?"

"Some. On his arms. One was an anchor, maybe. Couldn't tell you about the others. Too busy trying to get the knife away from him. Some kinda fucking hunting knife. He had me twice under the ribs before I even knew what was going on. Bastard cut me so deep." His tone had suddenly changed to that of a child about to ask for a wound to be kissed and so, healed. Then the hopelessness returned to his eyes as he remembered he was beyond childhood and beyond healing forever.

Nudger knew he had to get out soon. "What about Aaron?"

"What about him?"

"You kill him?"

Chambers closed his eyes and didn't answer. He wasn't the sort who'd feel the need for a deathbed confession. Or maybe a bathtub didn't lend itself to that kind of thing.

"Chambers?"

"You Catholic, Nudger? You got a key to heaven?"

"No. Why?"

Nudger stared at Chambers. There was no longer any discernible rise and fall of his chest, no longer the desperate faint whisper of breathing. All Nudger heard was the trickle of water-thinned blood finding its way down the drain. It made a regular ticking sound, like time passing.

Then he heard distant sirens.

He backed out of the bathroom and hurried across the living room, not looking at Mirabelle. As he left the apartment, he wiped the doorknob with the bottom of his shirt to smear his prints, realizing as he did so that he was tampering with evidence in a homicide. It had suddenly become doubly important that he get out of the building without being seen. He wished now he'd simply played by the rules and phoned Hammersmith, then put up with the complications, maybe even the suspicion, the hard line Springer was sure to take with him.

The elevator seemed to take forever reaching the lobby. Nudger kept swallowing, feeling as if he might vomit.

The sirens were deafening as he crossed the foyer and pushed opened the door to the street. He made himself slow down, walk normally. Though he saw no one around, he felt as if a thousand eyes were on him as he opened the black iron gate, strolled past the unconcerned stone wolf-hounds, and crossed the street to where the Granada squatted like a rusty safe haven in the sun.

The car's engine failed to start the first time.

It started on the second try, though. Nudger almost broke the ignition key twisting it to get the damned thing to kick over and power him away from there.

The motor clunked and sputtered as he fed it too much gas. Then it evened out and and continued to run, just as he was about to have a heart attack.

The sirens were screaming in his ears like taunting banshees as he drove to the intersection and turned the corner.

He'd driven only a few blocks when he had to pull to the curb while an ambulance and two police cars roared and wailed past, traveling in the opposite direction.

Instead of steering out into the flow of traffic again, Nudger sat there with the Granada's engine idling, sweating in the hot glare of sun blazing through the windows. The things his job brought him, he thought. He tried not to get involved in these kinds of cases, knowing it wouldn't be much different from when he was in the police department. Although it was possible to know too much about people, you still could never know enough.

He should have figured it out a long time ago. Norva had

mentioned that Luanne's real father had joined the Marines. Bobber Beane had a Marine anchor insignia tattooed on his arm. Bobber, Norva's cousin. Well, maybe it wasn't all that unusual in a place like Possum Run.

Nudger was sure that Bobber had killed Mirabelle and Chambers, and probably Aaron, and that he was Luanne Rand's biological father.

CHAPTER THIRTY-THREE

Nudger thought he understood. Luanne had soured a major drug deal, possibly by talking too much to the wrong party, so Chambers had instructed Aaron to make her pay with her life. Probably Chambers had seen it as a business decision, to guarantee future employee dedication. Norva had attempted to kill Dale Rand, and that made her a perfect patsy for the Luanne murder. Chambers had no way of knowing she was Luanne's mother. When he'd found out, he realized that eventually Norva would escape conviction and the case would remain open, so he deemed it wise to silence Aaron permanently.

After Aaron's death, Chambers probably thought he had control of the situation, when along came Bobber Beane. He'd known from the beginning that Norva hadn't killed her own daughter, and he was the one who'd originally tipped off Norva that Luanne was involved with the wrong people in St. Louis. If he'd known that, he probably knew about the aborted drug deal, and he'd figured out that King Chambers was Luanne's murderer. So Bobber had paid

Chambers a visit and worked his revenge, lost his temper, first with Mirabelle, then with Chambers.

It was possible that Norva Beane, Nudger's one and only client at the moment, knew nothing about what Bobber had done, possible that she was guilty of no crime other than taking a shot at Dale Rand. Possible.

Nudger decided to visit Rand and lay out enough of what he knew so that Rand would fully realize Norva hadn't killed Luanne. Maybe Rand would somehow get the police to ease up on their search for her. Then Nudger could locate her, or she would come to him, and he could put her in touch with Gideon Schiller. The savvy attorney could convince her to surrender herself to the law, and if she did know anything about what Bobber had done, to testify against him when he was caught. It was the only way for her to go now, Nudger knew, cut a deal so that charges against her would be dropped in return for her cooperation. She had a chance to walk away clean. She was his client and she was in deep water, and he needed to guide her in the direction of a life preserver.

He steered the Granada through a McDonald's and ate a Big Mac and fries for lunch as he drove toward Ladue. His stomach didn't approve of food on the run and let him know about it, so he chomped a couple of antacid tablets for dessert.

A black and orange Monarch butterfly was flapping around the shrubbery as Nudger made his way to the porch of the luxury house that cost more than he had probably earned in his lifetime. The butterfly got snagged in the thorny branches of one of the bushes. It beat its wings with a frantic and rhythmic speed. Monarchs migrated by the thousands to some remote place in Mexico, Nudger had read. This one had wandered into hostile territory, if it was indeed migrating. He didn't know what time of year the delicate and beautiful insects made their journey to Mexico.

As he watched, the butterfly tore itself free, but it didn't seem to be flying with the same elegant ease.

Sydney Rand answered his knock and stood silently, beautiful and delicate like the injured Monarch, only faded. She was wearing a pink robe and fuzzy pink slippers. Her eyes were pink, too. And not very focused. The gin on her breath explained why.

She peered at Nudger from the dim interior of the big house and said, "You work for that horrible woman."

"Yes. Is your husband home, Mrs. Rand?"

"Offish."

"Pardon me?"

"At the offish, downtown. He's always at the offish. He'll live in hish offish every goddamn day till Labor Day, is what he told me."

She was obviously very drunk, and he knew he shouldn't take advantage of her condition, but Nudger sensed opportunity here. "Why Labor Day?"

She stepped back and appraised him. "You don't know?"

He shook his head, smiling.

She smiled back. With one side of her face, anyway. "Well, neither do I. Some big kinda deal he's got cooking. Hish Labor Day venture, I heard him call it once. Businesh—ess. He lives for business in hish offish."

"He doesn't live for you?" Nudger the agitator.

"Hah! Not for me. Not for Luanne, either, Mr. . . . ?"

"Nudger."

"He doesn't live for Luanne or me or anybody but himself. Dale's what you'd call a selfish man, through and through. It's the buck. He lives for the almighty fucking dollar, and then for the next dollar." She was focused and angry now, not lisping.

"Mrs. Rand, I'm working even harder than the police to find out who killed Luanne. I know for sure Norva Beane didn't do it. But I need more proof. Can I come in, examine Luanne's room?"

"You mean search through her things?"

"No, of course not. I only want to look around and try to get a better idea of what kind of girl Luanne was."

"She was a damned fine girl. Confused, sure. But fine. The best." Her face contorted for a moment as if she might begin to cry, but she stiffened and gained control of herself.

Nudger flashed her the old sweet smile and squeezed past her into the house. She didn't attempt to stop him, but she almost fell down when he brushed her hip. She was even drunker than he'd first thought. Well, why not? Her adopted daughter was dead and her husband had been shot at. Here she was in the land of June Cleaver and living a horrible, lurid soap opera.

"You don't mind, do you?" Nudger said, already inside the cool house and standing as if he'd taken root.

She blinked twice, slowly, then closed the door to the bright heat outside. "No. Why should I mind? Nothing to hide. Not me." She teetered across the living room in her oversized slippers, almost stumbling twice. Leaning on a mahogany credenza in a corner, she poured herself a drink from a gin bottle that was almost empty. As if suddenly seeing herself in the role of hostess, she held the bottle out toward Nudger and raised her eyebrows. He shook his head no, and she finished her drink in three swallows and emptied the bottle into her glass, then added some ice from a silver bucket. "More where that came from," she said. Nudger didn't know if she meant ice or gin.

"Is Luanne's room upstairs?" he asked.

"Sure. Top of the shteps, to the right." She tried to walk away from the credenza but made it only a few feet and then stopped. For a few seconds she swayed dangerously, then she caught herself by leaning on the back of a dainty gray chair with elaborate wood arms. She took another sip from her glass and sat down in the chair. "You go on and help yourself," she said, not looking at him, losing concentration.

Nudger thanked her and went up the wide, curved stairway.

Seeing Luanne's room wasn't really what he had in mind, but while he was in the house he thought he might as well take a peek. In case Sydney quizzed him when he went back downstairs. Assuming she'd be conscious. She was working hard to crawl into the temporary refuge of the bottle. A trap, like so many refuges; easier to get in than out.

It was a typical teenage girl's room; the normal side of Luanne had lived here, not the doper and dealer and probable victim of incest. Everything seemed blue and white and fluffy, with a flowered, puffy comforter on the bed, stuffed animals lining the windowsill like helpless observers of inevitable tragedy. There was a Tom Cruise poster on one wall, a poster of a fierce-looking black man with dreadlocks and a guitar on another. A cross-eyed, stuffed bear was propped between perfume bottles and the mirror on the dresser, clasping a sign lettered "Just Say Yo!"

Nudger decided Yo, he'd have a closer look, since he'd made it this far. He might not have the chance again.

Luanne's dresser drawers revealed nothing unusual other than a pack of Zig-Zag paper for rolling joints. Well, even that wasn't unusual these days. In a corner was a mound of clothes, wadded pink socks, panties, and a pair of jeans, as if she'd hastily changed outfits and walked out a few minutes ago. Sydney must know she had to clean up after Luanne for the last time and hadn't yet brought herself to do it. Nudger felt a knife-thrust of compassion for her, along with guilt for what he was doing.

Still . . .

He left Luanne's room and looked into the rest of the upstairs rooms. He didn't find what he was searching for. Dale Rand's den or home offish—office.

He went downstairs and saw that Sydney was still slumped in the dainty chair, asleep. Gin had spilled from her glass, now empty and tilted in her hand, and darkened the lap of the pink housecoat. An ice cube was melting in the fuzz of one of her oversized slippers. Standing quietly, motionless, Nudger could hear her faint snoring. He should leave now, he knew. It was the only honorable thing to do.

Still . . .

A few minutes of cautious exploring was all he needed to find Rand's office. It was a large room with dark paneling and maroon drapes and carpet. In the center of the office was a large mahogany desk. Near it was a table holding a computer and printer. The desk was bare except for a fax machine with a built-in phone, a brass lamp with a black shade, and a sleek gray calculator with an intimidating number of keys.

The heavy drapes made the room dim. Nudger switched on the lamp and conducted a quick search of the desk drawers.

Most of what he found he didn't understand. Stock and mutual-fund information, mystifying charts and graphs. In a large bottom drawer was a Rolodex with hundreds of names and numbers. Nudger recognized none of them. He looked under *W*. No Horace Walling. Tucked beneath the

Rolodex itself he found a dozen or so sheets of paper, shoved toward the back of the drawer. He pulled them out and examined them. At first he thought they were confirmations of sales or purchases of stock; he'd received something like them from his own broker when he'd recently become a man of commerce. Then he saw that the forms were receipts for something called "puts," a term foreign to Nudger. They were all dated within the past month. He also saw the dollar amounts. Without even using the calculator on the desk, he thumbed through the forms and figured they added up to over three hundred thousand dollars.

Rand apparently intended to make big money out of these in some way. Money he probably needed to pay drug debts, or to finance what Sydney had referred to as the Labor Day venture.

Nudger switched on the computer and tried to get the thing going properly, punching this key and that, attempting to follow the cryptic instructions on the glowing monitor. It was as if Frankenstein's monster had somehow wandered into IBM headquarters. Nudger knew almost nothing about computers, but barely enough to come to the conclusion that some kind of password was needed to get into the thing's brain, and he didn't know the word. Or much of anything else about the humming, flickering object of progress before him. He switched it off before he caught a virus.

After leaving the computer, he wrote on the back of one of his business cards the names of the stocks on the forms in the desk drawer. They included his own stocks, Synpac and Fortune Fashions. This was something he had double reason to find out about.

He returned everything to the way it had been when

he'd entered the office, then walked softly through the quiet house, back to the living room.

Sydney hadn't moved. She was snoring louder, though, and her glass had dropped to the carpet. The ice cube, which had been caught in the fuzz of her slipper, had melted completely and left dewlike drops on the pink fibers. She would sleep the alcoholic's deep and dreamless slumber for hours.

Nudger stood for a moment watching her, a woman limp and remorseless in her boozy escape, which could only be temporary, and carried its own eventual, terrible cost. He didn't really know Sydney Rand, but he knew she didn't deserve what had happened to her already and what would happen next. No one did.

On some kind of inane, solemn impulse, he gently kissed her forehead before he left.

Her husband wouldn't mind.

CHAPTER THIRTY-FOUR

Nudger phoned Hammersmith and told him about his conversation with Sydney Rand, but not about his search of Dale Rand's desk.

"It could be this 'Labor Day venture' refers to a major drug deal that's going to go down during the holiday weekend," he said.

Hammersmith agreed. "That might have something to do with Chambers' murder."

"Maybe, but I doubt it."

"Your friend Bobber Beane might be heavily mixed up in the drug scene."

"As a user, maybe, or even a small-time dealer. But Bobber didn't impress me as smart or ambitious. He's not a planner. He's more the big, old country boy who muddles along in life buying lottery tickets and looking forward to deer season." As he spoke, it occurred to Nudger that he wasn't much of a planner himself. Of course, now he'd invested in the future with stocks. And maybe someday soon he'd go on a diet and become a new, sleek Nudger.

"You only got a snap impression, Nudge. That can be deceptive."

"I don't think so, in Bobber's case. He's not the sort who thinks with his head."

Then Hammersmith dropped his own piece of news on Nudger. "Dale Rand's disappeared."

"He couldn't have. I told you I talked with Sydney earlier today. She said he was at his office."

"He came home around four o'clock, went to his home office to do some work, and seems to have been abducted from there. Sydney was taking a nap, she said, but she heard what might have been a scuffle coming from the office, and when she went to see what was going on, Dale Rand was gone. His computer was still on, a lamp had been knocked to the floor, and the French doors leading out to a garden were wide open. She called the police."

Nudger sat back and tried to digest that information.

"What do you make of it, Nudge?"

"I'm not sure."

"What Massinger makes of it is that your client Norva sneaked through the wooded area and shrubs behind the house and abducted Rand at gunpoint."

"That doesn't sound right."

"But it doesn't sound wrong," Hammersmith said, and hung up the phone.

Nudger and Claudia were seated in a booth at Shoney's restaurant, down the street from his office. Nudger took Claudia to dinner there often. They were having the salad bar this evening, which was the cheapest meal on the menu. They always had the salad bar. It was understood.

Nudger said, "Do you know what a put is?"

Claudia finished chewing a bite of cold pasta and said, "Like in golf?"

"No, that's a putt. A put is when you pay for the right to sell a stock at a certain price by a certain date. So if the stock's price goes way up, you lose the relatively small amount you've paid for the put, but that's okay because you've made more on the stock itself. And if the stock falls, the put allows you to sell it at the higher, old price and not be too badly hurt financially. That's why some people buy puts, as a hedge, just in case the market falls drastically."

Claudia said, "Who told you this?"

"Benny Flit."

She took a sip of her iced tea and looked quizzically at him over the glass's rim.

"He's my broker. I mentioned him to you a few days ago."

"Oh."

Nudger told her about finding the receipts for puts in Dale Rand's desk.

She said, "So maybe Rand's protecting himself in case the market falls."

"But he's got a fortune invested in puts."

"Maybe he's got an even larger fortune invested in stocks."

"Could be. But nobody's *that* rich. Also, Benny says the stocks are all solid ones, and, if anything, they figure to go much higher. Two of them are the ones I own, Synpac and Fortune Fashions."

"Guided missiles and feather boas?"

"Right."

She spread butter on a roll. "Get out of the market, Nudger."

"There's no reason to do that. My stocks have low price/earnings ratios and sound management, and the interim and long-term outlooks are mostly on the upside."

"Get out while you can."

"That's bad advice."

"Almost all advice seems that way, or it wouldn't be advice."

"Anyway, you don't know anything about dealing in securities."

"I know this: No one makes money in the market if his broker's name is Benny."

"You're an English teacher. You shouldn't stereotype people like that."

The waitress refilled their iced tea glasses, then she hovered over the table and asked if everything was all right. Nudger could have told her a few things, but he simply nodded.

When the waitress had moved on, he said, "All that money in puts strikes me as a desperate gamble on Rand's part, unless he's acting on illegal inside information."

"It's also possible he's speculating with his clients' money. Maybe he suffered some unexpected losses and he's struggling to pull even. You said he seems to have disappeared. Maybe he only made it look as if he'd been abducted, and he actually left on his own with whatever he could salvage from his shady dealings."

Nudger hadn't considered that. It meant a new world of possibilities. "If Rand was secretly using his clients' money to make his personal investments, maybe one of his clients found out about it and abducted him."

"That could be. But they'd be much more likely to report him and try to get their money back through litigation."

That made sense to Nudger. He added artificial sweetener to his iced tea, stirred, sipped. Just right. Cool on a hot night. "Benny said some of the papers in Rand's desk were confirmations of short sales, too. Those are like puts."

"No, they aren't," Claudia said. "Selling short is when

you sell shares of stock that you don't yet own in the hope that they'll go down in price by a certain date. If they do, you buy the shares at the cheaper price to cover your sale, and the difference is your profit. There are two ways to make money in the market: Buy low and sell high, in that order. Or sell high and buy low, in that order."

Nudger was amazed. "How do you know that?"

"I'm repeating what my father told me, just before he lost the family fortune in the stock market. That's why it's painful for me to watch you."

"History doesn't always repeat itself. Anyway, I'm not your father. And I don't have a fortune to lose."

"My father didn't either, actually. It was only a figure of speech."

Nudger reached across the table and touched her hand, smiling at her. "I'm still not your father."

Claudia slid her plate near his and used her fork to edge some of a lumpy white substance toward a clear space on his plate. "Want some boiled eggplant?"

Nudger eyed the stuff with revulsion. It looked like something horrible that had been done to oysters. "No thanks. I've eaten enough. I'm not hungry."

"That never stopped you before, if something tasted good. You're less impulsive now that you've become a creature of commerce. But maybe that's one of the things you give up in order to get rich."

"I don't expect to get rich in the stock market," he told her, "just solidly middle class."

She stared at him. "Go ahead and have some," she urged, scraping half of the pale stuff onto his plate. "It'll make you smarter. It's brain food."

"Who told you that?"

"My grandmother."

"Eggplants aren't very smart."

"They don't have to be smart to make you smart. Besides, they're only brain food when they're boiled."

"When we leave here," Nudger said, docilely eating the bland and slimy eggplant and staying on Claudia's good side, "why don't we go to your place? We could, uh . . . forget about our worries for a while."

She used her fork to slide the other half of her eggplant onto his plate and said, "You'd better eat the rest of this."

He did. He was that smart.

CHAPTER THIRTY-FIVE

Smart didn't get him through the door. As he drove home after dropping Claudia off *outside* her apartment, Nudger thought about what she'd said in the restaurant. She made good sense, which was maybe the only annoying thing about her. Possibly he was in over his head, both in the stock market and in life.

He was more than aware of his immediate predicament. He was working for a woman who was wanted for suspicion of murder, and now, partly because of him, she was possibly mixed up in the abduction of her dead daughter's adoptive father. Or worse. Not to mention Bobber's murder of King Chambers and Mirabelle.

Nudger decided discretion was the better part of unemployment; he had no choice other than to go to the police with everything he knew.

Not to Massinger, though. Or to that hostile little ferret Springer.

Hammersmith.

He'd talk to Hammersmith and then go to bed early, and with a clearer mind get a good night's sleep.

Claudia's after-dinner kisses still at the top of his memory, he drove along steamy, darkening streets to his own more familiar but less exciting bed.

As soon as he got inside his apartment, Nudger went to the phone and sat down to call the Third District before he changed his mind. His stomach was grinding and he was getting a headache. He hoped it wasn't because of the eggplant Claudia had practically forced him to eat during dinner. Maybe he'd feel better after he'd talked to Hammersmith and unburdened himself. Confession, he knew, was sometimes a substitute for sex. He wondered if that vague but disturbing insight might be the result of the eggplant.

He hadn't quite touched the phone when it rang, startling him.

He waited two more rings, composing himself, before he lifted the receiver and said hello.

"Mr. Nudger. I been trying to call you all evening."

Norva! Nudger kept his tone matter-of-fact. "I was out to dinner, Norva. Then, uh, had some other things to do. Where are you?"

"I can't rightly say."

"You don't know?"

"I know, but I can't have other people knowing. Sometimes for their own protection I don't want them to know. I mean, if the police asked you my whereabouts, you'd be bound by your professional ethics to tell them. It's 'cause you're a good and honorable man. I know that and do understand it."

"I want to help you, Norva."

"You can. That's why I called, for you to give me a report about what all you learned since last we talked."

Oh, boy! She was his client, and he was a good and honorable man bound by professional ethics. Hopelessly entangled in them, in fact.

So Nudger told her about Luanne's connection to the drug world, a connection that was in part because of Dale Rand. And he told her about finding Mirabelle dead, and King Chambers almost dead, and what Chambers had told him about Luanne being responsible for a major drug deal not happening. Then about Chambers dying.

She was silent for a while, then she said, "Goddamnit, Mr. Nudger, if you'll pardon my French."

He said, "When something like the botched drug deal happens, the person responsible has got to pay, Norva. That's how those creeps do business. Chambers sent Aaron to kill Luanne, then he played it safe and killed Aaron so no one would ever find out. But now Chambers is dead. They're both dead, Norva."

"I got it all figured out that far, Mr. Nudger, since you turned over the right rocks for me and let in the light."

"Then why don't you give yourself up?"

"Not hardly, Mr. Nudger."

"Are you with Bobber?"

"How come you ask?"

"Before he died, Chambers described who broke into his girl friend's apartment, killed her, then attacked him with a knife. It had to have been Bobber."

"Hah! You serious, Mr. Nudger? Bobber ain't no killer."

"Chambers said the man had red hair and a Marine Corps insignia tattooed on his arm."

"Which arm?"

"Well, Chambers didn't say." Nudger searched his memory and couldn't recall himself which of Bobber's arms was tattooed with the insignia.

"Weren't Bobber, I'm sure. There's lots of ex-marines

out there walking around. Anyways, when were those people killed?"

"Early this morning."

"Well, see! I been with Bobber since last night. He was here all morning, right in my sight. Laying in bed in his Jockey shorts and the same shirt he always wears."

Nudger tried not to imagine that. "Norva, is Bobber Luanne's real father?"

"He wouldn't hurt nobody on purpose, much less kill them. He looks much gruffer than he is."

"Norva—"

A click like a gun's hammer falling on an empty chamber came over the line as she hung up.

Nudger stood up and went into the kitchen. He got a cold can of Budweiser out of the refrigerator and held it to his forehead as if it were an ice pack, rolling it now and then when his body heat began to warm the aluminum.

When his headache felt better, he opened the can and sat at the kitchen table to drink its contents and think for a few minutes before calling Hammersmith.

What if Bobber really had been with Norva at the time Mirabelle and Chambers were killed?

That would cloud everything again, just when Nudger thought comprehension was beginning to shine through.

He drank a second beer and discovered that his headache was gone. He felt calmer, and suddenly weary. Tomorrow, he decided, would be soon enough to call Hammersmith.

He made sure all the doors were locked, set the air conditioner on high, then stripped to his underwear, and stretched out on the bed. He tuned the small-screen bedroom TV to the ball game.

The Cardinals were playing the Dodgers on the west coast, so the game had started late and was only in the fourth inning. Nudger watched the Dodger lead-off man stride to the plate.

By strike one, Nudger's eyelids were heavy.

When the count was three and two, he was struggling to focus on the tiny glowing screen near the foot of the bed.

On the next pitch, the batter hit a high bouncing ball to the shortstop and was barely safe at first base, but Nudger was out.

When he opened his eyes the television screen was blank, the drapes were pulled wide open, and the room was splashed with bright yellow sunlight that brought with it a weighty morning heat.

And Norva Beane was sitting in a chair at the foot of the bed, studying him.

She was wearing a wrinkled gray shirt that looked like a man's dress shirt with the sleeves cut off just above the elbows. The shirt was tucked into Levi's that were creased and contoured to her body as if she'd been wearing them a long time. Life on the run had its drawbacks. She appeared exhausted, but the fire still shone in her eyes.

She said, "You look like you didn't sleep much last night, Mr. Nudger."

He swallowed the sour taste in his mouth, then cleared his throat. "You look like you didn't sleep much last week."

"Well, that's surely true."

He sat up straighter and rested his back against the headboard. He was glad he'd awakened without an erection and suddenly wondered how long Norva had been sitting there watching him. "Why are you here, Norva?"

" 'Cause after we talked on the phone, I spent the rest of last night thinking how it's definitely time to come to you with the entire story, the whole and nothing but the truth.''

"It's past time," Nudger said.

He wanted to get up and put on some pants, rinse his face, brush his teeth, and drink some strong black coffee. But he didn't want to interfere with Norva's inclination to tell him the truth, or something like it, yet again. She looked strangely innocent there in the harsh sunlight, pretty but haggard, a worn-out doll from someone's collection struck to life.

"After I took a shot at Dale Rand, I went and hid," she said. She wiped the back of her hand across her forehead quickly and lightly, as if brushing aside a stray wisp of hair. "I'm glad now you spoiled my aim and stopped me from killing him, Mr. Nudger."

"Everyone's glad, Norva."

"What I been doing is hiding, being a suspect in my own daughter's murder. You and I both know I wouldn't have hurt a hair on poor Luanne's head."

He nodded, thinking that was true.

Her Adam's apple worked in her sun-goldened throat; something beautiful about that, Nudger thought. She said, "I didn't do right by that girl, and I'll surely burn in hell for it."

"You did the best you could at the time," he told her. "Hell's when people can't let go of things and flog themselves with regret for the rest of their lives."

"She was my little girl and I coulda saved her from what happened. You can't change my mind on that."

"You had no way of knowing she'd be adopted by someone like Dale Rand. She might just as easily have landed in a happy enough family, been okay."

"Might have. World's full of might haves, though." She stared at the floor for a moment, then raised her head and looked directly at Nudger. Her Adam's apple bobbed again in her taut throat. "I didn't exactly tell you the truth last night about me being with Bobber. He was gone all that night I said he was with me, and I didn't see him till nearly noon yesterday."

Ah-ha! "Then he had plenty of time to murder Mirabelle and Chambers."

She worked her head around on her neck as if wearing a tight collar, looking miserable. "More'n that. He did kill them, Mr. Nudger. He told me so himself, thinking I'd be proud of him. He didn't plan on even hurting the woman, but she kept fighting him, and he had to take her down fast so's she wouldn't rouse Chambers. Bobber thought Chambers was in the bedroom, not in the shower. If he hadn't been under running water he mighta heard Bobber and the woman fighting and come out and shot Bobber."

"The world turns on those kinds of things, Norva."

"Don't it just ever? Anyways, you was right and Bobber surely did kill them folks. Not that Chambers didn't deserve it. And I can't hardly blame Bobber. 'Cause you was right about something else, Mr. Nudger: Bobber is Luanne's natural father. Not long after he learned I was expecting, he went and joined the marines and I never saw him for years. Not till he came back a few months ago to Possum Run and told me what had happened to our baby daughter."

Clouds must have moved across the sun. The bedroom dimmed for a moment, then gradually brightened to its previous intensity. Something was stirring uneasily in the back of Nudger's mind. "Why are you really telling me this, Norva?"

" 'Cause Bobber's not what I thought he was, not at all the boy I recollect."

"How so?"

"Well, he's got these demons in him now, and they cause him to do bad things."

Like murder, Nudger thought. He said, "What about Dale Rand? Did Bobber do something to him, too?"

"It was us that took Dale Rand. It wasn't a bit of trouble; Bobber just showed him the knife and Rand came right along with us. Rand's a coward, is what he is. Which ain't surprising."

Nudger swiveled his body and sat on the mattress. "Where's Rand now?"

She gnawed her lower lip, then the inside of her cheek. "Norva?"

"That's just the trouble, Mr. Nudger, I couldn't tell you."

He didn't want to play her word games. "Does that mean you don't know?"

"That's it. Rand got away from us, from where we was keeping him in this old house trailer. It was Bobber's fault."

"The abduction? Or Rand getting away?"

"I guess the abduction was purely my idea, though Bobber got right enthusiastic about it. He figured there'd be ransom money."

Nudger remembered the empty attaché case on the floor in Mirabelle's apartment. Had she been forced to reveal where drug money was hidden, then killed? "Did Bobber take money from Mirabelle Rogers' apartment?"

"Some. He didn't tell me how much. Wasn't enough, though."

"What do you mean?"

"Well, Bobber started listening to Rand where we had him tied up in this little room. That Rand is smooth, and pretty soon Bobber started saying to me how Rand really didn't hurt nobody, and he'd treated Luanne pretty well, considering. I mean, Bobber had these demons himself, so he wouldn't hold it against a man for getting involved in narcotics."

"What about the rest of it?"

"Bobber wouldn't believe the rest of what you told me. Not after hearing Rand's lies. Which is what I told Bobber they was, only he wouldn't listen. Me and Bobber had us a big argument, and after that's when Rand got real persuasive. I went in the next room and heard him offer Bobber lots and lots of money if Bobber'd only help him escape." Norva bowed her head and pressed her palms to her temples, as if she had a terrible headache. "Bobber told him to shut up, but Rand kept promising more and more money. Bobber stormed outa there then and found me eavesdropping, so he whapped me in the ribs. I don't put up with no man doing that to me, and I told him so."

"What did he do then?"

"He went on outside and started drinking. I laid down and went to sleep, and when I woke up, Rand was gone. Bobber said he musta slipped his ropes and snuck out whilst I was asleep and Bobber was passed out drunk, but I knew better. Rand finally offered enough money, so Bobber let him go. When I said that to Bobber we argued again and he made like he was gonna hit me, only he didn't. He just got in his truck and roared away, and I ain't seen him since."

"You sure Rand got away?"

"Yeah, and probably he'd of died if he hadn't. The trailer didn't have no air conditioning. It was hot enough to burst into fire there in that room where he was, and I think he was sick when we took him from his house. We went into his office through some French doors and made him walk with us right out through those same doors and through the backyard to where we had a car parked in the next block. We knew cops was watching the front of the house, but we got him anyways. We coulda killed him right there, which shows you how smart the cops are. Country folks can move through yards and trees so there's no way a city cop can figure we're there. Bobber had a good laugh outa that.''

"Sick?"

"Huh?"

"What did you mean, Norva, when you said Rand was sick when you abducted him?"

"Well, we hadda wait till he was done with a phone conversation before we went in and got him, and I overheard him talking to his doctor.''

"You're sure?"

"Yep. Called him Doctor Walling. They was talking about some kinda virus.''

Nudger sat still for a moment, staring at the patterns of sunlight and shadow on the carpet, at the dust motes swirling in the hot, heavy air.

Then he said, "Norva, it would be best if we found Dale Rand."

"If you say so.''

"Wait in the living room while I get dressed, then we'll go see if his wife knows where he is.''

"We could just call.''

"No. If Rand happens to be there, he might run. He's probably still afraid, and if he promised Bobber money, he won't go to the cops.''

"I suppose you're right." She stood up, stretched with her arms above her head, then gave him a smile, as if somehow he'd reassured her. "I got no desire to see you naked, Mr. Nudger." She walked from the bedroom and closed the door behind her.

Nudger called Hammersmith and pulled on some clothes.

On the drive to the Rand house, Norva sat calmly and silently beside him while he consumed half a roll of antacid tablets.

His stomach hardly noticed them.

CHAPTER THIRTY-SIX

As Nudger steered the car into Rand's driveway, he saw a stocky figure bending over the shrubbery that bordered the shaded concrete. He felt a wash of relief; if a gardener was pruning the shrubs, things must have returned to something like normal. Or, if not normal, at least more manageable. Routine could be a bulwark against grief.

He parked the car near the house and climbed out. Norva got out on the passenger's side. It wasn't yet unbearably hot, and the grassy, well-tended grounds lay as peaceful as a cemetery. A squirrel darted madly across the lawn and clawed its way up the trunk of a maple tree. A bird Nudger couldn't see was nattering away in an attempt to establish territorial control. Probably no one but Nudger was listening.

"Mr. Nudger!"

Norva's soft but alarmed voice made him turn, poised with one foot on the first step to the porch. She was facing away from him, staring down the driveway.

Nudger saw that the man he'd assumed was a gardener

was wearing a dark business suit, not coveralls, and was now on his hands and knees. He was vomiting blood, his body quaking with each painful, prolonged heave.

Nudger started down the driveway toward him. Norva was beside him but trailing a foot or so behind, as if she didn't want to look any closer at the man, or at what his presence might mean.

When they were halfway to him, he shifted position and Nudger saw his face. Despite the blood-smeared features, he recognized Al Martinelli.

He knelt beside him. One of Martinelli's eyes was rapidly swelling shut and his nose appeared to be broken. Those were the least of his problems. The front of his white shirt was red with blood, and the material was slashed as if by a knife blade. For a sickening moment Nudger was back in Mirabelle's apartment, watching King Chambers' life disappear like draining bathwater. Blood was such a terrible reminder of mortality.

"What happened?" Nudger asked, his stomach reeling at the sight, and at the stench of blood and bile.

Martinelli made a strangled, helpless sound, rolling his eyes. A hard guy who'd given up all pretense of toughness.

"We'll get help for you," Nudger assured him.

The wounded man made the same strangled sound, blood dribbling from the corner of his mouth and down his chin to spatter on the concrete driveway. This time he pointed to the house. Then he collapsed onto his side and seemed to hug the ground, as if embracing his shadow, shifting about until he lay curled in the fetal position. His breathing was rapid and unsteady, his gaze fixed inward. One hand rose feebly, sunlight glinting off a gold ring, and Martinelli pointed again toward the house. Briefly there was accusation and rage in his eyes, then they assumed their same shallow stare. The bleeding had let up enough for him to murmur, "House . . . inside."

"Hang on and we'll phone for an ambulance."

"Fuck that . . . Just get . . . "

As his voice trailed to silence, his eyes closed and his breathing evened out. Unconscious, he seemed to have achieved some delicate equilibrium on the thin edge between life and death.

Nudger stood up and strode through the brilliant heat toward the house.

Norva was trying to keep pace, breathing heavily. "That man's gonna die, Mr. Nudger."

He didn't say anything. His stomach was gnawing on the lump of fear in his gut. He was terrified of what he might find inside the house, but he knew he had to look.

"Mr. Nudger—"

"You better stay out here, Norva."

"No, sir!"

Nudger might have argued with her, but just then the door opened and Dale Rand burst from the house. He was gripping a brown leather briefcase and striding with his head down toward the rented blue Cadillac Nudger had seen him in earlier.

He suddenly looked up, spotted Nudger and Norva, and gazed at them with an odd detachment, a busy man without time to trifle with underlings, and continued toward the car without hesitation. Martinelli he didn't seem to notice at all.

Nudger took several quick steps to the side and grabbed his arm. "Rand, wait!"

Something slammed into the side of Nudger's head and he was on the ground. His right knee had banged against hard concrete but his upper body was on grass. He rolled onto his back and heard himself groan.

When the world stopped whirling, he realized Rand had struck him with the briefcase.

There were objects on the ground all around Nudger. Someone was cursing. Rand. He was bent over, scooping up hundred dollar bills and slips of paper. Money and evidence.

Norva came close to him as if to grab him and he shoved her away, then continued scooping up papers and bills from the ground.

He was in such a hurry that he lost his grip on a handful of bills and they scattered at his feet. He shouted, "God-damnit!" and slapped his briefcase closed, as if he couldn't spare any more time to gather what had dropped.

Nudger clutched the cuff of Rand's pants, then his ankle. Joined his other hand to that one. He wasn't going to let Rand leave.

Rand disagreed. He swung the briefcase at Nudger's head again, but the angle was awkward and the case only glanced off Nudger's shoulder. It hurt, but Nudger held on to Rand's ankle. Rand took three lurching steps, dragging Nudger with a strength born of panic. Nudger clenched his teeth and tightened his grip. Rand grunted with effort, and again the briefcase crashed into Nudger's shoulder. The case sprang open on the backswing as Rand prepared to strike another blow at Nudger. Slips of paper, white, pink, and green, littered the air in a wide and graceful arc above Rand's head as he brought the case down, missing Nudger entirely this time. He sobbed and hurled the briefcase into the shrubbery, then reached inside his suit jacket.

"Mr. Nudger, he's got a gun!"

Norva was on her feet and screaming.

Rand glanced at her as he pulled an ugly little snub-nosed pistol from his belt. Then he drew back his upper body as far as he could and aimed the pistol at Nudger.

Oh, Christ! Nudger immediately released Rand's ankle and scooted away from him, giving him room to run. *Run!* Nudger screamed silently at him. *Run at top speed forever!*

The pistol followed Nudger. Rand was glaring at him with puzzlement and disgust, his lips twisted and his eyes wide and unblinking as he sighted down the barrel.

"Nooooo!" Nudger heard himself yell.

The explosion rang in his ears, through his skull, so loud it seemed to come from inside his head, and he clenched his eyes tightly shut. He felt something wet and warm spreading beneath his body.

There was no sound in the reverberating aftermath of the shot.

No movement.

Nudger slowly opened his eyes. He saw blood on his stomach and right arm.

There was more blood on Dale Rand, who was lying next to him. They were almost nose to nose. Nudger stared over at Rand, who only seemed to stare back at him through opaque, puzzled eyes.

"Don't you try'n go away from here!" Norva was shouting.

Nudger craned his neck and saw Bobber standing in the doorway, a gun in his hand. He swaggered down off the porch, past Nudger and Rand. Norva yelled something at him again and leaped on his back, wrapping her arms around his neck like a lover unable to let him walk out of her life. Bobber spun several times and shoved her away so hard she was airborne for a long few seconds. She landed on the driveway and Nudger heard her head bounce off the concrete.

Bobber, his chest heaving and perspiration streaming down his face staining his jeans and sleeveless red shirt, ambled over to her and kicked her in the ribs. He drew back his foot to kick her again. Then he seemed to think about it and yanked the gun from where he'd tucked it his belt. It was a semi-automatic. He used his free hand to work its mechanism and pump a round into the chamber. That didn't seem right, but Nudger couldn't quite figure why at the moment. Bobber leveled the gun at Norva. She was where Nudger had been only minutes before, under the round, dark eye of death.

Nudger picked up Rand's gun and shot Bobber in the leg.

Bobber roared and fell hard to the ground, thrashing around as if energized by a thousand volts. He scrambled furiously with his arms and good leg, making it all the way to a low crouch, then dropped onto his back, all so abruptly it looked like an inane break-dance step. Then he stopped trying to get up. He lay on his back, clutching his upraised thigh with both hands as if trying to prevent his leg from dropping off. His gun had flown from his hand and was in the grass only about six feet from where he lay, but he didn't seem interested in retrieving it. He stayed very still, trying to stem the stream of blood finding its way between the fingers clamped to his leg, writhing like black snakes down his arms.

Nudger struggled to a sitting position, then to his feet. He knew he'd better get the gun before Bobber got his pain under control and remembered it. In the corner of his vision he saw Sydney Rand standing on the porch. She was looking at something beyond him.

Nudger turned and saw Hammersmith charging up the driveway, trailing half-a-dozen uniforms. Two of the uniforms tended to Bobber. A couple of plainclothes types were standing over Martinelli farther down the driveway.

Hammersmith glided over to Nudger with that odd grace of certain fat men, as if floating in a dream. He gripped Nudger's elbow to help him remain standing. Nudger pushed the supporting hand away, took several unsteady steps, then leaned back against the sun-warmed fender of Rand's rented Caddy. He could still hear the gunfire and smell the cordite hanging in the air, still feel the weighty jump of the gun in his hand, like something alive that had suddenly awakened. He'd shot someone. In the leg—but he'd shot someone. Bobber would live, he was sure. Unless the bullet had severed a main artery.

Sirens wailed out of unison, like an insane choir in practice, and two ambulances and another police car braked at the foot of the driveway and parked at angles blocking the street.

Hammersmith had followed him over to the Caddy and was staring intensely at him. His wide, flesh-padded face looked old, and there was concern in his pale blue eyes, compassion. "You shot or anything, Nudge?"

"I don't think so."

"Not hurt?"

"Not bad."

Hammersmith's expression changed. He was the deadpan cop again. "Then what is this, with people all over the ground, a rehearsal for the last act of Hamlet?"

"Huh?"

"Your idea of a practical joke?"

The stench of gunfire, the blood all over him, all around him, the steep and dizzying drop from his adrenaline high, made Nudger's stomach lurch. Trembling, he sank to his knees. He bowed his head as if praying, and vomited, remembering Martinelli's pain-distorted mouth emitting blood from an interior wound, like one of those gargoyle drains on medieval castles.

He felt Hammersmith's hand rest softly on his shoulder, as if a gentle bird had lighted there.

"No," Hammersmith said, "I guess it's not a joke."

CHAPTER THIRTY-SEVEN

Hammersmith sat across from Nudger in Nudger's office. Despite the fierce outside heat, it was more than cool enough with the window unit pumping out cold air, but Hammersmith had removed his jacket and sat overflowing the small chair in front of Nudger's desk. Nudger studied the impassive and obese lieutenant and was sure he was looking at the only fat man in the city without perspiration stains beneath his arms.

After drawing a cellophane-wrapped cigar from his shirt pocket and absently tapping it on his knee a few times, as if maybe checking his reflexes, Hammersmith said, "Martinelli cut his deal with the prosecutor. He's telling everything about everything. It was pretty much what you figured, Nudge. A major illegal drug shipment was hijacked a few months ago because Luanne Rand whispered something in the wrong ear in the sack. That world being what it is, somebody had to pay in human life. Martinelli left that task up to King Chambers. Dale Rand had been involved in the deal with Martinelli's money, so Chambers decided the sacrifice could be either Luanne or Rand himself. It made little difference to him, so he gave Rand the choice. Either way, the survivor would be in no position to make any more mistakes or commit acts of disloyalty. It didn't take Rand long to decide he wanted to live, even on the condition that if he didn't repay the lost drug money, he was going to die anyway."

Instead of satisfaction at having been right, Nudger felt a seething anger at Rand, tinged with a deep sadness. Incest had begotten murder. What chance had Luanne ever had in life? "Some decision."

"The narcotics trade causes people to make those kinds of choices, Nudge. The lure of wealth is a narcotic itself. It overpowers humanity and judgment. Then it becomes a question of survival." He tapped especially hard on his knee with the wrapped cigar. "So the admirable Dale Rand murdered Luanne to save his own skin."

Nudger wondered what Luanne must have thought in her final moments, when she'd known what was about to happen. Had she been surprised?

Probably not. That was the crux of the tragedy.

Hammersmith said, "When Bobber went with Rand to Rand's house to get the money Rand had promised him in the trailer, they met Martinelli in the driveway. He was worried about the money Rand owed him for the aborted drug deal and had come to the house to talk to Rand. So there stood Martinelli and Bobber, each with a claim on Rand's money and future, each dangerous in his own way. And Rand could only pay one of them. So he ran a bluff and went into the house while they waited outside. That was when Bobber got insistent and physical with Martinelli about Luanne's death. Martinelli let slip to Bobber that Rand had killed Luanne. Bobber's own daughter. Bobber knew who'd initiated the order, and he flew into a rage and beat Martinelli. But that was only an appetizer. When he was finished with Martinelli, he ran into the house after Rand."

"That was when Norva and I arrived," Nudger said.

"More or less," Hammersmith said. "There was a big argument between Rand, Bobber, and Sydney, then Rand broke and ran outside, carrying money and incriminating paperwork on the stock swindle he was working to get the rest of what he owed. That was when you and Norva tried to stop him in the driveway."

Nudger said, "Did Martinelli tell you about the stock swindle?"

Hammersmith shook his head no. "Sydney did."

Nudger was astounded. "She knew about it?"

"In her way. Like she knew and didn't know about what her husband was up to with Luanne."

Nudger understood her denial, not blaming her but feeling again a hot and futile rage about what Rand had done to Luanne, and to his wife.

"To pay his overwhelming drug debt to Martinelli," Hammersmith said, "Rand convinced Horace Walling, one of his investment clients and a hard-core user he supplied, to utilize Compu-Data to introduce a computer virus into Kearn-Wisdom Brokerage software, an electronic glitch that would, through computer linkage, soon spread to other brokerage firms as well as institutional investors such as mutual and pension funds. It was set to trigger automatic sell orders and cause select stocks to plunge the Friday before Labor Day. On the next trading day, Rand, having sold short or bought puts, would exercise his options and reap huge profits so he could pay King Chambers and have enough left over to regain safety and solvency."

Nudger leaned back and felt the cool air from the window unit like an icy human touch on the side of his neck. "Sydney really knew about this?"

"Knew most of it, Nudge."

"She did a good job of playing dumb."

"The lady isn't dumb, Nudge. She's into it with the bottle and doesn't think straight every waking hour, but stupid she's not. She was unable to face losing her wealth and station in life, so she decided to do nothing."

"Booze can do that to people," Nudger said, "cause them to accept whatever's going on and the hell with it."

"Well, it was that way with Sydney until she overheard Bobber confront Rand with the truth about Luanne's birth and death, and heard Rand admit he'd murdered her."

"Which set Bobber off."

"Until Rand went to work on him. Rand was persuasive and rich, a potent combination. Bobber, Luanne's real father, calmed down, then agreed to Rand's offer of a six-figure bribe to buy his silence. The girl was dead and going to stay that way, so Bobber figured what did it matter. The final betrayal of Luanne."

"Six figures, high or low, is a lot of money," the chronically poor Nudger said.

"Rand must have thought it was too much. After stuffing most of it into his briefcase with whatever else of value he could grab from his desk while Bobber was watching, he made a run for his car. That's when you and Norva stopped him."

"And when Bobber shot him."

Hammersmith smiled, but with no hint of humor. "No, Nudge, it was Sydney who shot and killed her husband."

Nudger went hollow inside. He was silent for a long time, thinking about the Rands, thinking back over the years.

Finally he said, "Family life."

Hammersmith unwrapped his cigar and heaved himself to his feet to leave.

"And death," he said, and flicked the lever on his flame-thrower lighter.

CHAPTER THIRTY-EIGHT

Nudger watched a piece of lettuce drop from his fork. It landed on the edge of his plate, but it splattered a stitch of oil-and-vinegar spots across his lap, leaving him looking as if he'd been careless in the restroom.

He was having the salad bar with Claudia at Shoney's. He'd told her about everything, evoking in her the same pity for Sydney Rand that he felt. Bobber was a killer and deserved what he would get. Norva was a tragic figure, but she was a *cause celebré* and would doubtless soon walk away free and return to the Ozarks. Sydney was staring at conviction and lengthy imprisonment.

"Aren't you gonna eat your salad?" Nudger asked. He took another bite, more careful this time, spearing a manageable tomato wedge.

She gazed out the window at the rain hitting the surface of Manchester Avenue and steaming in the hot summer air. "I lost my appetite." After a moment she turned back and met his eyes. "What happened about the computer virus?"

"It was deprogrammed before it could trigger automatic

sell orders. The stocks won't plunge after Labor Day. And Horace Walling was taken into custody."

She toyed with a breaded lump of something that might have been fish, might have been chicken. "At least that should give you an idea of the risks you're taking in the stock market. If you hadn't worked through to the end of this case in time, you would have lost money when the share prices plunged."

Nudger took a sip of iced tea and looked away. "I'm out of the market," he told her, but not very loud.

"What?" She was feigning mild interest, he knew. She'd heard what he said.

"I'm out of the market," he repeated, louder. "Benny Flit phoned me and said the Bundesbank had raised interest rates in Germany."

"Do you know what the Bundesbank is?"

"Sure. It's this big bank in Germany. It has something to do with interest rates in this country. And that has something to do with the stock market. Benny advised me to sell everything as soon as possible."

She looked at him for a while with something like pity, then said, "Well, how were you to know? You're an expert in stocks, not interest rates."

He said nothing in the face of her sarcasm.

"So how much did you make on your investments?"

Pushing now. Rubbing it in. "I took a loss, but I might have lost a lot more."

"You could say that about all losses," she pointed out. "They might have started with Marie Antoinette's fingers and toes. Jimmy Carter—"

"So you were right," he interrupted, trying to shut her up. Sometimes total capitulation would do that. But her expression of mild disgust didn't change. "You were right about the stock market, anyway," he said, getting angry and forgetting about total surrender. "But you were wrong about my broker not being competent or not having my best interest at heart. He called me and got me out before I lost everything."

"Okay," she said, apparently sensing she'd gone too far. "You were right about the Rand case, and that's what's most important. That kind of thing is your life's work, and you do it well."

He felt better. Took a sip of sweetened tea.

Now she did begin to probe at her salad with her fork, building up to taking a bite.

"Nudger," she said, "did Benny Flit explain to you about commissions?"